PHARAOH ADOLF

A Dirk Beretta Novel

Edward M. Grant

Banchixi Media
Canada

First Edition, 2017

Paperback
ISBN-13: 978-1-927549-33-9

Mobi ebook
ISBN-13: 978-1-927549-34-6

Epub ebook
ISBN-13: 978-1-927549-35-3

Revision: #4226 - February 17, 2018

Published by Banchixi Media, **www.banchixi.com**

<PROLOGUE>

For the first time since he left boot camp, 'Big' Dick Beretta was glad the boys in the platoon had been joking when they gave him his nick-name. He crouched as low as he could in a shallow shell hole that the Russki artillery had blown out of the rubble of what had once been the centre of Berlin. At a mere five feet tall, Dick's eyes barely rose above the pile of dirt and debris the exploding shell had tossed up around the edge of the hole. Gunfire cracked nearby, over the constant boom of the massed artillery on both sides. The armies of Nazis and Russkis were fighting through the ruined buildings of Berlin all around him. Shooting, or blowing up, anything that moved.

The ground shook as another artillery shell landed nearby. The front of a mangled five-storey department store a hundred yards to his left collapsed in a shower of bricks and broken glass as the shell exploded inside it, and threw out a thick cloud of white dust that spread in all directions. Dick ducked back into the bottom of the hole. He coughed as the dust burned his lungs and dried out his mouth. It was worse than smoking those damn Russki Makhorka cigarettes that he'd had to survive on for most of the last week, which tasted they were made from old rope. And, knowing the Russkis, they most probably were.

2 · EDWARD M. GRANT

He wasn't even supposed to be in Berlin. A few days before, he'd been happily getting drunk with the Russkis near the Elbe. After which, he fell asleep in the back of a big, green army truck with a very friendly Red Army blonde, and a bottle of vodka. The next thing he knew, the truck was rattling and bumping over rough ground in the orange glow of the early morning light as the Russkis raced for Berlin. He could either join the attack, or be shot as a spy, they said. He'd left his own rifle behind in his tent when he went to the party, but there were plenty of dead Nazis to borrow a weapon from.

And they wouldn't miss it.

He adjusted his grip on the Schmeisser he'd borrowed, and peered over the edge of the shell hole, past a cylindrical tower topped with a conical roof about thirty metres away that looked too much like a machine gun tower for his taste. Nazis moved near the ruined, grey stone building beyond it, which would have been a hundred yards long and ten high if the Russkis hadn't blown so many holes through it. He pulled his head back into his hole, before some Nazi put a bullet through that.

The German blonde who was curled up in the dirt behind him whimpered. When he arrived in the city, the Russki troops had rushed ahead, drunk, yelling, and eager for the honour of being first to die for Stalin in Berlin. The blonde had offered to let Dick hide in her cellar, to protect her from those very same Russki troops. She'd been so grateful that he'd have been quite content to spend the rest of the war doing just that.

Until he made the mistake of asking her where Hitler was. He'd been joking, and hadn't expected her to know, let alone tell him. But, after ten minutes of improvised sign language, she began leading him through the ruins toward this building. Then the first shell had exploded beside them, and she'd cowered in the hole ever since.

Why had he ever said anything? He could have been nice and safe back in that basement, in the arms of the blonde. All he'd have to do is keep the door locked and discourage any randy Russki who came their way looking for a bit of fun. It had to be better than being shot at or blown up.

But he'd come this far, and he couldn't turn back now. He carefully slid rocks and small lumps of concrete from between the large pieces of shattered concrete and rebar that the masses of artillery and bombs had scattered on the ground around the shell hole, until he cleared a gap large enough to look through without being seen.

Nazis strode along the rear of the building, checked their guns, then dragged a old man from an open metal door in the concrete wall nearby. The man wore loose grey overalls, all crumpled and dirty as though he'd slept in them for days, and he carried some kind of fancy radio with a circular antenna protruding from the top.

The Nazis pushed the man forward, away from the rubble that had fallen behind the building, and into the open patch of dirt near the tower. He struggled against them, and tried to pull himself out of their grip, but a Nazi wearing a fancy officer's hat shoved a pistol into his back. They pushed him on, then the officer shouted and slapped the man on the back of his head. He put the radio on the ground.

The officer shouted at the other Nazis, and stood guard over the man while the others strode past him and clambered over the rubble, heading away from the building. They disappeared into the streets beyond, and Russian and German yells and the rattle of gunfire soon followed.

The Nazi officer prodded the old man again. He flicked switches, turned knobs, and adjusted sliding controls on his fancy radio. It hummed as it warmed up, and red and green lights began to glow on the top, then flashed intermittently. Dick clenched the Schmeisser's grip tighter, and watched as the man adjusted more controls, flipped up a red cover on the side of the box, then flicked a large switch beneath it.

The air twisted, wobbled and warped in a three-yard-wide circle above the antenna, until a shimmering blue sky and piles of sand replaced the rubble of Berlin inside the circle. Beyond that warped vortex hanging there in the air, a man led a camel across the sand. He stopped and stared through the vortex at the Nazi.

Who raised his pistol, and fired.

4 · EDWARD M. GRANT

Blood spurted from the man's head, and he fell to the ground. The camel lunged toward the Nazi, who fired a second shot. Blood sprayed from the camel's leg, before it jumped out of the air above the box, and slammed into the Nazi's chest.

The Nazi flew backward onto the rubble pile behind him. The pistol rattled down onto a pile of broken concrete blocks, and the camel jumped on top of him. The Nazi screamed as the camel's hooves crushed his chest into red mush.

The man wearing the overalls leaned toward the switch that had opened the vortex. Another shot rang out. and a bloody patch spread slowly across the back of his overalls.

He fell forward, and slumped across the machine.

An older man stepped into the space between Dick and the vortex, with his back to the shell hole, and a smoking pistol in his hand. He reached out his right foot and kicked the overall-clad body away from the machine, then stared into the vortex.

The blonde girl pushed herself to her feet beside Dick. Her hair slapped against his arm as she peered through the gap in the rubble.

"Hitler," she muttered, and pointed at the man.

Could that grey-haired old fart really be the monster who'd dragged the entire world into years of war, and devastated most of Europe? And brought Dick all this way to Berlin?

The camel grunted and trudged across the rubble, passed the shell crater, and disappeared around the corner of the building. Dick watched as the old man stared at the desert through the vortex. The man's hand twitched where it gripped the gun. He was hunched over, and grey hair protruded from beneath a funny hat. He wasn't the Hitler Dick had seen in the newsreels, but, when a man has just lost his empire and is going to be hung by the Soviets if he survives that long, he probably doesn't look his best.

Dick pushed himself up over the edge of the shell hole. There were no more Nazis nearby. Just him and Hitler.

He raised the Schmeisser, and aimed at Hitler's back. Dick Beretta was about to make history, and there was no way he was gonna get suckered into a fair fight.

He pulled the trigger. The Schmeisser rattled, flames burst from the barrel, and the bullets punched red holes across the back of the man's suit. Blood flew through the air in front of the man, and splattered across the sand beyond the vortex.

He dropped the pistol, and collapsed among the debris. Dick dropped the Schmeisser, and punched the air. Then he grabbed the girl, stood on a rock to raise himself up to her height, and planted a big, slobbering kiss on her lips.

"I did it," he yelled. "I killed Hitler."

Dick Beretta—the boy who always wanted to be a Marine, but had been rejected for his height every time he applied, until Uncle Sam drafted him into the Army—would now go down in history as the man who killed Adolf Hitler. There would be ticker-tape parades in New York, girls would fight over him, and he wouldn't have to pay for a drink for the rest of his life.

<1>

Deep Space, Speer 8869 A.H.

The Pharaoh-size bed smelled of sweat and flowers beneath the pink sheets, and the thick straw mattress sank beneath Dirk Beretta's bare, muscular back as he reached out his arms, stretched, and yawned. Even though he was the tallest human on the Vixen College ship, his hands still didn't reach the edges of the bed from where he lay in the middle, with his head on the thick pillows, and full of pleasant, sweaty memories.

A cloud of hot, sweet-smelling steam oozed through the part-open doorway in the room's tan-coloured walls. The steam swirled in the air as the door opened wide, releasing the heat from the tub beyond. Bambi and her roommate Brazen stepped out, their naked bodies wrapped in damp white towels, and bulging and wobbling in all the right places as they moved.

Hot water from the tub dripped from their blonde hair, and ran down the perfectly tanned skin of their long arms and legs before it fell to the grey plasteel floor of their cabin. Shiny, gold microbots emerged from holes in the wall, and rushed around, cleaning it up.

"We're going for swim practise," Bambi said as she rubbed a second towel over her wet hair. "Why don't you join us there after breakfast?"

After two weeks on the Platypus Planet helping to move the platypoids' nest to a safer area, dividing his free time between Pokaplatus, Floozie, and sundry now-ex-maidens, even Dirk's nano-enhanced ex-Space Marine body was exhausted. He had almost been relieved when Bambi's ship arrived to give him a lift home... until he discovered that she and her Vixen College swim team friends had their own plans in mind for him.

Now he just hoped he would survive the trip.

But breakfast sure sounded good right now. After the rocket exhaust from Bastado's personal escape pod burned out much of the interior of his mining ship, *Pooper-Scooper*, and left Dirk and Floozie stranded on the Platypus Planet, they'd raided the ship's burned-out kitchen for supplies. But, after those ran out, Dirk had lived on leaves and jungle fruit for the last week.

He could kill for a bagel and cream cheese.

He climbed out of the bed, and lowered his feet to the floor, which was toasty from the under-floor heating. He flung his long, white toga over his naked body, then wrapped his sword belt around it. He'd used swords before, but he didn't recognize the short-bladed gladius hanging from his belt.

And he wasn't entirely sure how he knew that was what it was called. Thick black outlines of giant eagles with their wings spread and talons ready to strike were tattooed on his forearms, and he didn't remember doing that, either.

Had he done something he was going to regret, while he was drunk last night? The girls had fed him wine and grapes before bed, from what he could remember.

Which wasn't much.

He peered out of the doorway, into the corridor that led through the starship from the girls' bedrooms to the pool. Gold painted busts stood in alcoves between the doors. One of them was unlike the others, and he stepped out for a closer look. The other busts along the corridor were kind of ordinary-looking, distinguished men. But this one had piggy eyes, with small lips twisted into a sneer below a funny little moustache.

Dirk leaned closer, and checked the plaque.

Pharaoh Adolf I.

Why didn't he remember seeing that before? It didn't seem like the kind of thing he'd easily forget.

He wandered along the corridor to the kitchen, then peered into the fridge. He picked up a bagel and sniffed it. It didn't seem mouldy yet, but it wasn't as fresh as he would have liked. He should get the Robo-Baker to make some more next time he saw it. He sliced the bagel in half with the well-sharpened blade of his gladius, and dropped the slices in the toaster.

Then he poured himself a glass of mulled wine from the jug that was sitting on the stove. He sipped the warm, sweet-smelling liquid as he wandered along the corridor toward the starship's pool. Might as well see what was going on there while he waited for his breakfast.

Steamy heat and the burning stench of chlorine blasted his face as he stepped through the door to the pool room. Bambi and Brazen were swimming in the blue water. Half a dozen girls played volleyball in the sand that surrounded it. The rest of the college swim team lounged on blankets nearby.

Dirk looked from one Vixen College girl to the next, until he had seen them all. Then he looked at them all again in the opposite direction.

They were naked.

All of them.

Bambi swam to the edge of the pool, and put her hands on the marble tiles around the edge to support herself. Her chest rose out of the water as she stood. Water ran down her bulging chest, and dripped onto the marble from her bare breasts.

"Get that toga off, and join us."

"Are you sure? I mean, you're all... nude."

"We always train nude. You do too, don't you?"

Dirk frowned. What did he do? What would he train for?

He didn't remember anything about fighting naked, and it seemed a pretty dangerous idea. Far too many delicate parts of your body could get injured. But he didn't remember much of anything very clearly right now.

When he woke, he had been sure of who he was. But now?

"I don't know."

"Gladiators..." Brazen said. "He's been hit on the head too many times in the arena."

Was he a gladiator? He remembered fighting for a living, but where, and why? He examined his arms. Bulging muscles rippled under his skin as he flexed them. Perhaps he was. That could explain the tattoos.

Why couldn't he remember?

"Are you going to join us or what?" Bambi said. "I didn't think you'd be embarrassed by your body."

"I'm not embarrassed. I just don't feel right this morning."

"I'm not surprised, after the workout we gave you."

The other girls laughed.

Then a voice spoke inside Dirk's skull.

Dirk Beretta, come to me, now. The fate of the universe depends on you.

Swim practise and volleyball with a pack of naked college girls, or follow some weird voice claiming the universe needed him? What a decision for a man to make before breakfast.

Dirk turned toward the volleyball court and studied the girls' oil-covered bodies as they glowed in the light from the ceiling bulbs. As he watched their flesh wobble, he thought of what Brazen had said the previous night, about the tricks they could do that no normal girl could, because they had gills, and didn't need to breathe underwater.

Then he thought of the fate of the universe. It was a big place, with a lot of people, and he remembered travelling through much of it. And it had depended on him before.

But, somehow, he couldn't quite remember when or why.

Hurry, there is little time.

Dirk glanced toward a movement from the corner of his eye. That voice wasn't really inside his head. It was just a faint whisper from a guy who stood outside the pool room. He wore a black cloak and dark glasses, and was so short his head would barely rise above Dirk's waist. He waved a hand toward Dirk.

"Just a moment," Dirk said. "I think I must have left a bagel in the toaster."

"What's a bagel?" Bambi said.

"It's..." Dirk began. What was a bagel? The words were on the tip of his tongue, but wouldn't come out. "Something small and brown and crunchy. I think."

"Well, hurry up. After we finish our practise, we're having an orgy, and you're the only man on this ship."

"This won't take long."

"If you're not here, we'll just have to make do," Brazen said, then put her arm around Bambi's shoulders, and licked her ear.

<2>

Dirk strode out of the pool room. The girls' splashing and laughing faded as the glass door slid closed behind him, and he shivered in the cool air of the corridor after a few minutes in the heat around the steaming pool. His sandals clacked on the hard floor as he searched the corridor for the man.

This saving-the-universe crap had better be important, if it was going to tear him away from an orgy. He might be tired, but there were some things he would always find the energy for. He imagined a herd of happy bunnies bouncing along the corridor, and felt his chi power growing in his limbs.

The man peered out of the kitchen doorway, and waved his little hand in Dirk's direction.

"Hurry."

Enough with the damn hurrying everywhere. Just give him a relaxing cruise back to his girlfriend Felicia's villa, with no battles to fight, and no-one trying to kill him, and where he didn't have to do anything more stressful than keep a pack of naked, bisexual college girls happy.

Was that really too much for a man to ask?

He glanced into the kitchen. The toaster was on fire, and a mini-bot flew out of a hole in the wall, fluttered its shiny wings as it flew across the kitchen, and sprayed the toaster with fire-extinguishing foam until the flames went out.

But that wasn't the strangest thing going on. In the middle of the floor sat a metal box covered with switches, knobs and dials on the sides, and antennae on top. That hadn't been there when he left, had it? Or was it the microwave?

And even that wasn't the strangest thing. Two feet above the antenna, the air had warped into a whirling elliptical vortex, opening onto sand and blue skies. It looked rather like the pool room, just not so well maintained.

"What is this? Why did you drag me away from an orgy to show me a pile of sand?"

"Dirk Beretta, you must pass through this portal, and save history, for all mankind."

Giggles and moans floated toward them along the hallway.

"I'd rather pass through the door back to the orgy."

"You must right a great wrong committed by one of your distant ancestors."

"What did he do? Crap in the school sand pit?"

"This portal leads to ancient Egypt. In a moment, Adolf Hitler will step through another portal from 1945, bringing with him the secrets of future technology. He will take over the nation, become Pharaoh, wipe out the Jews, and conquer the world. History will be utterly changed."

"Who's Hitler?"

The strange man sighed, and shook his head. His face was turning red. "Did you see the gold bust with the stupid little moustache in the hallway?"

Dirk nodded. "Pharaoh Adolf I. I remember that much."

"That's him. Adolf Hitler began a vicious war that killed millions, hates people who make bagels, and wants to wipe them out. Does that help?"

"I guess. So Hitler is some asshole from this planet Egypt?"

The man sighed again, and rolled his eyes. "I guess that's close enough. Just remember that, if you fail to defeat him, you will never eat a bagel again. The historical changes your stupid ancestor triggered have been rippling through time for five thousand years, and have finally caught up with you. In just a few moments, the timeline conversion will be complete."

Whatever timeline conversion was, it didn't seem like such a bad idea, if it meant that Dirk would spend the rest of his life entertaining bisexual college girls. But naked sword fights? Not so much. Perhaps he'd better do this, for the sake of the body parts he'd prefer not to have hacked off.

"Watch," the man said.

The machine buzzed, and another portal opened. On the far side, Dick Beretta stood in the rubble of Berlin with a pretty blonde girl in his arms, and his lips on her face. He released her, picked up the Schmeisser that lay on the ground beside them, and strolled from the shell hole to the dead body of an old man, then rolled it over.

The man's face was wrinkled, clean-shaven, and smeared with blood. The eyes stared into the dark sky.

Dick said something Dirk couldn't understand, but he could tell it involved swearing in whatever language Dick spoke.

"Hitler! Hitler! Hitler!" the girl yelled, and pointed past the portal. "It's really him this time."

Her eyes bulged, and her mouth opened wide as a spray of blood spurted from a bullet hole in her chest. She fell backward into the shell hole.

Bullets hammered into the wall behind Dick. He dove to the ground, and fired randomly past Dirk's portal, in the direction the bullets were coming from. Then he began to crawl back to the shell hole.

Dirk peered around the edge of the portal, so he could see more. Two Nazi officers aimed guns in Dick's direction. An old man grabbed the officer's arm, and pushed the gun toward the ground. Dirk recognized him from the eyes, the crazy hair and the moustache.

Pharaoh Adolf.

Hitler pulled the officer's arm down. "Totenkopf, we cannot risk hitting the portal generator until we are through."

Another man joined them, carrying a briefcase, and a large green backpack. Another blonde girl, wearing a flowery dress and leading a big, grey dog, followed behind him. They strode through the rubble, toward the other portal.

"Why can't I just go through and stop him now?" Dirk said.

"This is a viewing portal. You can see them, but they cannot see us, and you cannot pass through. Besides, that would cause a temporal paradox even worse than we already face. Kill Hitler when he arrives in Egypt, and he will just be another nameless pile of bones in the desert, forgotten by history."

Dick watched from his shell hole as the Nazis approached the portal to Egypt. He raised his Schmeisser, but the officer turned and fired in his direction. Dick slid back into the hole.

Hitler spoke to Totenkopf, who raised his arm in salute, then led the group toward the other portal. Briefcase Man and the girl followed Hitler. The officer carrying the Schmeisser brought up the rear, covering them. Dick tried to get a clear shot, but bullets from the Nazi's guns hammered the debris around him whenever he raised his head.

They stepped through the portal. Hitler glanced back at Dick, then spat on the rubble. Dick peered out of the hole, and ducked back as the officer fired his Schmeisser through the portal at him. Briefcase Man reached back through the portal and grabbed the machine. As he leaned back into Egypt and flicked a switch on top of the machine, the portal shimmered, shrunk to a dot and vanished.

Dick leaned over the girl. He patted her face, but she didn't move. Dirk had seen enough dead bodies to know that she was one of them. Though there was that time with the renegade zombie army on Paradigm Three...

Dick lit a cigarette, stood, and looked around. He looked at the girl in the shell hole, then the dead body that had been by the machine. He looked at the building, where a jerrycan of fuel stood near the remains of a German car by one wall.

He dragged the man's body to the shell hole, and laid him beside the girl. Then he poured gasoline over the bodies, and threw his cigarette on top. Flames and smoke rose high into the air as the bodies caught alight.

"Why did he do that?" Dirk said.

"He will tell everyone Hitler and his wife killed themselves, and the Nazis burned their bodies."

"What's a Nazi?"

"Hitler's men. That's what they call themselves."

It was a dumb name. But he'd heard worse.

"Why would he lie about them burning the bodies?"

"Would you really want to be known as the man who let an asshole like Hitler escape?"

The man flicked a switch, and the portal to Berlin closed.

"Now, you must go. In a moment the temporal conversion will be complete, and you will not even remember why this mission is important."

He pulled a small, flesh-coloured metal disk from his toga and climbed up on a chair to attach it to Dirk's ear.

"This will translate Egyptian into German for you."

"But I don't speak German."

"What do you think you're speaking right now? The world has been speaking German since nearly two thousand years BC. Except it wasn't Before Christ, because the Egyptian Nazi Horde exterminated the Jews, and Jesus was never born."

"Who's Jesus?"

The strange little man slapped Dirk's back, and pushed him toward the portal to Egypt.

"Just go. Now."

<3>

The universe flickered as Dirk stepped through the portal. The whirs, clicks and beeps of the starship faded away. Hot sand crunched beneath his feet, and warm, dry desert air blasted his face. To his right, a man led a camel across the desert. Dirk waved at him. The man glanced his way, spat on the sand, then returned to pulling the camel's rope. The camel stopped and leaned back, and the man raised a stick and beat it on the ass. The camel grunted, leaned forward, and walked on.

Dirk suddenly realized that, in the rush to save the universe, he hadn't asked the strange man on the Vixen College swim team ship who he actually was.

Worse, Dirk hadn't asked how he was supposed to get back to the ship when the job was done. Maybe that would have been a good idea.

He turned to ask the man, but the portal back to the ship had disappeared. Bright yellow sand stretched out toward the horizon where the portal had floated in the air when Dirk stepped through it. The hot sun poured down on his body, and his exposed skin was already turning a deep brown. While he watched, the skin darkened further, until it turned almost black, as his bioengineered body adjusted itself to protect him from the strong ultraviolet light. The engineered lenses of his eyes darkened too, until they blocked out the worst of the glare.

With a familiar buzz, the air near the camel warped, and a portal opened. The portal was nearly sideways-on to Dirk, so he could see little through it. Camel Man stopped and stared into the hole in space. Then blood spurted from his head, and the crack of a pistol shot floated across the desert. The camel grunted, then rushed toward the portal. Another shot hit its leg before it disappeared through the vortex, and screams came from the far side.

Dirk strode across the sand toward the portal, taking care to stay behind it, so the bad guys wouldn't be able to see him when they came through. Blood spurted through the portal, and sprayed across the sand in front of it.

Yells and more gunfire came from the portal. Time must be running out. They'd be coming through it any second. Dirk stopped behind the portal. He could see straight through the air from that direction, as though the portal wasn't there. But they wouldn't see him when they stepped through.

A blob appeared in space, and grew rapidly into a severed hand holding a pistol, with red, bloody muscles around the truncated bone. A foot followed, hanging in mid-air for a second, then the rest of an arm and a leg joined them, followed by a plump torso that exposed the bloody mass of its internal organs to the world, until, finally, a complete man stood on the far side of the portal. Totenkopf looked around and waved his pistol in all directions. Dirk raised his arms, ready to pounce, before he remembered that the portal still hid him from view on the other side.

Totenkopf walked toward the dead man. Five more briefly dissected bodies appeared in front of Dirk, then became whole. Four human, and one canine. Another Nazi officer, Briefcase Man, Hitler, his girl and the dog.

They looked around the desert, and, for the moment, they couldn't see Dirk behind the portal. Hitler spat, and Totenkopf raised his gun toward Dirk's face, and fired. Dirk's heart jumped. They must have seen him there after all, and now the universe was doomed. But the bullet and Hitler's saliva vanished through the portal, instead.

Briefcase Man leaned into the portal, first exposing slices of his brain, then his lungs and intestines. He leaned back again, holding the machine, and flicked the switch.

The portal closed. Now Hitler stared straight at Dirk.

Dirk pointed his index finger at Hitler. "Stop right there, you bagel-hating bastard."

"What are you doing?" Hitler said.

"This is a laser."

"It is a finger," Hitler held up the fingers of one hand and wiggled them. "Finger, dummkopf."

"There is a laser in my finger."

Totenkopf stared at Dirk, but didn't raise the gun. Then glanced at Briefcase Man.

"Laser?" Hitler said. "What is a laser? Is this some kind of Jewish trick?"

Did they really come from a culture so backward that they didn't even know what a laser was? His first laser was a present on his third birthday, for hunting the mice in his uncle's barn. He'd always enjoyed the way they exploded when he shot them with it, or caught fire and ran around squeaking and trailing smoke until they fell over, dead. At least, he did until the day a burning mouse ran into the hay pile and set the barn alight. His uncle spanked his ass for that one.

"It's like a flashlight that fires a beam of light so bright that it burns. Now, put that gun down, or Adolf gets it right now."

Hitler shook his head, and pointed at Dirk. "Kill the stupid Untermensch. We have work to do."

Totenkopf raised his pistol. Dirk swung his finger toward the man and willed the laser to fire. His fingertip sizzled, smoke rose from it, then the maintenance light began to flash on his internal HUD.

Dammit, he'd been meaning to get that thing serviced for months. But when did he have time?

Totenkopf smirked, and fired.

Bullets slammed into Dirk's body.

Everything went black.

<4>

Pharaoh Khatty wriggled his ample ass on the hard, lumpy, straw cushion which separated his flesh from the wooden seat of the throne, whose back towered above his head, marking him as a child of the gods. His scraggly brown cat purred on the floor, and rubbed its tail around his feet. Khatty squealed as the fur tickled his skin, and pulled his legs up into the air until the cat settled down again.

He nervously scratched the arm of the throne, just to have something to do. Gold leaf had once covered the raised motifs of the gods' faces, and shone against the red paint. But his long fingernails had scraped most of the gold away over the years since he poisoned his father and became Pharaoh. Good years, but tiresome ones. Somehow, all the plotting to become Pharaoh had been much more fun than actually being Pharaoh.

Tall marble pillars flanked the dark, stone interior of the throne room. Busts of his ancestors lined the walls, and his guards stood at the far end, flanking the ornate doorway to the world of Egypt. Topless female slaves strolled across the throne room from side to side, out through the arches and back in again, carrying bowls of gold coins. Not because they needed to. He just liked to watch the glittering as the sunlight that oozed through the narrow windows reflected from the gold. His gold. The gold that could buy him anything.

If only he could think of something worth buying.

He scraped the throne again.

He hadn't had a good war with Thebes in months. No proper battles, just an occasional scrap on the border. The last plague of locusts was five years ago. The attempted slave revolt at the pyramid last week had been stopped in hours, with only a few hundred executions to entertain him.

What was the point of being Pharaoh, if you couldn't have any fun? Everyone expected him to tell them what to do, and he never got the time to just relax and enjoy himself.

A quiet cough distracted him. Oh, yes. Her again.

Bastet, his sister, lay prostrate at his feet beside the cat, where she had been for the last ten minutes with her bare chest pressed against the floor. He couldn't stand loud noise—it gave him the most horrible headaches—so she had been lying there silently all that time, not moving a muscle in case the rattling of her gold necklaces and bracelets upset him.

She stared at his bare feet, and whispered. "Why won't you marry me and make me your Great Wife?"

"Your sister is already my Great Wife."

"So?"

She had a point. Executing the wife had a certain appeal. It would definitely liven up the day, but it would be his third bloody divorce since he became Pharaoh, and he was worried that he was starting to get a taste for it. If he killed many more wives, he was going to run out of female relatives to marry.

Though, since they did little but nag him all day, that might not be such a bad idea. They couldn't do much nagging with their heads on spikes outside the palace.

"Not today," he said.

She raised her face far enough from the floor for her big brown eyes to stare up at his chest. "Then when?"

"Perhaps when the pyramid is complete."

Her round, red lips pouted at him. "I will be dead by then."

"If you continue to question me, that is quite likely."

"If you don't marry me and make me your Great Wife right now, I will never speak to you again."

Khatty frowned at her, and shrugged. She seemed to think that never talking to her would be a bad thing. He'd give his right ball for a few years of peace and quiet.

"I said..." she began.

"I heard what you said."

Her bare breasts wobbled as she climbed to her feet, the nipples big and stiff from being pressed against the cold stone floor. Then her high-heeled sandals stomped daintily across the throne room toward the door. Her shoulder slammed into the back of one of the slaves carrying gold. The slave gasped and tried to keep hold of her bowl as it wobbled in her grasp.

Then it fell, scattering gold coins across the stone floor. The noise echoed back from the walls, and the other slaves froze in place. The girl who had dropped the coins fell to her knees, and began to pile them back into the bowl.

The cat jumped to his feet, arched his back and hissed. Its claws dug into Khatty's foot, drawing blood.

Khatty yelled with the pain, then covered his ears against the echoes. He reached down and grabbed the cat. It continued hissing at the slave as he lifted it to his lap and stroked its back.

"You scared my pussy," he whispered.

The slave lowered her head, and lay almost flat on the floor. "I am sorry, master," she whispered. "It will not happen again."

Khatty stroked the cat, who began to purr on his lap.

Then he smiled. "No, it will not."

At last, thank the gods. Someone he could kill without any complaints from the family.

The guards had turned at the noise, and grasped the hilts of their swords. Khatty pointed toward the slave. "Take this one outside, and behead her. That will teach her to make noise in my presence."

A guard looked at him, then at the girl, then back at Khatty. "Me, sir?"

Khatty pointed to the nearest guard to his left. "Take both of these two outside, and behead them."

That guard didn't even think of arguing. He dragged the girl and the other guard out of the throne room.

"Please, Pharaoh, I have a wife, and six children," the ex-guard whispered. "They'll starve."

The slave shrieked and yelled at the top of her voice, until Khatty's head began to thump at the sound, and he stuffed his fingertips into his ears to block it out.

She *so* deserved to die.

He waited for the noise to fade away as the guard dragged them outside, then cradled the cat in his arms as he strode across the throne room to the balcony which overlooked the palace courtyard below, and the brown stones of the city beyond.

The city was silent. All he could hear was the faint hissing of the wind. Men and women tip-toed barefoot through the streets. The camels were muzzled, with cloth wrapped around their hooves, and their heads.

Khatty pushed his shoulders back, opened his mouth wide, and breathed in the refreshing silence. The thumping pain in his head slowed, and began to die away.

In the distance, the first few levels of his pyramid now rose above the city walls. Hundreds of slaves crawled over them, dragging stones up sand ramps so slowly they made no sound.

His overseers whispered orders to the slaves, then hit them with ostrich feathers that made far less noise than the whips he used to hear cracking across the sand as a child. Building the pyramid might take decades longer than the old methods, but it was better than decades of headaches from the bloody noise.

Guards dragged the man and girl into the courtyard below. The ex-guard was still yelling as they forced him down to his knees, and two guards held his arms so he couldn't move.

The guard that Khatty had made executioner pulled his sword from his belt. He raised it high above his head as the ex-guard yelled louder. Then he swung it downward.

The man's yells stopped, replaced by a crack as his head hit the stone floor of the courtyard, and rolled toward the gate. Blood spurted from his neck, and the other guards let the dying body fall to the ground. Khatty sniffed in a deep breath. He loved the smell of blood in the morning, that coppery tang that cleared your nostrils like nothing else.

The guards pushed the screaming girl to the ground.

Then loud cracks came from the front gate of the palace.

What in Ra's name was that about?

Guards screamed and shouted, and men yelled in a harsh, guttural tongue that Khatty had never heard before. Even the men of Thebes sounded better than that.

The cat squealed as Khatty dropped it, and covered his ears. How could his guards make such noise in his presence? He would have them all killed for making such a commotion. There would always be plenty more where they came from.

Men draped in grey cloth stepped through the gate, and the guards raised swords and spears toward them. The hands of the grey men boomed and spat fire, and the guards fell in pools of their own blood.

As the grey men advanced across the courtyard, an old man, a woman and a dog followed a safe distance behind them.

The greys' booming hands spat fire again, and Khatty's guards died, or turned and ran. The greys marched toward the palace. Khatty's bladder began to ache. He had to go to the bathroom. And, anyway, he didn't want to be standing in the throne room when the greys reached it.

He turned away from the balcony. The cat flailed its paws toward him, and he kicked it across the throne room. It slid across the slick stone floor, then jumped to its feet and ran for the doorway.

Booms and cracks echoed up the staircase from the hallway below, followed by loud screams. The greys were coming for him. His head was pounding again at the noise.

This wasn't fair. When he'd fought battles before, he stayed at the rear with his slaves, so he didn't have to hear the sounds of fighting, and the screams of soldiers dying.

Now, all the slaves stood as still as statues, listening to the fight down below.

"Protect me," Khatty yelled.

Some of the slaves ran for the steps. Others dropped their bowls, and cowered at the back of the throne room.

He would execute them all when this excitement was over.

Feet tapped up the steps. Khatty raced toward the throne. Perhaps he could hide behind it, and the greys would just take the gold and leave. They couldn't really mean to harm him. Not Khatty, the Pharaoh of Egypt. The gods would never allow it. He was of their blood, after all.

And relatives wouldn't kill their relatives.

Well, except for all the ones he'd had killed. But every one of them deserved it. What had he done to upset the gods?

He pressed himself close to the floor, until the stone sucked the heat from his body. He peered between the legs of the throne, beneath the cloth of gold that hung below the seat. Black shoes and grey trousers stepped into the throne room through the doorway, and the stomping soles echoed back from the walls. He pushed himself lower, and held his breath.

They greys barked like dogs. What were they saying? Were they they emissaries of Anubis, returned to Egypt? Perhaps they had come to reward him, not kill him? After all, he'd made his sister perform the rites of Anubis every year, to honour the god.

He'd enjoyed it, regardless of whether Anubis did.

He peered around the edge of the throne, and looked up. No, they were men, with human faces. They just sounded like dogs. His heart thumped as one of the slave girls pressed her bowl of gold against her cleavage, and pointed to the throne with her free hand.

Bitch. He'd have her executed by sunset. He'd have them all executed. They should have given their lives to save him, not helped the grey men to find him. He'd teach them not to rebel.

Two of the greys approached, their eyes flicking side to side as they moved, with scowls on their faces. His body shook with the noise as the stomps grew louder. He had to get away. But the only ways out were through the door, or over the balcony.

There were too many men between the throne and the door, and they held the booming, flaming sticks that they had used to kill the guards. There was only one way out.

This must be a test from the gods. They would give him wings to fly from the balcony, and he would return to smite the grey men in their name, and prove his divine nature.

He pushed himself to his feet. The grey men barked at him, and raised their sticks. He ran for the balcony. The sticks boomed. He squealed at the noise, covered his ears, and closed his eyes. Just a few steps, and he would be free.

Then something smacked into his ankle. His feet left the ground, and his body arced through the air. The gods were there, they were going to save him, and make him fly after all.

He smacked into the floor face-first. The world grew hazy as he raised his face from the stones, with blood pouring down his broken nose, and teeth rattling loose inside his mouth. He glanced behind him, where Baster held his right ankle.

"Perhaps we could marry after all," he tried to say, but all that came out was a spray of blood and teeth.

Baster smiled at him.

"I think I have a new Pharaoh to marry."

The grey men grabbed Khatty's arms, and dragged him back toward the throne. They tossed him to the floor as the old man shuffled toward them.

Khatty climbed to his knees, and lowered his head. "Please. I have gold," he muttered. "Take it, and let me go."

The greys barked at each other. Khatty covered his ears as his head pounded from the noise, and looked up at them. The old man barked back.

Then pointed his stick at Khatty's face.

It spat fire.

<5>

Hitler slumped down on the throne. A sense of relief flooded the muscles of his aching legs after all that shuffling across the desert sand, but the straw cushion was so hard and worn that the pain from his piles easily made up for it. He wasn't as young as he used to be, and his betrayal by the German people had taken a great toll on his health. If only that fucker Stalin hadn't vowed to make an ashtray from his skull, he'd have shot himself in Berlin, and be done with it. Those German cocksuckers didn't deserve a great leader like him. Let them chew on Stalin's kolbasa if they liked that Bolshevik bastard so much.

The heat was stifling, worse even than that fucking bunker in Berlin, and he was sweating like a pig. He grabbed the neck of his shirt, and pulled it forward, to try to get some air in there. He could feel sweat dripping down his back and arms, beneath the cloth. And he'd be able to smell it too, if this filthy, sand-strewn throne room didn't stink like someone had been raising goats in it. Fuck, they probably had.

Blondi lay on the stone floor beside the throne, her tongue dangling from her mouth as she panted in the heat. He should take the bitch for a walk, but his legs would have to recover first. He reached down and rubbed her between the ears. Then smiled for the first time since he arrived in this shitty place.

"At least you haven't deserted me," he whispered.

A brown-skinned girl crawled across the floor toward him, wearing only a loose skirt, with her tits swinging free below her chest. What did she think she was doing? Unlike the others, there were no chains around her ankles; she wore gold bracelets and necklaces instead. They rattled and clanked as she crawled toward the throne, then dropped to the floor at his feet.

She mumbled something as she lay there.

"What is she saying?"

"Jewish babble," General Totenkopf said.

The girl raised her head, smiled at him, and wiggled her chest, so her fat breasts swung from side to side like a pair of bulging, milk-laden udders. Then she pouted at him.

She babbled something else, winked, then licked her bright red lips with a long, wet tongue.

Then she screamed as Eva grabbed the girl's long hair, and heaved on it. The girl grabbed for Eva as her hair strained against her scalp. She continued screaming and writhing as Eva dragged her to a nearby doorway, stomping her feet on the stone floor for effect.

Eva yelled at her. "Leave my man alone, you bitch."

Speer unrolled a map of Egypt on the floor, beside the pool of blood and brains from the dead man. The corners of the map curled up, until Speer grabbed two half-full bowls of gold coins that lay on their side on the floor, and weighed down the map. Metal clinked as he dropped more coins into the bowls.

Hitler adjusted his glasses on his nose. His vision had been growing worse for years, and he could barely read the markings on the map. But he nodded as though he could. A Fuhrer should always look like he's in control, even if he isn't.

Speer ran his hand across the paper, along a wiggly curve that must be the shore of the Mediterranean, toward Sinai. He raised his voice over the yells, screams and thumps coming from Eva and the girl in the other room. "Here are rich deposits of iron and coal, well within reach of the technology of this time."

Hitler's hand shook as he leaned forward until he could see the map better. Pain stabbed his back, and he placed the hand on Speer's shoulder for support. "How do you know?"

"The British surveyed it before the war."

"Why do you think it is still there?"

"Mein Fuhrer," Speer said, with a sigh, "we are now four thousand years before the British ever reached Egypt. We will dig out the iron and coal, and build an army the like of which this world has never seen. In months, we will have rifles and tanks, take the oil fields of Arabia, and conquer Russia while it is still the land of barbarians wearing furs. In a year, we will begin to build a whole navy of ironclad steam ships. We will conquer America before it even is America. The world will be ours."

Hitler pushed himself to his feet, and rubbed his aching ass. His legs wobbled, and he leaned on the arm of the throne for support. Speer grabbed him, and helped him back to his feet. Hitler shuffled over to the balcony with Speer at his side, and stared out at the dead guards lying in pools of blood in the courtyard, and the half-finished pyramid rising above the palace walls. This rotten city smelled like a blocked, broken toilet after a bad wiener schnitzel. He wafted a hand in front of his face, but it merely moved the stench from one side of his head to the other. He held his nose, instead.

"Make me some tea."

General Totenkopf clicked his heels together and saluted. "At once, mein Fuhrer."

"There is no tea," Speer said.

"No tea? What kind of stinking cesspit did we come to?"

The screams grew louder. The girl with the golden bracelets clawed at the stone floor of the throne room as she tried to pull herself through the doorway on all fours. Eva yelled and lunged forward, grabbed the girl's legs, and pulled her back.

"Tea comes from China," Speer said. "There will be no tea again, until we conquer China."

"China," Hitler said, and huffed. "I can conquer a shit-hole like China with two platoons of SS."

"They would take a year just to walk there."

"What about Rome?" Totenkopf said.

Rome. Now that would be a worthy enemy. Or ally, if the greasy fuckers didn't change sides this time.

"Why did you not take me to Rome? Rome has eagles, and gladiator battles, and giant legions. Rome conquered the world. Egypt has stinking Arabs... and Jews."

Speer leaned on the balcony rail beside him. "The Roman Empire will not begin for another two thousand years. It will not begin at all, now we are here. Italy will become just a small part of the German Empire."

Hitler slapped his hand down on the rail. Rome might have been full of Italians, but it would have smelled less bad than...

Wherever they were.

An olive-skinned, raven-haired slave girl approached them, shaking and looking down, as she held out a bowl of grapes.

Totenkopf stared at the girl as she stopped beside them. She glanced up as he reached out slowly, and took a grape from the bowl. As her eyes met his, she pouted, and looked down again. Then glanced up at Totenkopf as he ate.

Will that man never stop leching? Eva had spent half her time in the bunker complaining about Totenkopf hitting on the girls they'd taken down there to do clerical work. But at least they'd been good Aryan stock. Not these Untermensch.

Speer grabbed a handful of grapes from the girl's bowl, and tossed one into his mouth. "Mein Fuhrer, you will have legions, and gladiators."

"What about eagles?"

"You can have eagles, if you like."

Hitler glared at the slave. That nose alone marked her as one of the undesirables. "And the Untermensch?"

Totenkopf interrupted. "We came here to exterminate them before they can bring down the Reich." His fingers tapped his pistol. "I will start with this one."

"They are already enslaved," Speer said. "They will work for us to build the new Reich. It is a fitting fate."

"Then we will kill them?" Hitler said.

"Of course we will kill them," Totenkopf said. "We must eliminate them now, every last one of them, before they can spread across the world. We should not make the same mistake we did last time. Not one of the vermin can survive."

Speer scowled at him. "Mein Fuhrer, we will need many, many workers if we are to conquer the world. Millions of them, working in the factories day and night."

Hitler sighed, and rubbed his chin. The rough bristles scraped against his fingers. He really needed a shave. But Speer was right. The Jews would serve the Reich until they were no longer needed, then they would be exterminated. It was only fitting that those who had destroyed the Third Reich would be instrumental in building the Fourth.

Although, in this world, perhaps it would be the First.

He nodded. "You will have your workers, Speer."

Eva stepped up beside them, rubbing her hands together and flexing her muscles. She wiped blood from her knuckles onto her palm, then wiped that on the railing. "Where's the pool?"

Ah, dear Eva, always the swimmer. "There is no pool, my little sauerkraut."

"I want a pool. And I want it now."

Totenkopf huffed. "We're in a desert. Where do you expect to find a pool?"

Hitler peered out past the half-constructed pyramid, and across the desert. Sunlight glinted from a river in the distance, beyond the city walls. Masts moved slowly along it, where boats were sailing. How could he deny her a pool, when water was so close? Bringing it to the city may be hard, but doing the impossible was what he brought Speer with him for in the first place. If not for that, he'd have executed the insolent little shit years ago.

"My sweet leberknödel wants a pool. She will have a pool by tomorrow morning."

"I'll see to it," Speer said, with a sigh.

<6>

Everything was still black. Dirk's body burned, and his skin was covered with sweat, but his forehead still felt cool. He could hear faint music, and smell things he wasn't sure he wanted to smell. Several seemed to involve camels, so he was pretty sure he wasn't in Heaven. But, from the smell, he couldn't be so sure that he wasn't in Hell.

People were mumbling somewhere, but he couldn't make out the words. He seemed to be lying on something soft that crunched below his back as he breathed. He stretched out his fingers beside him, and scraped them against the ground.

Sand. He should have guessed that much.

He opened his eyelids, and stared into the shadows above him. A pair of pretty green eyes in a brown face hung a few inches above his own. A young woman, no older than the swim team girls, held a wet towel against his forehead.

He glanced down at his black-skinned body. He was naked, and the girl was topless. Not that he was going to complain about either of those things. Particularly not about both of them happening at the same time.

Her breasts pressed against his chest as she leaned forward and ran the cloth over his face. She mumbled a few words in a language Dirk didn't understand, but glowing, green subtitles appeared in his HUD.

Dammit. He'd always hated subtitles. Couldn't the strange man who sent him there at least have programmed his translator to convert the sound of her voice into German?

"You are alive."

"I hope so."

The girl shook her head. "I'm sorry, but I don't understand. Do you speak Egyptian?"

"I guess not," Dirk said. The crappy translator must be one way, unable to translate his own speech to hers. If the fate of the universe really depended on Dirk, the strange man could at least have spent a few bucks on a proper translator. The more time Dirk spent on planet Egypt, the more this whole thing felt like a put-up job to get him off the ship. Maybe the strange man was hoping that, with Dirk gone, he'd be the only one the girls could invite to their orgies. But he was a bit short for the job.

"We found you in the desert. You have been asleep for weeks. We thought you would die, but your body healed."

Dirk nodded, slowly. The bullets might have put him down, but his bioengineered body had retained the greatly increased powers of regeneration the medics had built into him during his years in the Space Marines. Bullet wounds would heal, so long as they didn't hit something vital enough to kill him first.

"You are Nubian, I think," she said.

Dirk tried to connect his skulltop computer to *Infogalactic* to see whether it had any idea of what she was talking about, but the computer found no wi-fi signal. Planet Egypt must be even more primitive than it first appeared.

He settled for nodding. Whatever a Nubian was would be easier to explain than who he really was, and where he really came from. Particularly when he didn't speak the language.

She leaned closer. "An escaped slave?"

Dirk shook his head. As much as he needed a cover story, he would be slave to no man.

A woman, maybe.

She frowned. "I am sorry. I had hoped you might be able to help us escape from this place."

"I don't even know where I am."

The girl might not understand his language, but she seemed to understand what he meant. She leaned back, and her breasts wobbled as she moved. They were bigger even than Brazen's, nicely rounded, and tanned from the sun. But, despite those distractions, Dirk still had a job to do, if he could just remember what it was. Something about chasing some asshole.

Ah, that was it.

"Adolf."

"Your name?"

Dirk shook his head. He held two fingers against his lip like Hitler's moustache, and tried to replicate the salute he'd seen the men giving in Berlin.

The girl suddenly smiled, and nodded.

"The new Pharaoh? He killed the old Pharaoh just before we found you, and announced he is in charge." Then she pouted, and shrugged. "Life was much better under the old Pharaoh. They didn't use real whips on us back then, they just pretended, because he didn't like all the noise. Now, if any of us don't do what they say...." she swung her arm as though she was swinging a whip. "Crack."

Dirk looked around the room. His back was on a pile of straw in a rough hut lit by a few small oil lamps. The first hint of sunrise was beginning to appear at the open window.

"We are building pyramids," she said.

Dirk shook his head. What did she mean?

The girl made a triangle with her fingers. "Mountains of stone. The old Pharaoh was supposed to be buried in it, but now I guess the new Pharaoh will be. He's so old already."

Her arm barely seemed large enough to lift a single stone, let alone a mountain. Dirk flexed his arm muscle, and tapped his hand against it.

She blushed, and looked away. "No, I don't carry stones. I cook and carry, and... serve... the overseers."

Being an overseer wouldn't be all bad, if she was a perk of the job. But Dirk had a mission. He tried to push his body up from the straw, but, as he raised his head, the world twisted and wobbled around him, and he dropped back.

"You have hardly eaten in weeks. We hid you here from the overseers, and fed you whatever you might eat in your sleep. I am amazed you survived so long."

She stood and strode to the door. Her long, dark hair banged against her back and the short loincloth twisted over her ass as she moved. A few moments later, she returned, and handed a round, brown object to Dirk. She held more.

"These are called bagels. Eat them, and start to build up your strength again."

<7>

The next morning, the girl led Dirk around the Pharaoh's slave camp, as the early morning sun cast a golden glow over the sand. The sun was only a finger's width above the horizon, but the searing glow was already roasting Dirk's skin. It would be hell by noon, when the sun was directly overhead.

The girl had returned late the previous night, tired and sweaty, then slept beside him until breakfast. She wore only sandals and a loincloth, which swung behind her as she walked, exposing her ass as it moved. She'd found him the same to wear, to keep the sun and hot sand off his most vulnerable parts. Which it barely did, as the loincloth was obviously made for someone much smaller than Dirk's hard-muscled body. Just about everything swung beneath the loincloth as he moved.

Rough leather tents and mud huts stretched from the river on one side of the walled camp to a half-finished stone pyramid about a kilometre away on the other. Wood creaked quietly as a shallow boat sailed past the camp on the glittering water of the river, and the boat's tall, white sail twisted in the wind.

The slaves ate outside their tents and huts, and pulled their ragged clothing on for the new work day. Overseers with long, dark whips wearing sandals and cleaner clothes patrolled through the camp. Swastikas were crudely inked on their shirts, like the Nazi flags he'd seen in Berlin.

Slaves and overseers were already scuttling over the sides of the pyramids, and the long, tall sand ramps that led up to them. When a man fell behind the others, an overseer cracked his whip. Most of the men ran at the noise, but that one slumped down onto the ramp. The overseer whipped the man's back until blood ran into the sand, then kicked him over the side of the ramp. The man fell, bounced off the side of the pyramid, and became a red splat on the sandy rocks below.

These Nazi overseers weren't nice people. No wonder they worked for a bagel-hating asshole like Hitler.

Dirk tapped the girl's arm so she looked at him, then he pointed at his chest.

"Dirk."

"Your name?"

He nodded.

She pointed at herself. "Nefert."

An overseer with a crocodile tattooed poorly on his arm cracked his whip beside a family eating bagels outside a tent.

"Eat faster. Pyramids don't build themselves."

Dirk and Nefert approached the tattooed overseer, who cracked his whip between two kids sharing a bagel. Dirk tried not to look at the man. He needed to find out what Hitler was up to here on planet Egypt, not get into a fight.

The overseer stared at Nefert's body as they passed.

His whip cracked.

"You," he said.

Dirk stopped. He tensed his body, and thought of cute little gerbils and hamsters running across the sand with lettuce in their mouths. He felt a faint hint of chi power building in his muscles, ready to smash the overseer's bones if he had to fight.

He turned. The overseer strode toward them, taking time only to push a young boy off his mother's lap as he passed by. The boy smacked face down into the sand, and cried.

The overseer flicked his whip toward Nefert, and rubbed his loincloth. "I have something down here for you."

Nefert nodded and stepped toward him. He put his arm around her shoulder, and pushed her toward a nearby tent.

Dirk tapped the overseer's shoulder.

When the man turned, Dirk punched him in the face. The overseer's nose cracked as Dirk's knuckles smashed it flat, and the man slumped back against the tent.

"Leave her alone."

The overseer swung his arms wildly, until he grabbed the side of the tent. He pulled himself back up to his feet. Blood dripped down his top lip from his nose. He wiped it away, then flashed Dirk a twisted smile.

Dirk raised himself to his full height, at least a foot taller than the overseer.

The overseer raised his hand to try to hit Dirk with the whip. Dirk's own hand flew out, grabbed the whip and pulled it from him, tossing it to the ground behind him. He didn't need a weapon to fight a lowlife who'd take advantage of a sweet girl like Nefert.

The overseer grabbed Dirk's arm. Dirk wrapped his fingers around the overseer's forearm, twisted it, and threw him to the ground. The overseer landed face-down, and Dirk put a foot on his back.

"No," Nefert said, and grabbed his other arm. "If you fight, they will kill you."

The overseer raised his face and smiled at her, revealing the few rotting, yellow teeth he had left.

"Besides," she whispered, "I know this man well. Trust me, serving him will not take long."

More hands grabbed Dirk from behind, and pulled him away from Nefert. Three more Nazi overseers held his arms, and pulled him back. He struggled to haul his arms away from them, but his body was still too weak, and his muscles lacked their normal strength.

The tattooed overseer stood, spat out a broken tooth, and chuckled. He put one hand on Nefert's waist, and swung a punch with the other. Dirk dodged, and the blow smashed into another overseer's face behind him.

"Dumb Nubian," the overseer said. "I got better things to do, anyhow."

He pulled Nefert's loincloth from her hips, and tossed it onto the sand. Then pushed her on, naked, toward the tent. A woman and child sat inside, and they hurried out. The overseer lifted the door flap and pushed it aside.

He smirked as he pulled aside the front of his own loincloth. "Your boyfriend can watch." He turned to Nefert, then smiled a crooked, lecherous smile. "Just for him, we do it camel-style."

Nefert got down on her hands and knees inside the tent, and frowned. The overseer crouched behind her.

"What is this?" a voice said from behind Dirk.

A brown-skinned man wearing grey shorts and a jacket that looked like a rough approximation of the Nazi officer's uniform from Berlin strode through the camp. A dozen men followed, wearing bowl-like metal helmets, and carrying crude rifles.

The overseer stood. and adjusted his loincloth. "I was just showing the Nubian how to treat a woman right."

The officer glanced into the tent. "Pharaoh has issued new orders. Work on this pyramid will stop. Send the women and children to the factories, and the men to the mines." He stared at Dirk. "If this Nubian has too much energy, the coal mines will make good use of it."

Nefert glanced toward Dirk, and her eyes grew wide at the news. The overseer slapped her bare ass and cackled. "Don't worry, Nubian. I will keep your girlfriend warm for you."

<8>

Dirk swung the rough stone hammer at the dark wall in front of him, in the dim light of the candles that filled the hot, clammy air with thick clouds of black smoke that smelled like burning pigs. The stone wall crunched as the hammer landed, cracking the crunchy black rock, and throwing a cloud of dust into the air. The impact broke away chunks of rock that slid to the floor of the tunnel. He grabbed the lumps of black rock, and tossed them into a cart alongside him. They smacked down onto the pile he had already built up there on this long shift.

The temperature was high on the surface, but, down in the mine, with almost no ventilation and the sweat of a thousand men in the air, he was glad his engineered body could survive extremes of climate which would kill many of the natives. Since he now spent most of the day in the depths of the mine, and was outside it only at night, his skin had reverted to his natural colour. But, with a thick layer of black dust ground into it from work underground, he barely noticed the difference.

A whip cracked, and slammed into his back. It would have cut a gouge in the flesh of a normal man, and made him scream for his mother, but the rock dust absorbed much of the impact, and Dirk's bioengineered skin merely winced beneath it.

"Enjoy your work like I enjoyed your woman," the overseer said. "She was better than any camel."

Dirk glared at the man. Surely he must be joking about the camel? No, with a face like his, it might have been all the action he could get, before the Pharaoh gave him a swastika shirt, a whip, and the power to take any slave girl he fancied.

In the weeks Dirk had worked in the mine, he had learned to speak enough Egyptian to get by, and attempted to find out why the Nazis had sent them there. What he had learned did nothing to make him like the overseer more. The man's name was Seth, and his broken nose had healed into a twisted, flat mess three times as wide and a fraction as long as it had been before Dirk broke it. Seth's snorting breath and twisted laughter echoed along the dark tunnel as he strolled away, randomly whipping the backs of other men as he did so.

Dirk continued hammering until he could no longer see Seth. Then he crouched. He'd found a lump of flint among the rocks outside, and used any spare moments he could find where no overseers were nearby to turn it into a weapon. He carefully knocked a few more chips from the edge, then pressed it against his palm to test the sharpness. The rounded end of the rock felt good in his other hand, and would make a decent handle. The blade would soon be sharp enough to cut deep into a human body. He was used to shredders, lasers, or planet-busting nukes, but any weapon was better than none.

The overseers blew whistles.

About time.

Dirk dropped his hammer, and joined the long line of slaves shuffling toward the entrance, crouching low in the tunnel whose roof barely reached his shoulders. Another line of slaves crept in the opposite direction, entering the mine to take their place for the next shift.

"What we do this for?" Dirk said, in Egyptian.

"We dig up rocks that burn," the man ahead of him said.

"Rocks don't burn. That stupid."

"What they say, we do, or they hit us. If they say rocks burn, rocks burn." The man glanced over his shoulder at Dirk. "You want to get hit?"

"I want to kill Pharaoh."

The man sniggered. "I want to get out of here and eat. I hear we might get a bit of dog in the pot today."

"Me Dirk," Dirk said. He would need to find some men to help him escape and kill Hitler, and this was as good a time as any to start finding them.

"Thoth. You Nubians have strange names."

The line shuffled forward. The men leaving the mine stared at the ground as they moved, most of them probably thinking of little more than their next meal. The men of the new shift coming in the opposite direction didn't look much better.

The line emerged into the fading daylight. Dirk's stomach rumbled as he watched the girls preparing stew around the fires on the sand, and the line of men turned in that direction. Ahead of them, the first few hundred men had already collected a small bowl of food, and slumped down to eat it.

Thoth waved toward another man who walked past them.

"Osiris. Where you been?"

Osiris joined the queue beside them, and smirked. "Digging grave pits out by the cliffs."

"Lucky dog. Give my right ball for a cushy job like that."

Osiris stretched his arms. "Fresh air, plenty of work. On good days, they're even dead before we bury them."

"What if not dead?" Dirk said.

"The overseers hit them until they stop moving. Easier for us, better for them, Don't want to be burying them alive."

How much longer would Dirk last if he failed to escape from the mines? How long before he became too weak to work, and was thrown in the pits? How long before Osiris was burying him? A week? A month?

He waited to collect his food. A wild dog howled. There seemed to be fewer around the camp than he had seen in earlier days. Perhaps even they had tired of the food.

At the canteen tent, a pregnant slave girl poured water into his bowl, with a few lumps of dark, fatty, meaty stuff floating on top. A short, wide man with muscles the size of tree trunks, stood beside the tent with his arms crossed and whip ready. Ammon, the head overseer. Too tough for Dirk to fight. Yet.

Dirk, Thoth and Osiris found a spot to sit as far as they could from the overseers. At the far side of the mine, a caravan rolled in from outside the camp. One overseer prodded another, and they strode across the sand as the carts slowed and stopped. Dirk chewed on a lump of what he hoped was, at worst, dog meat, and watched them. Seth pulled a topless girl from the back of one of the carts.

Could that be Nefert? Dirk stared as Seth threw her over his shoulder, then turned around. No, her hair was too long, her chest too flat, and her face too young.

The overseers swore at each other for a moment, then one of them grabbed the girl's arms, pulled her away from Seth, and led her to a hut. More overseers approached the cart convoy, removing men and girls from the carts, and lining them up.

"How many overseers you think are?" Dirk said.

"Two dozen, maybe three," Thoth said.

"And slaves?"

"Lots."

Dirk was going to suggest about five hundred, but he didn't know the words. Besides, would any slaves know how to count that high? Lots was enough.

He finished the bowl of water with chewy lumps. So far, his body's engineered regeneration was working faster than it was decaying from lack of food. He was stronger now, and would soon be ready to make his move. If he didn't, in a few days, he would be past his peak, and would become a starving weakling like some of the other slaves, struggling to survive just one more day before the overseers threw him the grave pits.

But he couldn't beat dozens of overseers and soldiers by himself, with just a sharp stone to fight them. He had to find help, and needed a plan for what the slaves would do after they escaped. He had to find Hitler and kill him, then return planet Egypt to its rightful owners. Whoever they might turn out to be, by the time the war was done.

Three overseers led the newly arrived men toward the mine. Others picked girls from the line, and led them to the tents.

"I'd kill for some of that," Thoth said.

"Try it, and the overseers will kill you," Osiris said.

The men were thin from over work and under eating, but perhaps a few dozen working together could have a chance, if they had some brains behind them.

"Serious about killing for girls?" Dirk said.

Thoth scoffed. "What chance do we have against those overseers? Maybe if every one of us joined together we could beat them, but just a few? They'd kill us one by one."

"Got a good job," Osiris said. "No need to fight."

"Until throw you in grave pit," Dirk said.

Osiris shrugged. "Happens to everyone soon enough."

"Not me."

"It will very soon, if you pick a fight with the overseers."

Dirk's integrated weaponry still needed a service, and wouldn't be much help. But they had other options. There were at least ten times as many slaves as overseers, and, with only whips and swords against them, the odds of success were much better than they would have been when fighting against the kind of weapons he was used to. Ten sick men with knives and rocks could kill one fat, happy overseer with a sword, if Dirk could get everyone to join him.

"If we start fight, others might join."

A man sitting in a group nearby turned toward them. "If they saw us winning, maybe. If we were losing, they would hang back so they wouldn't be killed too."

Grunts and moans floated across the sand from the tents. "You fight them, I'll take care of the girls," Thoth said.

"Given me idea," Dirk said.

Thoth chuckled, then stared at the tents. "Those girls give me plenty of ideas."

"No. Listen..."

<9>

Dirk crawled through the sand in the faint moonlight, away from the fires near the mine entrance. To his eyes, with his augmented Space Marine vision, the desert night seemed almost as bright as day. To the Egyptians, it would barely be enough to see by whenever they moved more than a few metres from those fires. The overseers who ventured further afield were easy to spot by the light of the burning torches they carried through the darkness.

At least a dozen overseers were occupied with the girls in their tents near the edge of the camp. The miners were sleeping on whatever piece of sand they could find, for the few hours before their next shift began. More overseers patrolled between them in the narrow, yellow ovals of torchlight, but they were fat, lazy, and inattentive. If Dirk's plan worked, that would be the very last mistake they made... but, for now, they would live to see another day.

He'd been watching them for a couple of hours since the sun set. Studying their patterns, learning their procedures, to the extent they had any. Security at the camp was hopeless, and relied on whips and fear keeping the slaves in line.

And sun. And sand.

Which were the only things they really needed to stop any slaves escaping from their clutches.

He could just crawl past them, and out into the desert. But then what? All he could see around the mine were sand, rocks, and more sand. He had no idea how far the nearest town might be, or in which direction. If he tried to escape the mine alone, with only what he carried, some historians would dig up his bones thousands of years in the future, and puzzle over the high-tech gadgetry they found buried inside his ancient body.

Two overseers strolled across the desert. Dirk stopped, and pressed himself flat against the ground as they approached. Their feet crunched across the sand barely five feet ahead of him as they passed him in the night, then strolled away.

He waited for them to reach a safe distance before he crossed their path and risked crawling toward the tents beyond. He avoided the tents with the loudest grunts and squeals, didn't even want to know why barking and howling was coming from another, and aimed for the one from which he could hear loud snoring. He wasn't likely to find any opposition there.

The squealing stopped in the tent to his left. The flaps opened, and Seth stepped out, adjusting his loin cloth. He strode across the sand back toward the camp, passing another overseer on the way, even shorter and fatter than he was.

"How's the new girl?" the overseer said.

"Worth the wait," Seth said.

"Maybe I'll give her a try."

"I'd do it now, while she's still tight."

The overseer chuckled. "Good point. New ones never are for long, are they?"

Seth disappeared past a sand dune, and the other overseer stepped into the tent. Dirk rose to a crouch, and crept across the sand toward the snoring. He needed to talk to a girl, and at least he knew someone was in there.

He grabbed the tent flap and raised it. He stared into the face of an overseer, eyes closed in sleep, and snoring like a hog.

A girl lay naked beside him, on her side, facing away. Dirk knelt and put his hand over her mouth. She squealed as she woke, but his hand blocked the sound. She shook her head, and twisted it toward him.

"Nefert," he said in a low whisper, and pulled his hand back.

"You are alive. I had no idea you were here."

"Alive for now. Won't for long, if don't get out of here. Need your help."

"What can I do?"

"Few men can't fight dozens overseers. Girls distract them, can kill others, take weapons, get other miners join fight before overseers react."

"When?"

"Tomorrow night, when moon above sand. Will begin dealing with overseers, kill them, ready men to fight, soon as you distract others."

Nefert nodded. "We can do that. I will tell every girl I see."

Dirk reached down to his loincloth and pulled out his flint knife. He held it out to her. He would find himself a real weapon once the fighting started.

"Perhaps you help fighting too."

Nefert took the knife, hefted it in her hand, then smiled. She glanced toward the sleeping overseer.

"If we have a means to fight, we will put these pigs out of our misery."

<10>

Dirk swung the stone pick, dug more chunks of black rock from the walls of the mine, and piled it up in the cart. He wiped the sweat from his face, but it did nothing to clear the smoky, sweaty stench from his nose. He wished he had a better means of picking the time for battle than moon rise, but his skulltop computer still thought he was in deep space in the far future, and had no idea what the time was on planet Egypt, or when the moon would come up. For his plan to work, he needed to be out there, ready to strike, when the time came.

A whip cracked behind him, and one of the miners grunted as it slapped across his back. Seth had returned for a patrol through the tunnel. Dirk had a few scores to settle with him that night, if Nefert didn't get to him first.

"It's another lovely day in the mines," Seth said, and whipped a passing miner. "A day in the mines is like a day in the steaming pits of the Netherworld, being shit on from the divine assholes of the gods."

For now, Seth could be useful. Dirk raised his pick and swung it at the wall again. More crunchy black rocks fell, and he threw them into the cart. The whip cracks moved closer as Seth approached. Just let him follow his usual routine...

"Work hard, Nubian, like your girlfriend did last night. She'll be walking crooked this morning."

The whip cracked again, and smacked into Dirk's back, tearing away skin. He dropped the pick and fell forward, then lay on the floor of the tunnel, groaning.

"Tired, Nubian? I have a way to wake you up."

The whip cracked on Dirk's back again. He twitched and groaned. Seth whipped him again. And again. And again.

Then he laughed. He kicked Dirk's side.

Dirk lay there, as motionless as he could, despite his great urge to lunge upward and rip Seth's head from his body. It would be satisfying... for a few moments, until the rest of the overseers ganged up and killed him.

"Not so tough now, are you, Nubian?" Seth said. "Looks like we've got another one for the grave pits."

Seth pointed the whip at Thoth, then at the slave beside him. "You and you. Dump this garbage in the grave pit. I'll let his girl know where to find him when I'm done with her."

He whipped once more, then continued along the tunnel, laughing and whipping as he went.

"Which of you slackers wants to join him?" he yelled.

Thoth and the other slave grabbed Dirk's arms. They grunted and struggled against his weight as they tried to lift him from the ground. Dirk tried to help by pushing a little with his legs, but not enough to give away his real condition.

"You're not dead, are you?" Thoth whispered.

"How you guess?"

"What are you doing?"

"Be ready for fight."

"Now?"

"When time right, you know. Tell everyone."

They dragged him out of the tunnel. Golden light shone across the sand as the sun sank toward the horizon. They panted and groaned as they dragged him toward the pits.

"Stop," a voice boomed. Dirk wanted to look, but would give himself away. He let his head slump down.

"What are you doing with him?"

"Overseer Seth told us to take this sack of garbage to the grave pits," Thoth said.

"Seth is dumber than a camel, and this man looks as strong as one," the voice said. "Let me see."

Something grabbed Dirk's hair and pulled his head up. He relaxed his muscles, playing dead.

Then something hard poked his eye.

"Ow," Dirk said and pulled his head back. He looked into Ammon's smiling face.

"Not so good at pretending," Ammon said.

"We thought he was dead," Thoth said. "He fooled us."

"A blind camel could fool you slaves." Ammon pointed at two nearby overseers. "You two. Take this fool slave to the punishment ground." He turned to Thoth. "Think yourself lucky you're not going with him."

The overseers grabbed Dirk's arms.

"Heavy bastard, ain't he?" one of them said.

Dirk stood. If he was going to be punished, he'd take it like a man. As they led him away, he winked at Thoth. The others had better be ready when the time came.

The overseers led him past the staring eyes of the crowd of slaves eating outside the mine, toward the girls' tents. Dirk smiled. If the overseers were trying to help him, they couldn't do much better than that.

They pulled off his loincloth, then pushed him down onto his back, near a set of large wooden stakes buried deep in the sand. Dirk whistled to himself as the overseers tied his arms and legs to them. More stakes stretched out across the sand nearby, but he would have been happier if two sets weren't tied to the yellowed bones of dead men, gnawed into and smashed open by animals, then blasted by the sand.

"Now what?" he said as they tied the final cord from the stakes around his ankle. and pulled until it dug into his skin.

"If you're lucky," the overseer said, "the boss may let you go in a day or two." He nodded at the bones. "If the dogs don't eat you first."

"They usually start with the tender parts, if you know what I mean," the other overseer said.

The overseers chuckled as they strolled toward the mine.

Dirk lay back, and looked for dogs. So far they were still hanging around the food tent, but, when the food ran out, they might come looking. That was an unexpected problem.

"Hello there," a voice said.

Overseer Seth strode across the sand toward him.

"Oh boy, did I catch some shit from the boss for that one. Pretend to be dead so you can try to escape. Very funny."

"No more than deserve."

"Your girl's gonna get a good rogering for that one. Her butt will ache tomorrow."

Dirk struggled against the cords. The stakes creaked, but held him tight.

Seth stared up at the sun. "Bet you're getting hot out here."

The sand was warm against Dirk's back, and the sun was shining brightly on his skin, but his body had quickly adjusted again, and was now almost as black as it could go. The heat would have killed a normal man after after a day or two, but he would last longer than that.

"Been worse."

"Well, let me cool you down," Seth said. He lifted up his loincloth, and began to pee.

<11>

The sun sank slowly toward the horizon, and the dunes turned an even brighter shade of orange than they were during the day. The cool night air chilled Dirk's skin as the shadows spread across the sand, and reached out across his bare body. The sun had dried up the urine, but he was definitely going to kill Seth the next time he saw the man.

When was the moon going to rise? And how would he get away? He'd tried pulling on the stakes, but they were solidly buried. If any stakes had been loose enough for normal human strength to pull out, the earlier prisoners had probably found them long ago, and they'd been replaced after the escapes.

He grunted as he heaved on the leather cords. They dug into his wrists, and the stakes strained. Sweat dripped down his forehead, and into his hair. But the stakes held. He slumped back on the sand. Besides, if he escaped too quickly, they would just tie him up again. He needed to be ready, not to run away.

The wild dogs were keeping their distance, but creeping closer. Half a dozen of them watched him from the dunes.

Another padded toward him across the sand, taking long, slow steps, pausing to sniff and stare between each movement.

"Get away," Dirk yelled. "Not dead yet."

The dog turned and trotted away. But they would probably become more adventurous after dark.

With nothing better to do, Dirk watched the sun disappear behind the dunes. A scorpion crawled across his face, snapped its claws in front of his eyes, then crawled off again. A gerbil hopped across the sand, and stared at Dirk with its bulbous black eyes. Dirk took a deep breath, then blew sand toward it, but it dodged out of the way.

"How's it going?" the gerbil said.

"Could be better."

The gerbil hopped around him.

"Got any seeds?"

"Don't have pockets."

The gerbil hopped onto Dirk's shoulder, then onto his chest. It sat up on its back legs, and stared into his face.

"What are you doing here?"

"Getting tan."

It tilted its head and stared at him. "Shouldn't you be, like, thousands of years in the future?"

"Here to kill Pharaoh," Dirk said. Why he was talking to a gerbil who knew seemed to who he really was? Was he just hallucinating in the hot sun? Or...

"Delhi Llama?"

"I was, once, before I achieved true enlightenment. In this reincarnation, I prefer to be known as the Jerusalem Gerbil. Not that they have built Jerusalem yet, of course."

"Thought reincarnation was to future?"

The gerbil tapped its tail on Dirk's chest. "Reincarnation has no concept of time. Besides, all life is one. I just remember my other lives, unlike most."

"If all life one, you me, right?"

"You are one of my sadly unenlightened and very distant past lives, yes. Perhaps dying here would cause us to be more enlightened next time."

The dogs howled on the dunes.

"If helped me... us... get away, help yourself."

"I suppose."

Dirk nodded toward the cord tying his right hand to the stake. "Chew through cord, and me go? I untie rest."

The gerbil hopped across Dirk's chest, then down his arm. It sniffed the leather cord, then hopped down onto the sand, across to the stake, and began to nibble. The cord vibrated as the gerbil pulled chunks away with its tiny, sharp teeth. Dirk looked back toward the camp. None of the overseers seemed to be looking their way.

"Thanks. Owe for this."

"If all life is one, all debt is repaid," the gerbil said, then began to chew again.

Then barely had time to squeak as a pair of furry jaws lunged forward and wrapped their sharp teeth around its body.

"Fuck," the gerbil said, with its head sticking out between the teeth of a wild dog. The gerbil's bones crunched as the dog pressed its jaws together, then gulped down the remains.

One of the dog's eyes glared at Dirk, the other was just a dark hole in its scraggly face. Its side was scarred where claw marks were slowly healing.

"Nice dog," Dirk said. The dog crept closer, staring at Dirk with the remaining eye.

Sand crunched on the far side. Three more dogs approached through the twilight. They were thin, with bones beginning to show through their fur. Being nice to them probably wasn't going to help. If Dirk could remain healthy and well fed, any missing body parts would regenerate eventually. But he still didn't want to see any bitten off.

Particularly not the delicate ones.

Dirk tugged at the strap the gerbil had chewed. The creature's teeth had weakened the leather, but it just stretched as he heaved on it, and still wouldn't break. He twisted his arm, trying to tear apart the cut section of cord, but the stake just creaked under the strain.

The one-eyed dog growled at the others, who stopped as though unsure whether to risk a fight for the sake of a meal. It barked at them, then stepped toward them and growled. A dog fight was probably Dirk's best chance to avoid injury himself. But he couldn't imagine it lasting long.

Nor did he want to be the battle ground.

He lifted his shoulders from the ground, twisted his body toward the pack of dogs, and gave them his best war face. He opened his mouth until his jaw hurt, and roared until his lungs were empty. They stopped in shock, and one turned and backed away. One-Eye barked again, then jumped across Dirk toward the other dogs. The cowardly one ran, but the other two growled back.

Thinking happy thoughts wasn't easy in the circumstances, but Dirk imagined a rainbow rising above the sand dunes, and unicorns prancing on the top. He closed his eyes, and imagined a herd of gerbils racing across the sand, singing happy songs. Hamsters stood on their back legs and spun in a happy dance.

His muscles glowed as the chi power charged them. If only the Delhi Llama, or whatever he was now calling himself in his next reincarnation, could be there to see it. He ignored the fighting dogs, and concentrated on the image of the dancing hamsters and prancing unicorns. His muscles tensed, his arms glowed bright. He pushed all the power into his right arm, where the weakened strap was tied, wrapped his fingers around it, and pulled. The imaginary hamsters squeaked at him as he struggled against the strap, and the leather dug into his wrist and hands. The stake creaked, and the leather stretched.

A dog squealed to his left, but Dirk didn't even stop to find out which one it was. He heaved on the leather, and it stretched further, becoming thinner as it did so. Feet padded toward him over the sand, and, as the dancing hamster music reached its crescendo, he pulled one more time. The leather strap snapped where the gerbil had weakened it, and his hand flew back from the stake, his body twisting as it moved. The hand flew up above his chest, still holding the remains of the strap.

And punched a dog in the face as it lunged forward to bite at his groin.

The dog yelped, fell back, and slumped onto the sand. It shook its head, spraying blood from its nose, as Dirk untied the strap that held his other hand. One-Eye lay down on the sand, nursing fresh wounds, while the other two dogs stood back and watched cautiously.

The dog Dirk had hit climbed to its feet and lunged toward him, mouth open wide. Dirk punched it again. This time it fell back, and lay yelping on the sand.

The stake he had pulled the cord from leaned toward him at a crazy angle. He grabbed it and pulled until it slid from the sand. A half-metre-long pointy stick was a poor weapon, but it was better than nothing.

He froze as he realized he wasn't seeing the night-time world with his enhanced vision, but with normal, everyday light. He glanced to his right. The edge of the moon was rising over the horizon.

And a long, painful scream filled the night.

<12>

Dirk untied the remaining leather cords as fast as he could. The dogs raced up a dune, away from the screams. Dirk bounded to his feet and charged up the sand dune on the other side of him, racing toward the screams. He stopped at the top, and looked down at the tents where the overseers kept the girls.

A naked overseer stumbled out of the tent where Dirk had seen Nefert, with blood oozing from dozens of stab wounds on his back and chest. Nefert followed him, holding the bloody flint knife in one hand, and cracking the overseer's own whip across his back with the other.

Another overseer stumbled out of a tent on the left, with blood spurting from where his genitals should be. A short girl stepped out behind him, with blood around her lips, and a smile on her face.

"Freedom!" Dirk yelled, and raced down the dune. Slaves lying on the sand near the mine looked up at the shout. A group of overseers who had been marching toward the mine from the tents turned and looked back.

More girls fought with overseers around the tents. One tried to whip an overseer who already had cuts on his chest, but the man grabbed the whip and pulled her to him. The girl screamed as the overseer wrapped his hands around her neck.

Another girl grabbed the overseer's arms and tried to pull them away from the other girl's neck. But he was too strong.

Chi power oozed into Dirk's muscles. He raised the stake above his head, and pounded his feet against the sand as he ran. The girl went limp as he reached her, and he smacked the stake into the back of the overseer's head. The stake broke, and chunks of wood flew through the air. The overseer's skull cracked, his eyes bulged, and he fell to the ground.

The girl gasped for breath. Dirk picked up the whip and threw it to her, then pulled a flint knife from the overseer's belt.

Slaves shouted from all around the mine entrance. One of the overseers tried to whip Thoth, but Thoth stepped toward him, ignoring the lashes, and swung his stone hammer. Blood exploded from the overseer's head as the hammer connected.

He fell to the sand, which turned red around him.

The surviving overseers from the tents all had at least two girls thumping, biting, stabbing, whipping, or clinging onto them and trying to strangle them. Dirk wasn't needed there. He ran toward the mine.

Three more overseers lunged toward Thoth, but a dozen slaves leaped on them and beat them, holding them down while Thoth finished them off with the hammer. By the time Dirk reached them, Thoth stood with a blood-covered hammer in his hands, and blood-soaked sand around the bodies at his feet. Overseers swung whips and knives. Slaves dodged the blows, some successful, others falling to the sand with cuts and slashes.

The slaves still standing swung back with picks, hammers, and rocks. Two overseers went down with smashed skulls as Dirk approached, but four of the attacking slaves fell with them, soaking the sand with their blood. Dirk jumped for the first overseer he reached, grabbed the man's neck, and slammed the knife deep into the man's back. The overseer dropped to the ground, and a slave finished him off with a rock.

Thoth laughed. "It's actually working."

Dirk dodged as an overseer swung a whip toward his head. "They can't beat all of us together."

He punched the overseer in the stomach as the whip swung again. Then kicked him with a chi-powered foot that crunched bone and threw him twenty feet back into the sand.

"To me, fools," Ammon shouted.

The remaining overseers backed toward Ammon, forming a circle of whips and knives. Every time a slave tried to approach, the cracking whips and flashing flints pushed them back. The slaves outnumbered them, but couldn't attack in large enough numbers to overpower the mob of overseers.

Dirk strode toward the overseers. He had to break up this standoff, somehow. Some of the slaves backed away to clear a path for him.

"Surrender," he said. "You live."

Ammon spat into the sand, and glared at him. "I will never surrender to a slave."

"Hoped you say that," Dirk said. After the way these men had treated the people they enslaved, he would have hated to see them walk away unpunished. But he wanted to give them the chance to see reason before he killed them.

Some of the slaves tried to close with them, carrying picks and hammers. But the overseers continued to crack their whips, and the slaves backed away. The slaves could rush the group, but many would be wounded or killed by the whips and knives.

One gauss rifle, or even a longbow, and the fight would be over in seconds. A flint knife wouldn't even be stable enough in the air for the point to stick into one of them if he threw it.

Ammon broke the stalemate. The circle of overseers began to move away from Dirk, their whips and knives flashing in the moonlight. The slaves on the far side backed away from the weapons, making room for them.

The one-eyed dog sniffed at Dirk's ankle. Fresh blood ran from new claw marks, where he had come off the worse in the fight. The other three dogs raced across the sand toward him.

Screw it.

Dirk grabbed One-Eye, who yelped as Dirk lifted him from the sand. Dirk pulled his arms back, thought of happy, smiling puppies as he took aim, then threw the dog at the overseers.

One-Eye flew high into the air, barking as he tumbled. Overseers flicked their whips at him, but he was too high for them to reach. He twisted and turned as he descended, and Ammon stared at the flying dog in bemusement until One-Eye smashed into his face, and sent him flying backward.

The other dogs raced away after One-Eye, leaving a cloud of flying sand behind them, dodging the whips, and darting through gaps between the overseers' legs. Overseers fell, and the dogs began to fight on Ammon's chest.

Dirk raised his knife. "Attack!"

Overseers flicked their whips, but the surging mass of slaves pushed their way through. The line of overseers was broken. and they could only make an uncoordinated defence.

A whip cracked across Dirk's chest, pushing him back, but three of the overseers to his right lay on the sand, kicking and punching at the slaves as they struggled back to their feet. Dirk dodged through the gap in the line, swung his knife, and stabbed the overseer who had attacked him. Then kicked one in the chest, and sent him flying backwards across the sand.

Now, the formation broke into a mass of individual fights, each overseer against many slaves. And those uneven battles were short. By the time Dirk reached Ammon, the wild dogs were fighting over his intestines. The other overseers either fell under the massed attack—their knives no match for the mass of picks, hammers and rocks—or were knocked down onto the ground, and disarmed.

A dark shape raced away from the mine, toward the distant dunes. Seth.

One-Eye glanced at Dirk, who pointed at Seth. "Get him."

One-Eye raced after him. Seth glanced back, saw the dog and picked up his pace, but One-Eye rapidly gained on him.

By the time Dirk caught up with them, whistling a happy tune in a slow stroll, Seth was screaming for his mother as One-Eye ripped a chunk of meat from his ankle.

<13>

A thin girl with a twisted smile on her face whipped one of the male slaves in the shadows by the fire burning just outside the mine entrance. Dirk grabbed the whip from her. She scowled at him. He tossed it away into the dark night around them.

"From now, until end of time, we slaves to no man," Dirk said. "Or woman. Live free, or die."

He sat on the sand, and stared into the fire. He'd won this battle, but there would be many more before he could get home. Would the slaves be up to the job?

Perhaps he could find more at the other mines. There must be plenty willing to fight for their freedom.

Nefert sauntered across the sand toward him, her loincloth and bare breasts swinging as she moved. She knelt behind his back, and rubbed his shoulders.

"Thank you," Dirk said. "If girls hadn't surprised so many overseers, we lose fight."

"Here," she said, and handed him a loincloth. "You might want to put this on, before the other girls get ideas."

Dirk took it from her, and strapped it around his waist. Spots of blood were splattered across the leather. He didn't ask where it came from.

"Can I ask you a favour?" Nefert said.

"Saved my life. Owe you one."

She rubbed his shoulders again, then leaned forward to whisper into his ear. "Let us have the overseers."

Dirk shrugged. He didn't like to mistreat prisoners, but he'd seen these bastards whip enough slaves to death that he had no sympathy for any of them.

And the girls had plenty of reasons to hate them.

Nefert giggled. Dirk pushed her hands away, stood, and strolled across the sand. They'd staked out the few surviving overseers where those overseers had previously staked out their prisoners. It had only seemed fitting at the time.

In this case, however, two slaves with whips stood guard, keeping the wild dogs away while Dirk decided what to do with the men. A long-haired girl picked up a rib bone that lay beside the stakes, and threw it to One-Eye, who jumped in the air and caught it in his mouth. The girl laughed as he ran to her, and dropped it at her feet. She threw it again.

Nefert whistled. The surviving girls climbed over the low dune between the stakes and the tents. Many were splattered or smeared with blood. One of them limped over the dune with her arm on another girl's shoulder for support. Another nursed a bleeding, limp and broken arm. Most carried whatever weapons they had found.

Nefert waved at them, and they descended the dune.

Dirk stepped over the first row of the staked-out overseers, ignoring their taunts. Beyond them, Seth stared up at him from the sand, his hands and feet tied to the stakes.

"What are you going to do, Nubian? Piss on me?"

"Not that kinky."

Seth laughed. "I am not afraid of death."

"Have friend you like to meet."

Nefert stepped past Dirk, with a big smile on her face. Dirk had never seen her so happy. Seth's smile faded.

Nefert tested the the flint blade against her finger. A drop of blood oozed out.

"Where shall I cut first?"

"Leave you to her," Dirk said. "Seems very skilled."

Seth struggled against his bonds. "You can't."

"Just get what you deserve."

"Kill me."

Dirk shrugged. "Done enough killing today."

He turned away, and strolled back to the mines, ignoring the screams and laughter that filled the night behind him.

Thoth sat by the fire outside the mine entrance. The slaves had looted the overseers' tents, and now passed the food and drink around. Thoth grabbed a bottle of wine, and held it out toward Dirk.

"Should we stop them?" Thoth said.

Dirk shrugged. "Overseers knew risks when took job. Let girls have fun."

"I can't sleep with all that noise," Osiris said.

Dirk raised the bottle and knocked back a good slug of the wine. The cool liquid soothed his throat after the heat of the day. "Be over by dawn. When Nefert done, don't think I sleep much, anyway."

<14>

Dirk lay in the tent in the cool morning air. The tent flaps fluttered in the cool wind, slapping against the wooden poles that supported the tent. The first rays of sunlight shone through the door, casting a triangular, orange glow over Nefert's back as she lay naked on top of him, snoring in his ear.

He'd stayed awake long after she fell asleep, thinking of a plan. The screaming, laughing and moaning outside had faded into silence an hour ago. The freedom celebrations were over, and reality would be starting to sink in. As the old stores of food and drink ran out, the remaining slaves would need to find a way to survive. They couldn't stay at the mine, and, if they did, they would be attacked as soon as Hitler discovered they had revolted and killed the overseers. Dirk needed them to follow him, and had to convince them to take on the rest of Hitler's forces, until the whole of planet Egypt was free.

But how? A revolt against people who abused you every day was one thing. A war, quite another. People who'd lived as slaves for years before he arrived wouldn't be eager to die to save their planet from Hitler.

The sand outside exploded. Hot metal flew through the air above them, tearing gashes in the tent. Men and girls in the nearby tents began to scream.

Nefert jerked awake. "What is it?"

The slaves might never have seen artillery before, but Dirk had seen more than he ever wanted to in dozens of wars across the galaxy. As he grabbed his loincloth and pulled it on, another shell whistled through the air above them. He poked his head out of the tent in time to see the shell fall beyond the dune and explode, spraying sand high into the air. The front half of a skinny dog twisted in the sand cloud, with a puzzled look on its face as it stared at the entrails dangling behind its front legs.

Dirk climbed up the dune, staying low as he reached the top. Another shell flew past him, and exploded near the mine. Two slaves near the explosion fell to the ground, screaming and bleeding. Nefert slumped down on the sand beside him.

"Who is attacking us?"

Dirk pointed toward a cloud of dark smoke passing a dune a couple of hundred metres away. The metallic rattle and screech of metal treads preceded it, and, as they watched, a boxy, grey tank rolled around the end of the dune. Men with Nazi swastikas on their loincloths followed the tank, holding rifles.

"Must have heard about revolt, sent more men."

"We killed every overseer. How could they have heard?"

Dirk shrugged. "Were enough that one could get away."

Or maybe it was just all the noise during the night. It did travel far across a desert. But that wasn't important, now. The tank turret turned toward them, and a cloud of smoke billowed from the barrel as it fired again. Dirk pressed himself down into the sand as the shell whistled low over their heads. It exploded just past the tents, and one of the girls squealed in pain.

"What is that?"

"It a..." Dirk said. Egyptian had no word for tank, or, if they did, it wasn't one he'd learned at the mines. "Don't matter what called, just how stop it."

How do you fight a tank with rocks and whips? They had to get in close, where the tank gun would be unable to hit them, without being hit by the soldiers' rifles.

The tank rolled slowly between the dunes, leaving a thick cloud of black smoke behind it. Dirk motioned to the girls to join him. They began to scramble up the dune.

"What are those men carrying?" Nefert said.

"They..." Egyptian probably had no word for rifle, either. "Loud killing things. Like slingshot, with metal rocks."

He was going to have to invent some words, and teach the Egyptians something about modern technology. But that could wait for later. None of it would matter, if they didn't survive this attack.

Girls slumped down on the sand on each side of them, and peered over the dune. Dirk motioned for them to stay low, and whispered his plan to them. Slaves screamed near the mine as more shells exploded there, and the soldiers fired their rifles.

Should he shout at the slaves to take cover? They seemed to have worked it out for themselves, and shouting would just give away his position. The slaves who still could were running toward the dunes or the mine, while the rest lay bleeding on the sand in between.

Smoke rose past the dune, only feet away. Dirk looked over the top. The tank was passing just below them.

One of the wild dogs padded out from the dunes. and sniffed the tank. Then it lifted a leg, and began to pee on the drive wheels. A soldier raised his rifle, and fired. The dog yelped, and blood spurted from its side, before it slumped down on the sand.

"Move fast," Dirk said to Nefert. "Keep moving, they not hit you. Get close to smoking thing, it not boom you up."

She nodded at him. He waved to the other girls.

"Attack," he yelled, then lunged forward, over the top of the dune. He screamed as he raced down toward the tank, and the girls followed, yelling and screaming insults at the men below.

The soldiers froze at the sight of a muscle-clad, black-skinned man and two dozen naked or topless girls racing down the sand dune toward them, swinging whips, knives and stone picks. Then one finally reacted, raised his rifle and fired, and a thick cloud of smoke billowed from the barrel. The bullet cracked past them, and threw sand into the air behind Nefert. The soldier worked the bolt to load another round, and the others raised their guns.

The tank turret clattered as it began to turn, and more rifles fired. Dirk jumped into the air near the bottom of the dune, and his feet smacked into the chest of the nearest soldier. The man flew backward, and his spine twisted as he smashed into the side of the tank. His ribs cracked under the force of the impact, and his chest deflated like a burst balloon. He slumped down, and didn't move again.

One of the girls fell to the sand with a bloody bullet hole in her chest, but the others reached the bottom of the dune and jumped on the men, knocking them to the ground. Dirk climbed to his feet, grabbed the dead soldier's rifle, and swung around just in time to shoot another soldier who was aiming at Nefert. The long-haired girl howled like a mad dog as she jumped onto a soldier's shoulders, then pulled up his chin and slashed her flint knife across his throat. She jumped free as he fell, gurgling and spurting blood.

Nefert pushed away a soldier's rifle as he tried to hit her with it, and rammed her knife into his groin. A girl grabbed him from behind, pulled his helmet away, and smashed his head into the side of the tank, again and again until blood ran down the metal to the sand. The tank crew began to shout, but their voices were muffled through the tiny vision slots.

Dirk dodged through the melee as the girls overpowered the soldiers. He shoved the barrel of his rifle into the driver's vision slot, cocked it, and fired. Blood spurted out through the hole, and the tank began to turn. Girls dodged out of the way as it rolled toward the dune to the left. One of the soldiers wasn't as fast as they were. He screamed as the track rolled over him, and his bones crunched beneath the treads.

The tank gun fired. The shell smashed into the sand dune and exploded harmlessly, showering them with sand. Men and girls stood stunned and shaken by the noise and muzzle blast. Dirk's ears had shut down automatically when the blast hit, and he jumped onto the front deck of the tank, just before the gun punched into the dune, and the rest of the tank followed. It rolled to a stop with several feet buried in the dune. Sand slid down on top of it, and poured over the sides.

Dirk heaved on the hatch. It didn't move. Must be locked from the inside. Made sense, but he'd have to find another way to get in there.

All around him, the melee resumed as the soldiers and girls recovered from their shock. The soldiers swung their rifles, but, after the losses in the initial fight, the girls now outnumbered them two to one. One soldier tried to fire his rifle, but Nefert knocked it aside. The long-haired girl jumped off the back of the tank, howling, and bashed the soldier's skull in with a rock.

The tank jerked backward. Someone must have taken the dead driver's place inside, and was trying to reverse away from the dune. Nefert climbed up beside Dirk, just as the turret began to turn, and the barrel pulled free of the dune.

"How do we get in?" she said. The other girls had finished off the remaining soldiers who weren't running from them, and climbed on the tank, ducking as the turret turned and the barrel swung around toward them.

Dirk motioned to one of the girls. "Give hammer."

She handed him a stone hammer, and he pounded on the hatch. The long-haired girl straddled the gun barrel and slid along it toward the muzzle, with her bare breasts dangling just above the metal.

The hatch bent under the hammer blows, but the lock held. The girls banged on the iron hull with rocks, hammers and picks, but it was built to survive much worse attacks. They knocked down the smoking metal chimney of the engine at the rear, but smoke just spewed out directly into the air from the hole beneath, and the tank rolled on.

Dirk glanced at the long-haired girl. What was she doing? She stopped at the end of the barrel, swung around so she was hanging underneath it by her legs, then pulled rocks from a pocket in a leather shoulder-bag and pushed one into the muzzle. She began to hammer the first rock with another.

The men inside shouted, and metal clunked on metal.

"Get down," Dirk yelled.

The girl glanced at him.

"Sakhmet," Nefert yelled. "Get down."

The girl let go, and fell into the sand. Then rolled away from the tank's treads.

"Cover ears," Dirk shouted, just before the gun fired again. The muzzle, and a metre of the barrel, split apart like a banana as the shell exploded inside the gun. Flames blasted out around the edges of the hatch, and the men in the tank screamed.

<15>

Dirk examined the still smoking tank wreck. The hull and treads were crudely constructed from soft iron, and wouldn't carry it far or protect it against RPGs. But the armour would be good enough against attacks from slaves with flint knives and stone picks. A smokey steam engine fuelled with black rocks from the mines drove the treads, and the gun fired rudimentary shells propelled by black powder charges that were stacked up all around the interior of the turret. If the flames that flashed back from the breech had set them all off, neither Dirk nor any of the girls would still be alive.

He climbed in through the turret hatch. The interior of the tank smelled like a barbecue. Four burned, blackened skeletons smoked on the floor. One was hunched over the long levers near the front of the tank that controlled steam power to the tracks. Even with the engine idle and the fire beneath the boiler burning down, the interior felt red hot in the desert sun.

But, crude as it was, it was an amazing achievement in the few months Hitler and his men had been in Egypt. The rifles, similarly, used sealed, black powder cartridges that would foul them after a few dozen shots, but would easily defeat opponents as lightly armed as the slaves were. At this rate, in a few years, Hitler would be able to conquer anyone who stood against him, until the entire planet Egypt was under his control.

Dirk and the slaves were going to need better tactics to beat Hitler's men. In close quarters battle, tanks were always at risk from courageous infantry attacks, but, out on the flat desert, the slaves would have little chance of getting close enough before the tanks or riflemen could kill them all.

He climbed out, and strode back across the sand toward the mine. The sun was rising toward noon, and, when the tank failed to return, the Nazis would know something was wrong. Would they wait for orders, or send more reinforcements?

He couldn't take that chance. He and the ex-slaves had to move out as soon as possible, and take the fight to Hitler.

Sakhmet played with One-Eye. She threw a bone, and he grabbed it and ran back. He jumped up at her, and knocked her down, then jumped onto her chest. She laughed and howled as they rolled in the sand.

Thoth lounged on the sand, one arm around the pregnant serving girl, the other around the girl with the broken arm, who now had a strip of bloody cloth wrapped around her wound, and a sling around her neck. Osiris sat beside him.

"This is the good life," Thoth said.

"I had a good life," Osiris said. "Until you lot messed it up. I could have gone places as a grave digger."

"You're free now," the pregnant girl said. "Isn't that better?"

"Free doesn't put food in your belly," Osiris said, then stared at her bulge. "No offence meant."

"Can't stay here," Dirk said. "They send more and more men. Soon, we lose. They cannot allow slave revolt succeed."

"We have the... smoking metal thing," Nefert said.

"Exploding thing broken, and they bring more. One smoking metal thing not beat twenty. Must take fight to them, find Pharaoh Adolf, kill him. Then we truly free."

Thoth kissed the girls. "I am free. I would rather stay and take my chances here."

"Would rather live. Not live long here when more smoking metal things turn up. I take dozen girls to kill Pharaoh. Thoth, take men, find other mines, free slaves and destroy tunnels."

"Why do you get the girls?"

"They vicious fighters. Hitler never think they threat to new Empire. Besides, cook great bagel."

Thoth pulled his girls closer. "Can I have these two?"

"Take them. But make chaos, cut off supplies, free slaves. To beat Pharaoh, you distract many soldiers as can."

"So I get to die fighting them, while you sneak around in safety with the girls?"

"Strike from desert, rescue slaves, take what need, vanish back to sand. Keep army busy looking, attack with surprise when outnumber them. You do that?"

The girls looked at each other. "We will do it if he won't," the pregnant girl said. "I would rather die than spread my legs for another of those monsters."

"Now, now," Thoth said. "I didn't say I wouldn't. I just wanted to be sure of the plan, before I agreed to it."

Nefert nudged Dirk. "I have a man to entertain me, but what about the other girls?"

"Pick one man with us. Rest go with Thoth. All ex-slaves collect everything can carry. We blow up mine with black powder from smoking metal thing, then go."

"Pick me," Osiris said. "I don't want to go with that lot."

"Could be a lot of graves to dig," Thoth said.

"I'd rather not be digging my own."

Thoth looked at Dirk, then nodded toward the tank. "Will you take the smoking metal thing?"

"Take if you want, not much use without exploding thing. Take all loud killing things. We travel quiet, try blend in, You be ones make noise and trouble."

One-Eye looked plaintively at Dirk. He really did owe the dog a favour, even if he had eaten the Delhi Llama. Besides, if the Llama was correct, One-Eye was just another of his many incarnations, teaching himself a valuable life lesson. Though what it was, Dirk wasn't quite sure.

He nodded. "You come too."

<16>

Hitler slumped back in the lumpy canvas seat of his new wheelchair. The iron bars of the frame creaked beneath him, even louder than his own old bones. One day, the damn chair was going to break, and he was going to crash down on the stone floor of the palace. It was all that fucker Speer's fault. He wanted the Reich for himself, and always had. Always thought he was the smart one, and looked down his nose at his Fuhrer. If only the shithead wasn't so useful, he'd be fucking dead.

The sun was low in the sky, sinking toward the horizon, but it was still far too fucking hot. There wasn't one tree in this palace courtyard, nor many more in the rest of the town. Sweat dripped down his forehead, and he wiped it off with a shaking hand. No food here worth the name, either. No sauerkraut, no liver dumpling. Just weird Jewish crap.

The courtyard gates towered above him, and they creaked and scraped as four slaves pushed them open, leaning against them and grunting as they pushed their weight against the heavy wood. Hitler picked up his glasses from his lap. His hands shook as he tried to find his nose. Shit-fuck. Even his fucking hand wouldn't obey him any more. He'd been the most feared man in the world a few weeks ago, now look at him. Fuhrer of some Jewish shit-hole in the desert. Barely an Aryan in sight, and no more coming for thousands of years.

"We'll breed another master race," Speer had said.

That old letch Totenkopf was already doing his best. Since Speer stopped Totenkopf killing all the Jews, he'd knocked up half a dozen of the palace Jewesses instead. But what was the point, if his bastard kids were all half-Untermensch? He'd take generations to breed a new race of Ubermensch that way.

"Forward... March," Totenkopf shouted.

Speak of the devil...

Hundreds of feet stomped on the stone of the courtyard, and the thumping sound of hordes of men marching through the gate echoed back from the tall, brown walls. Hitler almost wanted to cover his ears and block it out, but he was damned if he was going to show his age any more than he had to. Besides, who knew if his aching arms could reach that high any more?

He stared at his hand as the men approached. His fingers would barely move, and trying to force them just made it shake faster. A few years ago, he could make men worship him with one of his rousing speeches, but who was going to worship what he had become since then?

The men marched on. Not a bad formation, and they goose-stepped with enthusiasm. Not a patch on the troops he had commanded just a few years before, but a lot better than the rabble they had faced when they arrived in Egypt from the future. None of those idiots had been worth a damn, not since that stupid black Untermensch they killed in the desert when they stepped through the portal. He must have thought they were some kind of merchants he could bedazzle into handing over their money with his Jewish tricks.

Something moved to his right. That topless girl was there again. No matter how many times Eva told her to stay away, she came crawling back, muttering her Jewish nonsense. Her breasts rubbed against the stone as she crawled toward him. The women in Egypt had too much gold, and no shame. Eva would never behave like that slut.

Well, except when he'd taken her to Berchtesgaden to play Concentration Camp Guard and Jewess, long before they were married. And his back just wasn't up to that any more.

He winced with pain, and twisted in the chair to relieve the pressure on his aching vertebrae. Speer might be able to make a wheelchair, but he couldn't replace an ageing back.

Hitler glanced up at Speer, where he stood behind the wheelchair. Maybe that was the plan. Make the Fuhrer a cripple so he'd be easy to replace. At this rate, would he even live long to see the new Reich?

"Come here, you bitch," Eva yelled.

The girl howled as Eva grabbed her hair, and lifted her from the ground. On the one hand, he should send the Jewess to the camps, as maybe she'd be more useful making tanks and guns than creeping around the palace. On the other, she kept Eva occupied, and out of his hair. What was left of it, anyway.

Totenkopf raised his arm. "Heil Hitler."

The mass of men he led raised their arms in unison. Their "Heil Hitler," echoed around the courtyard, bouncing back and forward between the walls until it grew into an indecipherable rumble, then faded away into silence.

The girl yelled as Eva dragged her across the courtyard.

She had some spirit, Eva did. Not to mention jealousy. She was the only one who'd stood by him no matter what. Even now, she was willing to fight for him. Which was more than could be said of the rest of the German people.

Fuckers.

He huffed. Maybe he'd be better off with an army of Jews after all.

Totenkopf coughed to get Hitler's attention, then saluted, and nodded toward the lines of men behind him.

"May I present your new SS, mein Fuhrer?"

"Yes, yes. Very good. But these few will not conquer the world for me. Where are the others? In Germany I had armies of millions, not hundreds."

Totenkopf raised his hands, and clapped. Something rattled and roared outside the courtyard, and a thick cloud of black smoke rose above the walls. Metal clanked, and a halfhearted abomination that looked vaguely like a Panzer twisted and turned as it rolled through the gate.

The men stepped aside as it rolled across the courtyard, into the gap between them. It crunched to a stop in front of him, and wobbled slowly back and forward on the tracks. More of the tanks followed, and the men moved further apart as the tanks formed a line four abreast. More rolled in behind them. Speer followed behind.

He smirked at Hitler, "What do you think, mein Fuhrer? We already have the first prototype Panzers out in the field, and more follow them off the production line every day."

Hitler raised his hand, and motioned toward the tank. Speer grabbed the handles of the wheelchair, and pushed it forward. The axle squeaked beneath Hitler as Speer pushed him toward the front of the tank, then around it to the swastika painted on the side. Then he stopped.

Hitler looked at the metal wheels, then the solid vertical wall of iron above them. It was scored and dented, and held together by rough lines of rivets. So much for their superior German workmanship. He sniffed in the dark cloud of foul-smelling smoke that surrounded him. Then reached up and touched the swastika on the side of the tank.

For once, his hand didn't tremble.

Speer leaned closer. "Aren't they magnificent?"

What was the fool on about? "These tanks are too small."

"They are the most powerful we can build that these idiots to operate. If we gave them anything more complex, they'd blow it up more often than they blew up their targets."

"They look like something the French pansies would make. At home, we had real tanks. Tiger, Ratte, Maus. Tanks that roared, boomed, and crushed everything in their path. Tanks that spread fear wherever they went. Tanks that made men flee in terror at the mere whisper of their name. Not these crappy little things. My Mercedes was bigger."

Speer stood silently behind him. Did he not understand what his Fuhrer said? Or was he still plotting against the Reich? He'd done his best to stop the scorched earth policy that would have kept the fucking Bolshevicks from Berlin. Was he now working against the Fourth Reich, too?

Shouts came from outside the gate. The palace guards strode toward it, swinging spears, and pulling rifles from their shoulders. What was going on?

A man stumbled in, and leaned on the gate, panting. A thin beard covered the dark skin of his face, and his swastika-laden loincloth was torn, and hung loose around his waist. The guards grabbed his arms, and dragged him into the courtyard. Totenkopf scowled, and marched toward them.

"Mein Fuhrer," the man gasped, his voice breaking as though he hadn't drunk water for days. Then he muttered some of that Jewish crap.

Totenkopf listened intently, and nodded. Fucker must have learned some of the language from his Jewish whores while he was impregnating them. His face grew white, and the man waved his arms wildly, and muttered excitedly. Totenkopf turned toward Hitler, with sweat dripping down his forehead.

"Mein Fuhrer, he rode here to warn us that many slaves have revolted in the Maghara coal mine."

Hitler shrugged. What could be so important about a few revolting Jews? "Well, kill them. There are plenty more where they came from."

Totenkopf winced. "I don't think you understand. A patrol was sent to kill them, with one of the prototype tanks."

"Good. Let me know when they're dead."

"They're all dead, sir. The tank, too."

What did he mean? Oh.

Hitler leaned over the side of his wheelchair, and looked back at Speer. "So much for your tanks." He spat on the ground, and his saliva sizzled on the hot stone. "A few Jews are enough to destroy them."

"They are prototypes," Speer said. "And the new crews are inexperienced. Both will improve."

"You are building pyramids. Why do you waste your time on those things, when you could build me tanks worthy of the name? We must begin the new Reich this year, before it is too late. I cannot wait for you to piss away our iron and coal on your foolish pyramids."

Speer smiled a wide smile that lit up his face, for perhaps the first time since they had arrived in Egypt. "Mein Fuhrer, I am building a special pyramid just for you. Perhaps you would like to see it?"

<17>

Dirk shuffled through the hot sand, in the deep valley between two dunes that towered above their group. The sun had risen above the dunes, and the burning heat now beat down on his body. His skin had again turned black where the coal dust had been rubbed away in the battle, or in the night of celebrations afterwards. The change helped his body cope with the sun, but it wouldn't help for much longer, if they didn't find food and water. He'd fought on a few desert planets before. Dry, sandy rocks like Zeta Philosophie. But he wore an air-conditioned hazard suit back then. Now all he had was a loincloth.

He could taste the sand in his mouth, where the wind had blown it earlier in the day. It crunched between his teeth whenever he moved his jaw, and he would have spat it out, but his mouth was so dry he had no spit to spit.

"Are we there yet?" Nefert mumbled.

He glanced back. Osiris and the girls were stumbling along behind him. Since they'd lived on planet Egypt for years, he'd expected them to handle the heat and sun better than he did. But they didn't have the benefit of years in the Space Marines, and the many body modifications that came with it.

"We should have stayed back at the mine," Osiris muttered. "I had a good job at the mine. Now I'm going to die in this fucking sandpit, and get my balls eaten by wild dogs."

"We not die," Dirk muttered.

But was he right? He had no idea where they were. But, if they kept moving, surely they had to reach a town sooner or later. They'd followed the tank tracks away from the mine until a brief sandstorm blew through, carried the tracks away, and filled the pits with a fresh layer of sand. By the time the storm faded away, they'd probably been walking in circles for an hour. Now, he was just walking toward the sun, since that should keep them moving in something resembling a straight line. Until it set, then...

"Should never have listened to you," Osiris gasped. "What good is freedom, if you're dead?"

"Better die free than live on knees."

"You can say that again," Sakhmet said.

She laughed, then the laugh turned to a cough.

None of them would be walking for much longer, if they didn't find water soon. And, if Dirk failed, the universe would be doomed. He had to find a way to keep going, find the Pharaoh, and kill the bastard. He'd survived battles in far worse environments than this, with far more competent enemies than Hitler's Nazis trying to kill him. He wasn't go to die here, in this sand pit. Or let the others die, either.

Tall, brown rocks protruded from the sand up ahead. They rose high enough to cast a short, narrow shadow on the sand beside them. It wouldn't last, when the sun moved on. But it would provide a little shelter for the moment.

He nodded toward it. "Take break. I scout."

The sand sank beneath the weight of Dirk's muscular body as he stomped up the dunes. If he could reach the top, he could see the land that surrounded them. Maybe spot water or a town. He stomped on, panting and sweating as his feet sank deep into the sand.

One-Eye panted beside him. The dog seemed less worried by the lack of food and water than any of the humans. But, then again, he'd been living rough for... some time. It was hard even to tell quite how old the creature might be. Living rough could age anyone fast.

Dirk strode on, as fast as his feet could climb. The sand gave way beneath him, sliding in a sheet back toward the rocks. He slammed his hand deep into the dune, and the drag slowed his slide until he could dig his feet in deeper and climb on.

The sun was heading toward the far side of the dune by the time he approached the top. The others lay huddled together down below, in what remained of the shadows from the rocks. They'd have to move on soon. If they just lay there in the hot sun, in a few hours they'd never walk again.

The thought sent fresh power through Dirk's legs. It wasn't just the universe relying on him, the girls back there were, too. The top of the dune was only a few yards above him, and One-Eye was already pulling ahead, wagging his tail and spraying sand into the air whenever it hit the surface of the dune.

The hissing of the wind faded as Dirk approached the peak of the dune, and new sounds reached his ears, previously blocked by the sand, or overpowered by the wind. Creaking, and muffled voices.

Dirk slammed his body down into the sand, and crawled up the dune, toward the peak. One-Eye stared at him for a few moments, then turned and trotted up the dune.

"Come back, dog," Dirk whispered.

But One-Eye ignored him, and climbed higher, until he stood at the peak of the dune, with his tail wagging as he stared over the far side. He opened his mouth wide, and began to bark. Dirk crawled a couple of yards to the left as he climbed toward the peak. The voices on the far side were louder now, with constant muttering, and intermittent yelling.

Dirk carefully raised his head, and peered over the edge.

<18>

Cool, glittering water stretched from horizon to horizon. A river, and a big one, at least a hundred metres wide. Eyes looked up at One-Eye's barking, and stared at One-Eye and Dirk from a boat that sailed lazily past, its single mast towering over a pile of boxes full of fruit and vegetables. Dirk couldn't stay there for long, or he'd raise even more suspicions from the passing traders.

But he and his girls did need that water.

He yelled to the others, then raced down the far side of the dune as fast as he could, with One-Eye following close behind his heels in a cloud of sand.

Dirk dove into the river. His body shook with the shock of the sudden immersion in the cold water, but who cared? The heat immediately faded away, and a wave of relief flowed through his skin. He sank toward the bottom of the river for a few seconds, then kicked against it, and floated slowly back to the surface. His body came alive again as the water sucked the desert heat from his muscles and bones. He gasped in a deep breath as he broke the surface, then lowered his face and gulped down a mouthful of water. It cooled his insides now, just as it had cooled his outsides a few seconds before. He gulped down more. Then more still. Only moments before, he'd be almost sure they were going to die. Now, they were going to live.

The girls appeared at the top of the dune, howled, then raced down toward the river, their feet throwing up a cloud of sand that floated away on the wind. The girls tore away their loincloths as they ran, tossed them into the sand, then dove in beside him. Dirk gulped down more cool water as the girls floated all around him, giggling as they splashed water at each other. One-Eye watched from the shore for a moment, then looked down at the river as the waves rolled past him. He leaned forward, with his tongue stretched out toward the water.

Then fell in.

He splashed madly in the water as he tried to stay afloat. His head went under, then his legs paddled as fast as they could go as he pushed his snout high above the surface, and shook the water away. He paddled in slow circles near the shore, as he tried to find his way back. But the banks were too tall, even if he could get close enough to try to clamber out.

Dirk relaxed his aching muscles, and let his body float on the surface of the water. This was the first time he'd really had a chance to relax since he arrived on planet Egypt, and it wouldn't last long. He should make the most of it, before he had to clamber out and continue walking to his final battle with Hitler. He'd be lucky to get a chance to relax again before that.

One-Eye paddled past, toward Sakhmet. She splashed water at him, then reached out and grabbed him as he struggled. She giggled, and water sprayed into the air as they fought.

They all deserved a break for a few minutes after what they'd been through. He'd only been a slave at the mines for a few weeks, but the girls had been slaves all their lives. After he killed Hitler, he would free every slave on planet Egypt. And, in the meantime, they would give him an army to fight with.

A cloud of sand rose into the air near the horizon. A dark cloud, mixed with thick, black smoke. That couldn't be good. A low metallic clunking filled the air, then the nose of a tank appeared from the heat-haze in the distance. It rolled along the sandy riverbank in their direction. More tanks followed in a grey, smokey column, surrounded by dark dots that soon grew into men carrying rifles as the tanks approached.

Dirk sucked a long breath into his bioengineered lungs, and let himself sink into the water, holding air in his lungs, and staying close enough to the surface to watch the column pass.

The soldiers whistled and yelled toward the river. The girls giggled and waved at them. A scruffy, long-haired head poked out of the turret hatch of the lead tank, and shouted at them. The column slowly rolled on, too intent on their mission to stop to investigate a few girls swimming in the river.

But, where there were a few tanks, there'd soon be more. Dirk and his team had to get moving, away from the site of their last battle, before someone did decide to investigate.

They couldn't just walk to... wherever the heck the Pharaoh lived, while hoping to beat the Nazis every time they ran into a pack of them. He had to find another way.

As the column disappeared into the distance, leaving just a cloud of sand and smoke behind, Dirk paddled back toward the surface, lungs aching for fresh air. The Space Marine techs had upgraded his body to survive better underwater, but he couldn't stay there forever. He glanced up toward the sun.

Just in time to see a dark shape move across the water.

He tried to dodge aside, but a lump of wood smacked into the side of his head. He twisted around and slapped his arm against the wood, then used it to pull himself out of the water.

And found himself hanging from the side of a low sailing boat, maybe five metres long. It slowed under his extra weight, and the drag of his wide, muscular body. A wrinkled man who'd probably spent more years in the desert sun than Dirk had been alive leaned over the bow and stared down at him. Dirk bobbed up and down on the waves as the boat cut through the water, not even reaching walking speed. Another man stepped up to the side of the boat; a man wearing leather armour on his body and holding the hilt of a sword at his belt.

"Good afternoon down there," the old man said. "I do hope you're not pirates."

"If they are pirates," the swordsman said, "they're not very good at it."

"No pirates," Dirk said. "Just lost."

"And you fell in the river because you were lost?"

"Dying from thirst. Needed drink."

"Where were you supposed to be going?"

"I go to Pharaoh."

"You are travelling to New Berlin?"

What the heck was that? "If Pharaoh there, I go."

The old man frowned. "Well, I suppose the Pharaoh is quite the tourist attraction these days. I'm not sure why, he doesn't look much like a Pharaoh to me. The last one was so regal. So refined. So delicate. The new Pharaoh is so lower class. He's not descended from the gods, and he didn't even marry into the royal blood. Maybe that's the attraction? A bit of rough?"

"You give us ride?"

"Do you have food to eat?"

Dirk shook his head. "You have food. I trade."

"But how will you pay for it?"

Dirk grabbed Osiris, and pulled him closer in the water. Then Dirk clenched his fists, and bent his elbows up, until his artificially-enhanced muscles bulged from his black skin. He nodded to Osiris, who displayed the much smaller muscles he'd developed from his grave-digging days.

"You feed us," Dirk said, "we protect boats. Lots trouble these days."

"I have guards."

"Not like Dirk."

"What about the girls?"

The girls aimed their bare, wet flesh toward the merchant, and wiggled whatever they had to offer.

Nefert pouted, lay on her back in the water, and pushed out her chest. "We have other things to trade."

<19>

Dirk and his team floated down the Nile in the lead boat of the small trading flotilla. The mast and sail creaked above them, and river water splashed around the bow as the boat forced its way upriver against the current. Even One-Eye had grown fat on the scraps the traders had fed him. He lounged at the stern of the boat with his stomach basking in the sun, his legs spread, and his head on Sakhmet's lap. Nefert lounged beside Dirk at the side of the boat. She'd been teaching him more Egyptian, to help pass the time, but still laughed at his accent when he spoke.

They'd seen some more tanks lumbering along the banks of the river, heading in the opposite direction as fast as the steam engines could carry them, and accompanied by many soldiers. And learned the new words Hitler and his Nazis had added to the Egyptian language to describe their new weapons.

Travellers they met en route had passed on rumours of fighting in the East. Hopefully Thoth was doing a good job out that way, but news travelled only a little faster than the traders.

As they approached New Berlin, the number of boats on the river and carts alongside it rapidly increased. Coal, ore and slaves were only the most obvious cargoes they carried toward New Berlin. The sky was darker to the west, close to the city, and the stench of burning coal reached all the way to the river. Metal and stone clanked in the distance.

Whatever Hitler was doing there, it was taking a colossal amount of energy, and huge supplies of iron ore. Given he wanted to conquer the world, that could hardly be good.

Men unloaded cargoes from boats tied up along the river bank, transferring them to carts and camels. Soldiers with rifles, metal helmets and sand-coloured uniforms patrolled the bank and guarded the tracks that led through the dunes. They stared at the boats as they passed, and made lewd gestures at the girls. Some of them made lewd gestures at Osiris, too.

The leader of the trading flotilla sat at the side of the boat. Rai, a short, thin girl from the mines, crouched beside him, with her head bobbing up and down beneath his loincloth. The man smiled and hummed to himself as he looked out across the water toward the riverbank.

A row of tall dunes rose above the river, and men with rifles stood on top of them, starting down at the boats. The cracks and thuds of metal on metal and stone on stone came from the far side. Hitler was definitely up to something out there. From the sound of it, building up his army.

The trader groaned, and stroked Rai's red hair. Then moaned for moment before he spoke.

"Well, here we are. Though I must say I shall be sad to see you all go. Thanks to you, this has been a very pleasant trip."

The crew grabbed the ropes attached to the mast, and turned the sails until the boat slid toward the river bank, where at least a dozen more boats were already tied to palm trees while their crews unloaded their cargo. As their boat turned sideways toward the sand, the crew jumped up onto the riverbank, and pulled it in. The other boats of the flotilla pulled up in a row behind them, and tied onto the trees.

Soldiers strode along the riverbank, and an officer wearing a gold-rimmed, pointed hat was talking to a group loading carts with goods from the other boats.

"What's going on?" Dirk said to the trader.

The leader shrugged. "They ask lots of questions. Been like this ever since the new Pharaoh took over. It's almost like they don't want to buy from us any more."

The officer nodded to the group he was talking to, then waved them on. Their cart rolled past him, and away toward the city through a gap between the dunes.

The officer approached the trader's boat, stepped aboard and raised his arm in the air. "Heil Hitler. Papyrus. Papyrus."

"What does he mean?" Dirk said.

The trader grunted and sighed, then patted Rai's bare back. She pulled her head out from under his loincloth, gulped, and wiped her mouth with the back of her hand. The trader reached into his clothes and pulled out a light brown leaf with squiggles and pictures drawn on it. He handed it to the officer.

"You do not have papyrus?" the trader whispered to Dirk, as the officer studied the pictures on the leaf.

"I don't even know what that is."

"Ah, these days the Pharaoh's men make us all carry papyrus, proving that we are allowed into the city. They're not at all happy if you don't have some."

"Lot's changed with the new Pharaoh, then?"

The leader spat into the river. "You can say that again. All these new taxes, it's hardly worth bringing a cargo here these days. The Pharaoh makes more money from it than we do."

"You don't sound happy about it."

"I think next time, we're going to Thebes. At least it's not run by thieves."

Dirk was about to ask what Thebes was, when the officer handed the leaf back. He stared at Dirk with glaring eyes, and held out his hand.

"Papyrus. Papyrus."

"I don't have any."

"Then you go no further. What about these girls?"

"They are entertainers, if you know what I mean. We want to do our part for the Pharaoh, and we heard that your men were eager for some entertainment after work."

"Trust me," the leader said. "They are very entertaining."

The officer looked the girls over again. Nefert put her hands on her hips and wiggled her bare breasts toward him. Rai leaned toward him, and licked her lips.

"They still need papyrus. No-one approaches New Berlin without permission."

Dirk laughed, and put his arms around Nefert and Sakhmet.

"You're not afraid of a few girls, are you? Are you scared that they'll kill the Pharaoh, or that they'll steal your virginity?"

The officer blushed. Dirk leaned closer.

"Of course if you would like them to..."

The officer looked at the girls again. Sweat dripped down his brow. "No-one passes without permission. The Pharaoh would have my head, if he knew I let you in."

"He doesn't have to know."

The officer waved to the soldiers. "The traders can enter. The Nubian and the others stay here."

Dirk pointed at the girls with bulging bellies. "Two of these girls are pregnant. They shouldn't have to walk to another town, when they are carrying babies."

"Not my problem. Without permission, they don't enter the city. Pharaoh's orders."

"Where do I get permission?"

"You apply for papyrus at the Gestapo office."

"And where is that?"

The officer pointed west, toward the smoke clouds that rose above the dunes. "Prinz-Albrecht-Strasse, in New Berlin."

"But I can't get into the city to go to the office without my papyrus? Is that right?"

"Perhaps your trader friends can vouch for you. With the fighting in the east, we can't risk letting anyone close to the Pharaoh without permission."

Dirk nodded. They would have to find another way in.

<20>

Dirk sat in the shade below a small clump of palm trees that stood beside the river, as the sun sank toward the dunes between them and the city. He pulled a reed from the water, and chewed on the stalk. It crunched between his teeth, and filled his mouth with a bitter taste. He spat out the remains, and tossed it aside. The girls chattered on the riverbank beside him, with their legs dangling in the river, giggling as they kicked them in the water and splashed each other.

Sakhmet strode across the sand toward them, with her long, unkempt hair blowing in the wind behind her back, and One-Eye barking at her heels.

"What did you find?" Dirk said.

"One of the soldiers was very talkative, after I gave him a little entertainment. He said he was supposed to join the attack on Thebes very soon, but, what with the slave revolt and all, he's now stuck defending a pile of sand bags here, rather than raping and pillaging."

"What the heck is Thebes?"

"The City of the Sceptre. The capital of Upper Egypt." She pointed upstream. "Many days that way."

"So, if Hitler captures Thebes, he'll rule all of Egypt?"

"Yes. The Pharaohs have been fighting each other for many years, but none has ever held both cities."

"Then we'd better stop him before he gets the chance. Did the soldier say when they attack?"

She shrugged. "In a few days."

"Then we need to get into the city soon."

"The soldiers are only guarding the track around here. We could walk a few miles along the river, and just sneak in."

"No. They're sure to have patrols in the desert, looking for anyone who might do that. Let me scout it out first."

The shadow of the dunes stretched across the sand as the sun dropped toward the horizon. In a few minutes, twilight would fall, and, soon after, the desert would be dark until the moon rose. The wind was rising as the day cooled, blowing a thin layer of sand through the air. It was going to get cold.

Dirk shinned up the trunk of a palm tree, broke off most of the leaves, and threw them down. He had no idea how long they'd burn for, but they had to be better than nothing. With a pinch of black powder, a flint knife and a sliver of metal he had taken from the tank, he set the pile alight, then threw more leaves on top until a small camp fire warmed the darkness, and the girls formed a circle around it. He sat beside Nefert, who leaned against him for warmth.

"How about a sing-song?" he said.

"Shouldn't we be breaking into the city?"

Dirk looked up at the dunes. Soldiers were lighting torches along the top, where more of them stared out into the desert, and along the river. Even more stared down at the fire, and the girls around it. That should keep their attention away from him when he went scouting.

"You distract the guards, and I'll take a look around."

Nefert began to sing a slow, lilting song, and Sakhmet joined her. The blonde, and two of the other girls, sneaked up behind Osiris, grabbed his arms, then laughed as they dragged him along the riverbank, into the darkness. Squeals, moans, and groans followed soon after.

"Keep going," Dirk said.

"Come on," Nefert said, then returned to singing. The other girls joined in.

Dirk strolled along the riverbank, until he was far from the light, and hidden in the shadows. The noise should keep the soldiers' attention focused away from him, if the girls didn't. Something padded and panted across the sand behind him.

He glanced back. One-Eye ran after him. At least, with the dog following him, Dirk would have an excuse if anyone asked what he was doing. In fact, that wasn't such a bad idea. He should have thought of it earlier himself.

He pulled another leaf from a palm tree, stripped it down to the stalk, then strolled along the river. One-Eye ran at his heels, twisting his head from side to side as he moved, so his good eye could still see where Dirk was walking ahead of him.

Soldiers stood guard behind a sandbag wall near the river bank, beside the black, iron barrel of an artillery piece that pointed upstream, toward Thebes. The men stared suspiciously at Dirk as he strolled past the sandbags, and one slid his rifle from his shoulder, holding it ready at his side.

"Halt. What are you doing?"

Dirk stopped. These guys seemed more motivated than many of the Pharaoh's soldiers he'd met so far. Maybe Hitler kept the best of his men to protect his city. Dirk turned his head and nodded toward One-Eye.

"Just taking the dog for a walk."

The soldier crept to the edge of the sandbag wall, and peered over it. One-Eye sat on the sand and stared at him, with drool around his lips. Hopefully he wasn't getting hungry again. Eating the guard could interfere with Dirk's plans.

The soldier motioned Dirk away from the sandbags with his rifle. "Don't do it around here."

Many more artillery pieces were spread out along the river. The larger guns were protected by thick sand banks that had been piled up in front of them, and the smaller by piles of sand bags. Dirk strolled past them, waving at the wary soldiers, and throwing the stalk in front of him for One-Eye to chase and catch. Hitler was clearly building up his defences, ready for an attack from the river. Good, that meant he had no idea of what Dirk had planned.

He threw the stalk up a nearby dune. It smacked into the sand near the top of the dune, then tumbled slowly back down before it embedded itself in the sand about half-way up. One-Eye raced after it. Dirk looked both ways, but the soldiers were either asleep, or staring at the girls. He climbed up the dune, and stood at the top. One-Eye ran to him with the stalk in his mouth, and Dirk took it from him.

The clunks and thuds of metal and stone he had heard at the riverbank were louder without the dune to block them out, and the desert was illuminated by the orange glow from hundreds of fires. Molten iron glowed in huge melting pots. Leather tents, and rough stone and wood huts were spread in a chaotic mass behind tall rock walls outside the city. The overseers' shouts and the crack of whips filled the air as the slaves built Hitler's war machine behind the wall. Beyond the camp, on the far side, stood a tall, dark pyramid, and beyond it rose the walls of what must be the city itself, at least four or five metres high.

Small groups of soldiers patrolled the desert around the camp. Dirk could only see one set of gates through the outer walls, at the end of the track the caravan had taken through the dunes. He and the girls would have to sneak through there, or find a way through the wall. He couldn't see them climbing it.

"Come down," a voice shouted from below. An officer with a pistol, and half a dozen soldiers carrying rifles, strode toward him as they patrolled the river bank. Dirk waved.

He threw the stalk, and One-Eye raced across the sand after it. Dirk whistled, and pretended to ignore the soldiers, until he heard the click of the pistol being cocked.

"Now," the officer said.

Dirk stepped down the dune, then slid the last few metres as the sand gave way beneath him. The officer strode toward him.

"Papyrus. Oh, it's you. Where are your girls?"

Dirk studied the man's face. It was the same officer they had met at the gate. From the look of the scowl, Dirk was pretty sure the man was getting fed up with dealing with him.

Dirk pointed along the river bank. "Singing and dancing for your men."

"Then you should return to them while you still can."

One-Eye ran back to Dirk, with his tail wagging, and the stalk clasped in his mouth. The officer took the stalk, avoiding the worst of the dog slobber. He shook it, and dog spit splattered across the sand.

"If you aren't gone when the sun rises, you will enjoy the Pharaoh's hospitality. And there will be no singing or dancing in his dungeons."

<21>

Nefert followed Dirk downriver along the path into the desert, staying as close to him as she could. Dim moonlight shining through the clouds illuminated the riverbank ahead of her. The banging and clanking from the slave camp faded away, and the girls passed the last squad of soldiers leering and yelling at them from their posts at the top of the dunes. Then there was silence, aside from the waves tapping against the riverbank, and the hiss of the wind spraying sand into the air at the top of the dunes.

Where were they going? Dirk had taken that smelly old one-eyed dog for a walk along the riverbank, then returned and told them to leave the warm fire and head off back into the desert. She'd have been a lot happier back on the riverbank, with her man to keep her warm. Besides, she was tired. The traders had kept the girls busy on their trip along the river. And she'd been feeling sick for the last few days.

Maybe it was just from the boat ride.

Maybe.

"What is it with you people and pyramids?" Dirk said.

What was she supposed to say to that? How could someone not like pyramids? Even if they were a strange man from a strange place? You had to build pyramids. Everyone knew that.

"They raise us closer to the gods in the sky."

"I've lived in the sky. I didn't see any gods up there."

She giggled. "How can you live in the sky? You'd fall."

"They call it… I don't know how to say it in Egyptian."

"Well, then. It doesn't matter."

Sakhmet pushed through the mob of girls until she was alongside Nefert. The one-eyed dog panted as he followed her heels. He seemed to like her even more than he liked Dirk.

"Where are we going?"

Dirk looked back, over his shoulder. "Far enough away from the city that Hitler's soldiers won't suspect anything."

Nefert glanced behind her. All she could see was dark sand, and the moonlight reflecting off the waves in the river. She hadn't seen a soldier, or heard one shout lewd comments about her tits and ass, for half a mile.

Dirk held up his hands, and motioned the group to stop. "All right. I want you all to sneak into the camp outside the city, and organize the slaves. Disrupt production, delay Hitler's attack, and if you can get them to revolt, storm the city."

"Sounds easy," Osiris said. "I think I'll stay here."

"There'll be a lot of graves to dig when we're done."

Far too many. Nefert smacked her elbow into Osiris' gut. Couldn't the idiot see this was serious? Even if they succeeded, defeated the Pharaoh, and gained their freedom forever, many slaves would die in the fight.

"We'll do it." She said. Even if she died, it would be better than going back to being an overseers' entertainment. She looked up at Dirk. "What about you?"

"One-Eye and me will find a way into the city somehow, then find a way to stop Hitler. If I can kill him, you'll all be free anyway, once you beat the overseers."

Sakhmet crouched on the sand, and rubbed the dog's head.

"Be careful. I want you back in one piece."

"Good luck," Nefert said. She'd saved Dirk's life when they first met, and now she might have to save it again, bringing a slave army to fight with him. She leaned forward, and pressed her chest against his abdomen, squashing her breasts against his dark skin. She reached as far as she could, but her arms couldn't even stretch around his muscular waist.

"You come back too," she said.

Particularly if the sickness in her belly wasn't from floating down the river. She'd felt odd ever since that night after they fought for their freedom, and celebrated in the tent. She rubbed her belly gently as Dirk stepped away from her.

"Time to go," he said. "We must stop Hitler and his army, before it's too late."

She released him, and turned away.

She couldn't watch as he left for what might be the last time. She strode into the desert, instead, and Osiris and the rest of the girls followed. They didn't need much light to see by as they crossed the sand, because they could just follow the stench of smoke. And, as they strode up the nearest dune toward the city, the orange glow of the fires in the slave camp illuminated the dark plain in scattered ovals of light.

Hitler must be working the slaves all day and all night. At least, back at the pyramid, she'd only had to work twelve hours a day, and fill an overseer's bed at night. Here, they seemed to be working the slaves to death.

But not for much longer.

<22>

Dirk crouched in the deep, dark shadows behind a tall dune, and scanned the riverbank in the dim moonlight, looking for Nazi patrol. The girls had long ago vanished into the desert. He just had to hope they did their part, or his might all be in vain. Even if he killed Hitler, some other asshole might just take over if the slaves didn't revolt and take power. But, first, he had to find a way into the city, or he would never get a chance to deal with Adolf. And how the heck was he going to do that, when there were hundreds of soldiers between him and the gates?

The girls might get away with wandering through the desert at night, and could be very convincing to any soldiers who decided to challenge them. But a tall, muscular warrior like Dirk would have a hard time talking his way in.

One-Eye tapped his tail against the sand beside Dirk. Then jumped to his feet and barked. A long, shallow boat sailed along the moonlit river toward them, the shimmering, moonlit glow of the boat's wake barely visible against the ripples and waves in the dark water. Dirk adjusted his enhanced vision until he could see the boat more clearly. It was small, but low in the water and packed with men. A fat man wearing colourful, expensive clothes sat near the bow, while two dark-skinned, muscular men with sickle-shaped blades hanging from their belts stood at the steering oars at the rear.

In the centre of the boat sat a dozen men tied to wooden poles. Scowling, scarred, battle-hardened men with dangerous eyes. The ones who actually still had both eyes, anyway. They looked like the last men standing at the end of a raucous space-dock bar brawl.

Dirk waved as the boat sailed past.

"Where are you going?"

"The Pharaoh wishes to see men fight to the death for sport," the fat man said. "Seems a funny idea to me, but it takes all sorts, I guess. And it's good money."

"Who are these men?"

"Criminals, mostly. The cheapest I could find at the slave market. Don't see the point paying over the odds, when they'll be dead tomorrow night. Do you?"

Dirk turned, and walked along the bank beside the boat. One-Eye followed closed behind. "Can I join you?"

"We're only travelling a few miles to the dock. Besides, you were heading in the other direction."

"No, I will join to fight."

The man laughed. "That's a good one." Then his eyes slowly studied Dirk, and the laughter faded. "Oh, you mean it."

Dirk raised his arm, and flexed his muscles. "I fight better than any slave."

"But why would you want to?"

"I just want to please the Pharaoh. Is that so bad?"

"Most will die in the games. Probably you will, too."

Dirk nodded toward the men in the boat.

"They will die. Not me."

The fat man rubbed his chin, and motioned for Dirk to step into the boat. The crew pulled on ropes, and it steered closer to the shore. The guards at the stern put their hands on their swords as Dirk jumped in.

The man motioned for Dirk to turn around, and studied his body as he did so. "Nubian, eh? You could add some spice to the fight. Why not?"

Dirk whistled. One-Eye peered over the river bank, then jumped into the boat.

The man motioned Dirk to sit beside him. "Name's Snefru. Welcome aboard."

Whether or not he had really been a gladiator in the world he came from, Dirk definitely remembered training in various kinds of unarmed combat in the Space Marines, plus bayonet, machete and knife fighting. How hard could this be? If they could get him into the city within stabbing distance of Hitler, that asshole wouldn't last long.

<23>

The girls crouched low as they jogged the final hundred cubits through the darkness down a low dune, then across the moonlit sand, toward the wall around the slave camp. Shouts and smoke clouds floated over the hastily-piled rock wall, from the camp and the glowing iron works beyond it. They had crossed the desert toward the camp without any patrols seeing them, but the only way forward was to sneak through a gate in the wall, or climb over. And neither seemed like a good idea as Nefert stared up at the stones.

She studied it for a moment. The wall was at least six cubits high. Nefert was barely three cubits tall, and she was one of the tallest of the girls. Could they grip the stones with their hands and feet to climb? She reached up to a gap between the stones, and tried to push her small fingertips between them. Even those wouldn't fit, and the skin of her fingers slid over the smooth surface of the rocks when she tried to grip them.

"Who wants to climb?" Nefert whispered.

"I don't like heights," Sakhmet said.

Sheba pushed out her bulging, pregnant belly, and rubbed it with her hand. "Do you really think I'm climbing over there like this?"

Rai yawned. "I'm too tired to climb. And my legs ache. And my ass hurts. That trader kept me up all last night."

"He was rich. And he liked you. You should have gone off with him. He might have made you his fifth wife."

Rai chuckled. "I know his type He'd have sold me to the nearest slave market as soon as he got tired of me."

Nefert turned to Osiris. "Stand against the wall."

He stepped up to the wall, and leaned against it.

"Put your hands together," Nefert said.

He clasped his hands in front of his stomach. Nefert placed her foot in his grip, lifted herself, and grabbed his shoulders. Then she wobbled on his hands as she pushed herself higher, and tried to grab the wall further up. Her hands slid on the smooth surface, and Osiris' hands wobbled beneath her.

There was a ledge just a bit higher. If she could reach that, maybe she could pull herself up. She crouched for a second, then jumped up, and grabbed for it. Her fingertips caught the edge and she hung there for a moment, sliding her fingers from side to side as they took her weight, searching for a spot where they could find a good grip.

Then she yelped as they slid free from the rock. She tumbled backwards, and flew through the dark night air until she slapped down on something. Sakhmet and Rai had grabbed her just before she hit the ground, and lowered her to the sand.

Osiris stared up at the wall. "Why don't we just go through the gate?"

"Without their papyrus?" Nefert said.

"I can tell them I'm taking you in as slaves."

Sakhmet chuckled. "Even they aren't stupid enough to fall for that one."

"It's dark now. If I offer to let them try you out, you could distract them while the rest of us sneak in."

"Oh, gods," Rai muttered. "You can't expect me to pleasure another man tonight. Unless he doesn't mind me snoring while he goes at it."

Osiris shrugged. "Most men wouldn't mind. Some might prefer it."

"What if they want to try you out?" Nefert said. "Will you sneak off with them?"

Sakhmet slapped his ass. "Look at this big, fat ass. He sure would be a good one for them to sneak off with."

Osiris bit his lip for a second, then nodded.

"All right. Let's look for another way in."

"Just like a man," Rai said. "You expect us to put out for these assholes, but you won't do it yourself."

"I'm a grave-digger, not a whore."

"Nor are we."

"Other men would say different."

"We never wanted to be the overseers' playthings."

"I never wanted to be part of this revolution. I was quite happy back there at the mines, with a nice life out in the fresh air, and plenty of exercise from digging graves. I never asked to come here with you."

"Besides," Nefert said, "even if we talked our way past them without papyrus, someone would hear of it, and come looking for us in the camp before long. We need to pass through their wall without making them suspicious."

Muffled speech came from a gate about a hundred cubits to their right. A patrol of four soldiers strode out of the gate, and walked across the sand below the dune, heading their way. Osiris and the girls pressed themselves back into the shadows near the wall, until the patrol had passed by, then disappeared into the darkness.

Osiris nodded toward them. "Why not capture those guys and take their clothes?"

"There are many more of us than them. And they're men."

Sakhmet pouted. "I don't look good in men's clothes."

"But I can pretend to be the officer, and you can pretend to be my prisoners."

Rai nudged him. "You're really getting off on this whole soldier and slave-girl thing, aren't you?"

"A man's got to have his dreams. Have you got a better idea? Because I haven't heard one from any of you."

"It's still an idiotic idea," Sakhmet said.

But the idiot did have a point. And perhaps an idiotic idea was better than no idea at all.

They couldn't fail Dirk. He was alone against an army. His life might depend on them getting through this damn wall.

And maybe, with just a few more changes, this idiotic idea might work…

<24>

Nefert led the girls along the wall. She made no attempt to avoid being seen this time. The sooner the guards saw them, the better her plan would work. Boots crunched on the sand up ahead, much louder than the dainty hiss of the girls' bare feet as they sauntered toward the men, though not much louder than the noise of Osiris' big feet on the sand behind her, as he hunched over in the middle of the group, trying to pretend he wasn't there. She'd have left him behind rather than risk the whole group, but she was going to need him once they got through the damn wall. He may be an idiot, but he still made a better man than she or any of the other girls did.

Just not much better.

A dim glow appeared around the corner of the wall as a patrol of half a dozen guards walked around it. The man at the front held a flaming torch above his head that illuminated a small circle of sand around the men.

The guard with the torch put his free hand on the hilt of his sword, and stared at the girls as they approached. His eyes opened wide as the girls smiled back at him. He watched them in silence for a few seconds, before he came to a sudden halt. Then grunted as the guards behind slammed into his back.

"Halt," the guard said, as he recovered from the surprise.

Nefert waved. "Hello, boys."

"Who are you?"

"We're the new whores for the slave camp."

The other girls giggled, and waved at the guards.

A tall guard, whose shoulders were about level with the heads of the others, stepped around the group, and studied the girls with one eye. The other was sunken and sewn-up, as though lost in the wars.

"About bloody time. The old ones are getting worn out."

"Pharaoh sent us to replace them." Nefert said. She looked up at the wall, put her finger on her lips, and pouted. "But, silly us, we just can't find the way in."

Rai grabbed the guard's arm, rubbed her bare breasts against his elbow, and stared up at him with sleepy eyes. "Maybe you brave men could help us, before we fall asleep out here, and get eaten by wild dogs?" She pressed her body closer to his. "You wouldn't want that to happen to us, would you?"

The tall guard slapped his hand on her ass. She squealed, then giggled. The guards spread out, peering past each other for a better look at the girls where the glow from the flaming torch illuminated the group.

Osiris crept forward, pushing his way between Sheba and the other pregnant girl ahead of him, keeping his head low, and his face away from the light. Good. They might believe he was a tall, fat girl in the dark, but not if they got a good look at him from close up.

Then a spindly, pointy-nosed man wearing a swastika shirt pushed the guards apart, and slid between them.

"What in Ra's name is going on?"

Nefert pouted at him. "We were just asking for directions."

"To where?" the officer said.

"They're the new whores," the tall guard said, as he fondled Rai's ass. "They're looking for the gate to the slave camp."

The officer held out his hand, and stared into Nefert's eyes.

"Papyrus."

"Papyrus?" Nefert put her hands on her hips, spread her legs wider so her bare thighs slid from the sides of her loincloth, pushed her chest out, and frowned as she pouted at him.

"Where do you think we could carry papyrus?"

The girls giggled. Osiris started to giggle with them, but Nefert motioned for him to stop. His deep voice just didn't sound right among their high-pitched cacophony. Then he tried to hide. But, even hunched down, he still towered nearly a cubit over many of the girls.

"She's got a point," the guard with the torch said.

Then he yelped as the officer slapped his hand across the back of the guard's head.

"How do we know they're really whores?"

"What do you mean?" the guards said, and pointed toward Nefert. "Just look at them."

The girls smiled at the men, and wiggled their bodies.

The officer's eyes narrowed as he stared at them. "They could be spies. The Fuhrer says we should look out for spies."

The tall guard looked down at Rai, then grabbed her hand and pulled her toward the nearest dune. "Let's find out, then."

The officer nodded toward a dark-skinned guard.

"Go with him."

The other guard grabbed Sakhmet's hand, and followed Rai. The remaining guards stared at Osiris, and kept their hands on the butts of their swords.

Nefert took a step toward them, and wiggled her butt as she did so. She raise her arms above her head. "Why don't we give the boys a dance?" she said, and winked at them.

As the girls danced, the eyes of the men turned away from Osiris, toward the girls' bare, wobbling flesh. The girls sang as they danced, turning slowly on the spot, and waving their butts at the men. Giggles and grunts floated toward them from the sand dune. Sounded like they were doing a convincing job.

The officer nodded toward Osiris. "Who's that?"

"Oh," Nefert said. "That's just Isis."

"She doesn't look much like the rest of you."

The guard with the torch swung it toward Osiris, until the light shone back from his bare skin. "She's a cubit taller. She's got no tits. And a hairy chest."

"Some men like girls like that," Nefert said.

Osiris ducked down, and turned away. But the officer strolled around the mob of girls, heading toward him.

Nefert followed, and grabbed the officer's arm, but he pulled it away from her. Osiris put his hands on his hips, and tried to pout. The officer leaned forward and stared into his face.

"Ugliest whore I've ever seen."

Osiris smiled, exposing his battered, brown teeth. Then he belched out a burp that echoed back from the stone wall beside them. His breath filled the warm, desert air with the stench of the wine and fish they'd been eating and drinking for the last week in the traders' flotilla.

The officer coughed as he backed away. The other guards returned from behind the dune, with big smiles across their faces. Sakhmet and Rai followed slowly behind them, adjusting their hair and loincloths as they sauntered back toward the group, yawning as they did so.

"These two are definitely whores, sir."

The officer glanced at Osiris, who burped in his face again. Then he nodded. "Come on."

He led the way along the wall, and the guard holding the flaming torch marched alongside him. Osiris and the girls formed up in a mass, and followed them. The other guard brought up the rear, still holding their swords.

The guards at the gates looked up as the patrol approached. Then stared at the rows of girls between the men of the patrol. Osiris looked down, and tried to avoid their gaze.

"Papyrus," the guard at the gate said.

The officer pulled something from a pouch on his belt, and waved it in front of the man. The guard saluted, then stepped away from the gates.

The officer motioned toward the open gateway. "There, ladies. I hope you bring pleasure to many of my men."

And then they were through.

The gates scraped across the sand behind the girls, then clunked closed. Behind the walls, the orange glow of hot fires melting iron illuminated the sand, and the clunk and clatter of metal on metal filled their ears.

Men leaned over the fires, with sweat running down their bare chests as they hammered the red-hot steel into weapons and strange, twisted shapes. A few glanced up at the girls as they entered, but quickly returned to their work.

Overseers patrolled between the fires. They all looked up as the gates closed, and leered at the girls. But they didn't look away. One who was as wide as he was tall stomped across the sand toward them.

"Osiris," Nefert whispered, "join up with the men, find the leaders, and bring them to me. The rest of you, find out as much as you can about this place from the overseers and guards, and figure out how to fight them."

Then the overseer grabbed her arm. She smiled at the vile bastard as he led her toward a nearby hut.

<25>

Dirk stared out between the bars that blocked the window in the thick, stone wall of the barn near the middle of the city. Straw crunched beneath his feet as he shifted his weight from side to side. The smell of piss and crap filled the air. Whether it was from the city, the animals, or the other gladiators was hard to tell. A camel was glaring at them from the far corner of the barn. Its wet, soiled fur smelled better than most of the men.

Dirk's wrists were still red from where they'd tied him up and brought him into the city with the other gladiators. It hadn't made much sense to him, but they'd said they didn't want to show him special treatment, and maybe it had helped to get him past the guards. The other gladiators hadn't taken kindly to his arrival, throwing threats and insults his way ever since he'd joined them. For now, though, they seemed to have settled into their own thoughts, most likely wondering whether they'd live to see another day.

Dirk was used to cities that sprawled for a thousand or more kilometres from side to side, often crossed entire continents, and were packed with billions of people. New Berlin barely seemed to cover two kilometres, and the slave camp outside probably held more people than the city. On many planets he'd visited, this wouldn't even qualify as a village, let alone the home of the most powerful man in the world.

Now he stood in the barn in the early morning sunlight, near a large, open square where the builders had piled roughly-cut stones into walls four or five metres tall, to build an arena for gladiator fights. The rough iron bars covering the windows and doors of the barn felt too solid for even Dirk's augmented muscles to bend. If he wanted to get to Hitler, he wouldn't do so by breaking out that way. Even if all the other gladiators were on his side, they'd be lucky to pull one bar free.

And, right now, none of them were on his side.

One-Eye was entertaining himself with a mangy, stray bitch who had sneaked in through a hole in the far corner of the barn. She yelped as he panted and drooled on her back, his tail wagging hard, and hips hammering against her ass.

Dirk's stomach rumbled. He could murder a bagel and cream cheese. Even though he had been unconscious for most of the weeks since he'd set out to eat one on the Vixen College starship, he felt like he hadn't eaten one in years. He could barely even remember what cream cheese tasted like.

Soldiers patrolled outside the barn, passing the windows in pairs every twenty minutes or so. He'd been watching them for a couple of hours, learning their routine, first as they marched with flaming torches in the night, and now as they moved on through the orange glow of the rising sun. Occasionally he could hear them shout at someone or something out of sight, then silence returned. There was no sign of Hitler, but he would have to arrive soon. If Dirk couldn't get to Hitler during the fight, he would deal with the man when it was over, the other gladiators were dead, and he was presented for his prize.

"Hey, Nubian."

One of those other gladiators stared at him. The man's cheek was scarred, and a wide, red scar crossed the thick hair on his chest. He had muscles, and big ones. But his belly was flabby as though he'd filled it with beer, and he looked more like a bar fighter than a trained gladiator. Like Dirk, he was tied to a metal ring embedded in the wall of the barn, to keep them from killing each other in private. Dying behind closed doors wouldn't be any fun for the spectators.

"What?" Dirk said.

"I'm gonna kill you." The man opened his mouth in a wide smile, revealing the three teeth he had left, then laughed.

Dirk had hoped he might be able to convince some of the men to fight with him against Hitler, rather than against each other, but, the more time he spent with them, the less likely that seemed. These men wouldn't have to be forced to fight in the arena. They'd enjoy it.

At least until one of the other men ripped their head off.

A wide man with scarred arms and a broken nose stared at him. "What are you here for anyway, Nubian?"

"My name is Dirk. And I am here to kill the Pharaoh."

A cloud of sickly-smelling spit exploded from Three-Teeth's mouth as he laughed again. "That's a good one, Nubian. I can see you'll die with a smile on your face. Might even put a smile on mine as I kill you."

"Why don't you join me? When they send us out to fight, we'll break out, attack the guards instead, and then kill Hitler. And you'll be free."

Broken-Nose nodded toward Three-Teeth. "You see him? After I robbed him, he tracked me down, killed my sisters, and ravished my camel."

Three-Teeth laughed again. "Yeah, good times. Those were the days, eh?"

"You think I want to see him go free?"

"You could settle your personal differences after we free your country from Hitler."

"I don't give a damn about Hitler. One Pharaoh is the same as any another, so far as I'm concerned," Broken-Nose said, and pulled against the rope that held him to the wall, trying to pull himself closer to Three-Teeth. "But a camel is a camel. I just want to rip his throat out with my teeth."

"You get any closer, and I'll break your nose again."

"Not if I get to him first," a man with a black eye shouted.

Soon, half the men were shouting threats, or obscenities—or both—at the other half, straining against the ropes as they tried to attack each other. Co-operation just wouldn't work.

The door opened, and Dirk squinted against the bright glow of sunlight in the doorway. Snefru stepped in, and studied the chaos around him. He clapped his hands, then smiled and rubbed them together.

"Good, good, you're really getting into the spirit of the game. I think the Pharaoh will be well pleased when you lot get swinging at each other in the arena."

"What exactly is the plan?" Dirk said.

"Oh, it's a good one. A very good one. The Pharaoh wants to demonstrate what his army is going to do to Thebes." Snefru waved his hand toward Dirk. "So this half of you are going to be Thebes, and the other half are going to be New Berlin."

"I don't want to be New Berlin," Broken-Nose said.

"Of course, Thebes will lose. The Pharaoh would be most upset otherwise. And we can't have that."

"I will be New Berlin, then."

"Prepare yourself, men. I want to see a rough, tough, no-holds-barred fight. And I want to see Thebes lose, or I will kill you myself, if the Pharaoh doesn't do it first."

Snefru held his hand in the air.

"Death to Thebes."

The men at that end of the barn all raised their hands. "Death to Thebes," they repeated, and laughed.

The men around Dirk glanced at each other. They didn't look anywhere near as happy.

<26>

Nefert gasped and panted for breath as she hauled a roughly-shaped clay water pot on her shoulder between the long rows of red-hot coal fires and metal pots where slaves were melting iron into an orange, glowing mass. The weight pressed down on her back, and forced her feet deeper into the sand, which was warming as the sun rose higher in the sky. Cool water dripped from the top of the pot as she stumbled, and it soothed her hot skin. The men glanced at her with dark, dirt-smeared faces above bare chests slick and shiny with sweat in the light from the fires. Then the overseers whipped their backs until the men looked away, and returned to their work.

Whatever their work might be. Strange metal objects were scattered across the sand around them, slowly cooling. More men, the ones with fewer muscles or serious wounds, pulled carts between the fires, tossing the metal into the carts and grunting as they took the strain and dragged them onward.

What did the Pharaoh need so much metal for?

The sun had risen above the walls of the camp, and was casting long shadows across the sand. The girls had spent half the night in the camp, talking, exploring, and entertaining... and now it was morning. Had Dirk managed to enter the city, or was he still trying? Either way, she had to find a way to start a revolt against the Pharaoh if she wanted to see her man again.

"Over here, girl," a deep, male voice said.

The man gasped and wiped sweat from his brow onto the back of his arm as she approached. His bulky, muscle-clad arms reached out and grabbed her water pot. Nefert massaged her shoulders as he lowered the pot to the ground. Her legs and back felt like they were growing a cubit longer now the weight had lifted from her body.

The man shoved his face into the top of the pot, then pulled it back out, and shook his head from side to side. His matted hair flapped around his skull. He laughed as filthy water splattered across Nefert's face and chest, and she jumped back.

Then he picked up dark metal tongs and grabbed a piece of glowing orange metal from the fire. Steam hissed from the pot as he lowered it into the water.

He nodded toward another clay pot beside the fire. "You can fill that one, now."

Nefert grabbed the pot, put it on her shoulder, and strolled on through the camp, taking the long way back toward the river. There were pits on that side of the camp, below the wall, which let water run in from the river so girls could collect it and deliver it to the men who needed it. Carrying heavy pots of water all day wasn't a job her body was suited to, but it gave her a good excuse to be wandering all over the camp, talking to people, watching them, and studying the layout.

Someone whistled, quietly, from her right.

By Set's fat cock, not another one. She'd had men whistling at her all morning, thinking they could get some action. But she was Dirk's girl now.

The whistling came again.

Her head flicked round toward it, with her mouth open, ready to tell whoever it was to piss right off. But the words stopped in her throat when she saw Osiris waving toward her from the shadows.

She glanced around her, but the men working at the fires were much too busy melting iron to be looking her way. She shuffled across the sand toward Osiris.

"What do you want?"

He nodded for her to follow him between the nearby rows of rough, leather tents. She glanced back again, then did so.

"What's going on?" she whispered.

"I've got some men for you to meet."

She stayed, as much as possible, in the shadows between the tents as she followed him. She glanced behind them every few seconds, but no overseers seemed to be looking their way. Then Osiris lifted the flap of a tent, looked past her, and motioned for her to go inside.

She slid the empty pot from her shoulder, and crouched as she entered the tent. Her eyes ached for a moment in the dim light, as they adjusted after an hour trudging around the camp in the morning desert sun. Then the interior of the tent faded in around her as her eyes adjusted. Half a dozen men crouched in a circle around the leather walls, between piled clay pots. She sniffed. The whole place smelled of oil and fish. Which was better than she could say about the rest of the slave camp.

The men stared at her as Osiris stepped in behind and closed the tent flap behind him. Finally, one of them spoke. A tanned man with scars on his stomach, a bald head, and scraggly beard.

"So you're one of the whores who say they're going to kill the Pharaoh?"

"That's right."

The men laughed. "You? Maybe you're going to fuck him to death? Is that your plan?"

"He is an old fart," a short man whose ears reached almost to the back of his head said. "I wouldn't put it past them."

"We need your help," Nefert said. "If all the slaves revolt..."

"If we revolt," Baldy said, "the soldiers will kill us. We can't fight the tanks, and their guns."

"We have fought them. And beaten them."

"I hear some of the overseers like having whores beat them."

The men laughed.

"We have killed the Pharaoh's soldiers, and destroyed their tanks. It is possible."

"In your dreams," Big-Ears said.

"It's true." Nefert nodded toward Osiris. "He saw it."

Baldy studied Osiris. "Is that true?"

"We wouldn't be here if it wasn't," Osiris said.

Baldy huffed, then rested his chin on his hands as though deep in thought. "So why would we want to join you?"

"You could be free."

"Better to live hauling rocks than die a free man. This new Pharaoh won't live forever. When he's gone, who knows what the next one will be like?"

"Maybe with the next Pharaoh," Big-Ears said, "our life will be as cushy was it was with the last Pharaoh."

A scrawny man nodded.

"Yeah, he was alright, he was."

"Yeah, he was alright. Wasn't he?"

"I mean, he might have killed a few people now and again, but he didn't really mean it. He had to behead someone now and again, or who'd respect him?"

"So long as you didn't make any noise, he didn't make any trouble. That was alright, if you ask me."

"And, if you got lucky, you might get called to the palace to see his little sister. She was a bit of alright, too."

Baldy nudged him. "Real goer, she was."

"You never saw her."

"No, but I heard about it from the guys who did."

"Silence," Nefert yelled. They were running out of time, if they were going to help Dirk. "Which of you has the balls to help us kill the Pharaoh, and take back their freedom?"

The men stared at her in silence. Not one opened his mouth to say he would help. Until Baldy eventually spoke.

"Come on, girl. You know it's not going to happen. It's not a bad life here, once you get used to it. Sure, maybe you lose a hand or leg now and again hauling rocks, but who doesn't?"

"It won't happen so long as you refuse to make it happen."

Baldy leaned closer to Big-Ears. and they whispered to each other for a moment. Scrawny pointed at Nefert and whispered.

Then Baldy turned back.

"Tell you what. You kill the Pharaoh, then maybe we'll join in, and do some rioting."

Well, so much for that. Nefert stepped out of the tent, picked up her water pot, and walked away. What a waste of time. The men here had grown fat and lazy, and they wouldn't follow her the way they might follow Dirk. Even if the Pharaoh decided to kill them all, they'd just line up and wait.

Useless, the lot of them.

There was no way she was going to let Dirk down, when he was risking his life to free her people from the Pharaoh. She had to find some way to help him.

Well, fine. If the bloody men wouldn't help, she and the girls would have to start the slave revolt on their own.

Sakhmet and Rai giggled as they chatted to two soldiers who stood beside one of the tanks. They pouted at the men, wriggled against the metal sides of the tank, and pushed out their chests. The men stared at them, and muttered.

Nefert strolled on through the camp. Bright sunlight glinted from the tall, black pyramid near the city walls. She raised her arm to shade her eyes from the light. Was that marble it was coated with, or iron, like the tanks?

It towered above not only the slave camp, but the Pharaoh's city, and the stone pyramids the slaves had been building for decades for the old Pharaoh. Much larger than any pyramid she had ever seen before. Why would the Pharaoh set his slaves to build that, when he could be building more tanks? Why dig up all this coal and metal, just to build another pyramid? Was he trying to seek the favour of the gods for his coming war?

Or just showing off?

Probably. Men liked doing that.

Either way, she couldn't get any closer to it. A low stone wall surrounded the pyramid, and overseers guarded the only gate. Men dragged their carts through the gate, or carried chunks of metal on their shoulders.

Her heart thudded as she stepped in behind one of the carts, and tried to pretend she belonged there. If she could sneak in between them, maybe she could find out what was inside.

<27>

The crowd shouted and yelled outside the barn, in so many voices that Dirk couldn't distinguish their words. But he could make a good guess at what they wanted. Blood and death. He'd seen enough gladiator battles on backward planets around the galaxy during his time in the Space Marines that he knew the kind of fervour they brought out in the audience. And now he was about to perform for them.

Hopefully to give them a show they didn't expect.

And would never forget.

One-Eye peered out of the barn through a gap between the door and the frame. Three-Teeth tried to grab him, then screamed and pulled his hand back, covered in blood, as One-Eye bit off one of his fingers.

One-Eye slumped down on the straw beside Dirk and chewed. Dirk peered out through the bars. Hitler still wasn't there, and Dirk had lost count of how many hours had passed. Was that asshole even coming to see the fight? Had this whole plan been a waste of his time?

The barn door creaked open as Snefru returned, smirking and wobbling as he stepped through the door. His nose glowed red, and he smelled of wine. He slapped his hands against his belly. "Ah, today is a good day to die. I hope my brave warriors are ready to perform for their Pharaoh."

Broken-Nose turned, and nodded toward Three-Teeth, who had slumped down on the rotten straw to suck on the stump of his severed finger.

"Just give me a sword, and I will kill this one."

"But you are supposed to be on the same side."

"Then I will wait until we have defeated Thebes together, and then I will kill him."

Snefru's guards stepped into the barn, untied the gladiators from the metal rings in the walls, and led them out into the arena, with their hands still tied behind them. One-eye trotted behind Dirk, dodging from side to side behind his feet and looking up at the crowd who sat on rows of stone seats around the top of the arena walls.

Snefru and the guards made two teams, five men for Thebes at one end of the arena, eight for New Berlin at the other. That didn't seem fair, but Dirk had faced far worse odds in the Space Marines. If his integrated weaponry was still working, the fight would be over in five seconds. This way, it might have to take five minutes. If he could get the team to work together.

If not, it would be hard to take eight men on his own, even if they did just turn out to be a bunch of barroom brawlers with little understanding of real combat tactics.

Snefru's men lifted piles of cloth from the rocks around the base of the arena walls. They carried the cloth toward those fighting for New Berlin, and placed a jerkin with a swastika emblazoned on the chest over each man's neck. Then they placed jerkins with stars on them over the men fighting for Thebes. Dirk smirked. How apt the symbol was for a man who had come from the stars to fight against Hitler. And they didn't even realize what they were doing.

Flags with the same symbols hung at each end of the arena, and, at the Nazi end, seats were arranged on a balcony at the top of the wall, above a row of tall stone pillars. Hitler's girl strode across the balcony, wearing a golden dress that trailed far behind her, and a silly hat shaped like a half-metre pyramid. Hitler's dog was sitting in front of one of the seats. Hitler's girl kicked the dog out of the way, and sat.

A slave girl brought her a bowl of food. Hitler's girl grabbed a handful from the bowl, then waved the girl aside.

"Is this thing ever going to start?" Hitler's girl yelled as she chewed on her snacks. "I want to get back to the pool."

Snefru strode across the arena toward the balcony, and bowed in front of her. "We await the Pharaoh's arrival before we begin our blood-soaked spectacle today."

She turned in her seat, and peered into the shadows behind the balcony. "Adolf! Stop yacking with that bloody Jewess, and get out here."

The crowd around the top of the walls cheered as Hitler stepped onto the balcony, wearing a hat even taller, sillier, and more pyramidal than his girl's. A swastika was emblazoned on the front, high above his receding hairline. Hitler had never showed any dress sense any time Dirk had seen him, and didn't look like he wanted to change that habit today. He waved at the crowd, then walked to the front of the balcony. A topless, bronze-skinned girl covered with gold jewellery followed him, crawling on all fours.

The man who had carried the briefcase through the portal stepped onto the balcony behind her. Unlike the other Nazis, he still wore a dark suit, and sweat dripped slowly down his red face above it. He sat on a wooden throne in the shade of the balcony's cloth roof, and a topless slave girl fanned his face.

"Who's that with the Pharaoh?" Dirk said.

Snefru shaded his eyes from the sun with his hand as he looked at the man. "That's Spear. Stupid name, if you ask me, but he's the one who's been making all the metal things. The Pharaoh would be nowhere without him."

Hitler coughed. The crowd's cheers faded away as his piggy eyes scanned the crowd from side to side. Then he leaned over the balcony and began to speak, spitting out his words in short bursts like an overheated machinegun.

"In just two days, our army will march on Thebes." He slammed his fist into his open palm. "They will annihilate all who stand against the new German Reich. The sword of Nazism will destroy any who resist. We will..."

Hitler's girl reached into the bowl to grab more food, then stuffed it in her mouth and mumbled as she chewed. "Get on with it, Adolf. I'm bored."

Dirk tried to ignore both of them, and Hitler's droning words, and imagine happy little fluffy bunnies hopping through the desert. He had to centre his mind, and build up a reserve of chi power to carry him through the fight.

"Today you will witness our valiant heroes exterminate the untermensch in Thebes," Hitler said, "And, before the end of the week, you will witness it for real."

The crowd cheered. Hitler sat, then waved his hand toward Snefru, who motioned to his guards.

They untied the gladiators' wrists, and handed each a weapon, keeping their free hands on their swords as they did so. Not that there was any real chance of the gladiators deciding to attack the guards instead of each other. The men stared at each other with murderous eyes, and ignored Snefru and his men.

Dirk took one of the curved swords, and twisted it in his hand. The blade was flimsy and dull, but it should still make a bloody mess of anyone he hit. He glanced at the other men on his team. None of them looked like they had much idea of how to handle any weapon bigger than the knife they would slip between your ribs in a dark alley if they got the chance.

"We're all going to die," a short man said. He tested a short spear in his hands, adjusting their position on the spear as the poorly-balanced shaft tilted in his hands.

"You're only going to die if you believe you are," Dirk said.

"You heard the Pharaoh. We're here to lose."

"Dirk Beretta does not lose."

"That doesn't help the rest of us much."

Dirk watched the New Berlin team form up at the far end of the arena. It was much like the time he fought the Vermin on Santaganeous III. They outnumbered the Marines by hundreds to one, but by circling their ships and pouring down fire, they'd driven back attack after attack, as the Vermin were forced to fight through the gaps between the ships, a few dozen at a time.

He nodded toward the stone pillars below the balcony.

"Take up a defensive position behind those pillars. Make them come to you, while I go to them."

"That doesn't sound like an exciting fight."

"Would it be more exciting if they're killing you?"

At the far end of the arena, Three-Teeth smiled at Dirk, and swung his spear in his hand. Dirk imagined butterflies fluttering around his head in a rainbow. His arms began to glow with chi power, and his vision grew brighter.

"Fight!" Snefru yelled.

The New Berlin men shouted and charged. Knowing that they were supposed to win seemed to have invigorated them. Short-Ass and the other Thebes men finally took Dirk's advice and ran behind the stone pillars, forming a tight group where they could stab through the gaps, but no-one could get a good swing at them from outside.

Dirk planted his feet firmly on the ground, yelled, and ran straight toward Three-Teeth. At the sight of Dirk's powerful, musclebound body charging toward him, Three-Teeth's smile faded, and he began to slow. Dirk pushed the chi power into his legs, and raced across the sandy floor as fast as his feet could move him.

Three-Teeth dodged the attack, but Dirk had never really intended to collide with him. Dirk pushed his weight back, fell to the sandy, stone floor of the arena, and slid along on his side. He swung his sword as he passed Three-Teeth, and blood splattered across the stone as the dull blade slashed through the man's ankle. Three-Teeth yelled and slumped down as Dirk slid to a stop. One-Eye raced across the stone and jumped toward Three-Teeth with his jaws open and teeth exposed, but one of the other men kicked him in mid-air. The impact knocked One-Eye sideways across the arena.

Dirk climbed back to his feet, just in time to parry a blow from Broken-Nose. Three-Teeth moaned as he lay in a pool of blood that oozed from his ankle and spread out into a dark brown circle across the sand. Then he pushed himself up onto his good leg. The other New Berliners fell on the Thebes men in a flurry of uncoordinated attacks.

Good. They weren't working together, only as individuals fighting for themselves. Thebes had a chance.

Blades slashed, spears stabbed and metal clanged as the men fought for an opening. Short-Ass crouched, and rammed a spear through the knee of one of the New Berlin attackers. The man screamed and fell to the stone floor of the arena, then his screams stopped short as a sword rammed hard into his left ear, and emerged from the right.

First blood to Thebes.

"Bastards," Broken-Nose said. "I was gonna kill him."

Dirk swung his sword toward Broken-Nose, who dodged back, so the blade hissed through the air mere millimetres from his chest. Dirk stepped to the left, and Broken-Nose turned with him, until his back was toward Hitler. He swung at Dirk, who ducked beneath the blow, and lunged forward to smash his shoulder into Broken-nose's chest. Broken-nose dropped his dagger under the impact, and stumbled backwards.

Just in time, as Three-Teeth's spear stabbed the ground where Dirk had been standing. One-Eye barked, and jumped on Three-Teeth's back. His jaws snapped as he tried to bite into the man's neck. Three-Teeth dropped the spear and spun around on his good leg, trying to grab One-Eye, and pull the angry dog away from his shoulders.

Broken-Nose backed closer to the wall as Dirk pushed his shoulder hard against the man. If he could push Broken-Nose back to the stones, maybe he could jump on the man's shoulders and try to get up to Hitler's balcony. Broken-Nose swung his arms, trying to grab Dirk and pull him away, but Dirk pulled his head back and dodged the attack.

A slave girl fanned Hitler's girl with a giant leaf as she leaned over the edge of the balcony. "Can you men please get this damn thing over with, so I can get back to the pool?"

The men were certainly trying. The men of Thebes moved closer together and covered the gaps between the pillars that protected them from the swinging, stabbing and poking blades of the New Berliners. They dodged aside as the New Berliners attacked, and their weapons smacked into stone, not flesh.

Another of the New Berlin men went down with a spear in his guts as a bulbous Thebian shoved it out through a gap between the pillars. But the dying man stumbled back before he fell to his knees, pulling the spear from the hands of the man who had stabbed him. He tried to pull the spear back, but one of the New Berliners swung his sword toward the man, and blood spurted from his mouth as the blade slammed into his chest, and out his back. Then he, too, fell.

Broken-Nose grunted as his back slammed against the hard stone wall of the arena. He gasped for breath, and grabbed Dirk's arms. Then his head swung forward. Dirk dodged aside, to avoid the attempt at a headbutt.

Just as the point of a spear swung past Dirk's side, and slammed into Broken-Nose's chest. Blood gushed out around the wooden shaft as it punctured his heart, then slid through his body until it burst out of his back, and pushed him away from the wall.

Dirk twisted around and grabbed the spear shaft. Broken-Nose twitched and gasped as his life oozed away through the holes in his chest. Three-Teeth clung to the other end of the spear shaft, and looked into Dirk's eyes. Then shrugged.

"Well, guess killing him now is as good as later."

Dirk heaved on the shaft. It slid from Broken-Nose's chest, and Dirk tightened his grip. He heaved against Three-Teeth, trying to pull the spear away from him as Broken-Nose slid to the ground and groaned in a pool of blood. He couldn't use Broken-Nose as a step-ladder any more, but, if he could get the spear, maybe he could toss it at Hitler and end this whole thing right now.

One-Eye yapped, and ran for Three-Teeth's feet, then snapped at the man's ankles. Three-Teeh dodged, stamping his wounded foot madly on the ground as he tried to avoid One-Eye's teeth, and fought with Dirk over the spear.

Dirk imagined a furry carpet of hundreds of happy little gerbils racing across the arena toward him, trailing rainbows. He could feel the chi power growing in his body, and his muscles glowed with fresh strength.

Then he heard yelling up above.

A pair of soldiers strode onto the balcony, pushing a bald man in front of them. Two more followed, holding a topless, brown-skinned girl between them. She kicked madly as she struggled in their grip, and the soldiers dragged her toward Hitler and Spear.

"Let go of me," she yelled.

Dirk could hardly mistake that voice. Or that bare chest, and those plump, dangling breasts that swung from side to side as she moved.

Nefert.

<28>

Dirk stared up at the balcony as Hitler twisted in his chair, to look toward Nefert. Hitler fumbled with his glasses, pushing them up his nose with his shaking hands, and squinted through the thick lenses as he stared at Nefert's writhing body between the soldiers, in the shadows below the cloth that shaded them from the burning sunlight. She struggled as the soldiers pushed her forward. Two more soldiers pushed Baldy past her, then on toward Hitler. Baldy held up his hands as they pushed him down to the stone floor of the balcony beside Hitler's chair.

Hitler's girl slumped back on her chair, then looked Nefert over with a smirk. The soldiers who held Nefert clung tighter her arms, and she squealed as they lifted her from the ground, until her feet just kicked against empty air.

Hitler leaned closer, then adjusted his glasses again as he stared at her.

"What is this Jewess doing here? Don't we have enough of them already?"

"You can say that again," Hitler's girl mumbled, as she munched on scraps from her golden bowl. "Get rid of her."

Spear glanced absentmindedly at his watch, then crossed his arms over his chest. The soldiers pushed Nefert toward Hitler, and Dirk could barely hear their words over the murmuring of the crowd as they spoke.

"We caught her making trouble near the metal pyramid. She said she had permission to go in, but she had no papyrus."

Baldy pushed himself up to his knees, keeping his face low as he rose. "My Pharaoh, she came to us trying to start a revolt, but we told her to go away."

The solder slammed his knee into Baldy's back, and pushed him back down. "So why did you not come and tell us?"

"I was going to, as soon as I could. But you know how hard it is to walk with my leg the way it is. Besides, she is just an overseer's whore, how could anyone take her seriously? I didn't think she really meant it. Who would?"

Three-Teeth grunted, and brought Dirk's attention back to the reality of the arena. Three-Teeth grabbed the spear, pulled it away, and swung it at Dirk. He dodged, and One-Eye lunged for Three-Teeth's ankle again.

This time, Three-Teeth lifted his wounded foot, and kicked One-Eye aside. Then swore as he hopped on his good leg and held the wounded foot off the ground behind him.

The dog collapsed on the sand beside Dirk, panting as though he was out of energy after all the running and barking he'd been doing during the fight. He twisted toward Dirk, and stared at the man with his one good eye.

Dirk took a step toward Three-Teeth as he hopped.

Hitler turned toward the arena, and raised his shaky hand.

"Stop," he yelled.

The men ignored him. Three-Teeth swung his spear at Dirk again, and Dirk parried with his sword. Three-Teeth swung it again. Dirk lunged forward with the sword, and the blade slashed a shallow cut across Three-Teeth's forearm.

But Dirk was tiring, too. Every swing of his sword was slower than the last, and the dull blade seemed heavier every second he held it out. The New Berliners were beginning to tire of being wounded or killed by the remaining men of Thebes, who stayed behind whatever cover the stone pillars provided, and stabbed at anything that came close. Now, those same New Berliners were beginning to glance toward Dirk, and his fight out in the open with Three-Teeth.

Where he must look like easy prey for a mass attack.

He had to beat Three-Teeth fast, and get up on the balcony to kill Hitler and rescue Nefert. If not, he might never get the chance to do so.

He sucked in a deep breath as Three-Teeth stepped away and pulled the spear back to swing it again. The long shaft gave Three-Teeth at least a half-metre more reach than Dirk. And the point lunged toward him.

Dirk dodged back, and the spear point swung past him with centimetres to spare. But that move just took him closer to the New Berliners as they approached.

Four against one. Even Dirk's enhanced strength wouldn't be much help without enough energy to power it. He glanced toward One-Eye, and whistled. But One-Eye just slumped down on the ground and panted, with his long, red tongue dangling down onto the sand. He was done.

"Stop," Hitler yelled again. Louder, this time.

The New Berliners looked up for a second, then finally stopped their approach. They stared toward the balcony, and Dirk's gaze followed theirs.

"Let us make this more interesting," Hitler said.

He grabbed Nefert's arm. And shoved her over the balcony.

She shrieked as she fell into the arena, and slumped down into the sand below the balcony. She gasped for breath as she pushed herself up onto her elbows, and tried to stand.

Three-Teeth laughed, and rubbed the front of his loincloth, as it bulged away from his legs. "Now we can show them what we'll do to the women of Thebes."

But the bare, female flesh writhing in the sand distracted the others just long enough for Dirk to attack. He felt fresh power rush through his limbs at the sight of the New Berliners striding toward Nefert. He didn't just have to save the universe now. He had to save his girl.

Three-Teeth tossed his spear into the ground beside Nefert, then stepped toward her. She screamed and tried to dodge, but her legs were still wobbling beneath her after the fall. Her knees buckled and her legs collapsed, and she fell back to the ground.

Three-Teeth grabbed Nefert's hair, and she swung her arms wildly in his direction, with her tiny fists clenched. They slammed into Three-Teeth's stomach, but he just laughed as he twisted her hair and pulled her from the ground. The other men moved in around her.

Dirk pushed all the energy he could find into his legs as he lunged toward Three-Teeth.

Three-Teeth grunted as Dirk's muscular shoulder slammed into his back. Nefert shrieked as Three-Teeth tumbled forward. She rolled aside as Three-Teeth's face smacked into the sand. Dirk grabbed her and pulled her to her feet, then pushed her away as Three-Teeth pushed himself up and spat a bloody tooth out into the sand.

He grinned a two-teethed grin toward Dirk.

"Now I'm really mad."

The remaining New Berliners stepped toward Dirk. One screamed as the bloody point of a spear burst from his chest.

Then he went down on the sand.

Short-Ass laughed and danced from where he'd thrown the spear from behind the stone pillars. Then he reached out between them and grabbed a sword from a dead New Berliner who lay in a dark pool of blood on the sand with his severed head and arms scattered around him.

The dying New Berliner screamed as Nefert pulled the spear from his back. She swung it toward them, and they dodged away. They glanced at each other, then one took a step forward. Nefert swung the spear toward him, and he dodged it. He backed away, but she couldn't keep them all at bay for long.

The point of Three-Teeth's spear was still stuck in the ground nearby. Three-Teeth climbed to his feet. Dirk raced past him, and grabbed the shaft of the spear.

He heaved it out of the ground, and began to turn.

Too late. Three-Teeth's clenched fist hammered into the back of Dirk's head. For a second, as Dirk fell to his knees, he saw stars, and galaxies, and a mob of naked college girls. Then Three-Teeth pulled the spear from his grip, and slammed a fist into Dirk's chest.

Dirk slammed down onto his back. The impact knocked the air from his lungs. He tried to get up, but his arms and legs felt like rubber. He gasped down fresh air, and tried to imagine multicoloured unicorns prancing across the arena as the world spun around him. His muscles twitched with a hint of chi power. But not enough.

"I'm bored," Hitler's girl said. "I'm going to the pool."

"Stay, my sweet currywurst," Hitler said. "It's almost done."

Hitler's girl munched from her bowl. "I've seen more action at the opera. Better fighting, too."

Three-Teeth raised the spear high above his head. Dirk grabbed One-Eye. who yelped as Dirk threw him toward Three-Teeth. One-Eye's legs flailed wildly in the air as he flew, and his claws swung toward Three-Teeth's face.

Too late. Three-Teeth dodged sideways. The tips of One-Eye's claws scraped across Three-Teeth's cheek, tearing a long, red slash across his skin. But One-Eye flew on past, and slammed down onto the sand behind Thee-Teeth, scrabbling for grip on the sandy stone as he slid toward the wall.

Three-Teeth chuckled, and swung the spear down.

<29>

Dirk stared up at Three-Teeth's spear as it flew toward his face. Nefert swung hers toward the New Berliners, but one caught it, and pulled her toward him. She pulled up her knee, trying to slam it into his balls. But he twisted aside, and it slammed into the scrawny man's stomach, instead. Dirk willed what remained of his energy into his arms as he swung them up, to try to catch Three-Teeth's spear. He tried to twist away as the gleaming metal point swung down toward him.

Three-Teeth's mangled, two-toothed grin spread even wider as the spear descended, seemingly in slow motion. There was no way Dirk's hands could reach the spear in time. He could see that now. He stared death in the face as the spear point descended. The sharp metal swung toward his chest as his enhanced brain accelerated under the threat of death, and he watched his arms swing up in slow motion.

His hands would grab the spear, but too late.

And they were already moving as fast as they could.

Then the arena exploded inwards, and the smashes and crashes of tumbling rocks falling to the ground blocked out the screams and shouts of the spectators who had been sitting on top of the wall and were now buried beneath the rocks. Three-Teeth's smile became a jaw-dropping look of horror as he turned toward the wall.

The spear slowed its descent. Dirk's hands clapped together just behind the spear point, and the rough wood scraped against his palms as he pressed them together against it. The point stopped just centimetres from his chest.

Dirk heaved on the shaft, twisting it against Three-Teeth's hands, as he tried to pull it free.

"What the f...?" Three-Teeth began.

Then a wall of metal smashed into Three-Teeth's side. Dirk rolled away as a dark cloud of smoke spread across the arena from the hole in the wall. The chatter of clunking metal and hiss of escaping steam filled the arena, and echoed back from what was left of the walls.

Three-Teeth barely had time to scream before the metal treads of the tank that had just smashed its way through the arena wall rolled up his legs with a sickening crunch. His guts burst from his belly as his skin split under the tracks, and oozed out across the sand, as though someone had pressed too hard on a tube of red, gooey toothpaste until it exploded from the cap.

Bullets ricocheted from the metal side of the tank as soldiers fired their rifles at it from the balcony, and their positions on top of what was left of the arena's walls. The last of the New Berliners stared open-mouthed at the remains of Three-Teeth's body as it writhed on the sand, then ran as the tank rolled on toward them.

Dirk grabbed Nefert, and dove for the sand, covering her body with his. The men of Thebes crouched in cover behind the stone pillars, and the surviving New Berliners yelled as a hail of soldiers' bullets hammered into them; both shots gone wide, and those ricocheting from the tank. One-Eye sniffed Three-Teeth's splattered guts, then opened his mouth wide, and began to chew.

The tank hatch clunked as it opened.

Sakhmet stood up in the hatch and smiled. Then she put her fingers in her mouth and whistled.

One-eye's head spun around toward the noise, and he ran toward the tank. He jumped up the stone blocks, then onto the turret. Sakhmet rubbed his head.

A bullet smacked against the metal beside them. Sakhmet shrieked and ducked into the turret, and One-Eye clambered up the angled side of the turret, then jumped down into the hatch beside her. Sakhmet reached up and pulled the hatch closed as more soldiers fired at them, and a dozen bullets rattled against the turret.

Gears ground as the turret turned toward the soldiers on the balcony, and the tanks main gun rose until the muzzle was pointing their way. They yelled and ran.

The gun fired, scattering what was left of the crowd of spectators as a cloud of dark smoke billowed out around the tank, and rose into the seats on the walls. The crowd yelled and coughed as they barged into each other in their rush to escape, pushing and shoving to be the first to get away from the carnage in the arena below them.

This must be a show they hadn't expected to see.

The shell whistled through the air across the arena, until it impacted the wall below the balcony. Dirk and the Thebians dodged as stone blocks shattered and fell, while stone splinters ricocheted all around him, slashing his skin when they hit. As the dust cloud of the explosion cleared, it exposed a ruined wall of fractured blocks, leading up toward the balcony.

The Thebians ran. Dirk pushed himself up, pulled Nefert up by her arms, then nodded toward the tank.

"Go."

Nefert clambered to her feet, and ran toward the tank as bullets threw clouds of sand into the air behind her. The turret hatch clunked open again, and Sakhmet leaned out just long enough to help her inside.

Dirk ran toward the first stone block that had fallen into the sand below the balcony, then began to climb. Hitler was up there, and this was Dirk's chance to end this war once and for all, before anyone else had to get killed.

Shards of stone erupted from the blocks as bullets slammed into them. Dirk glanced toward the soldiers who stood on the far side of the arena with rifles raised, then willed more power into his limbs, trying to climb faster.

Bullets slammed into the stone again, and his loincloth fluttered as one passed right between his legs. He jumped to the fallen stone pillar on his right as he climbed, and the next volley of shots hammered into the stone where he'd just been hanging.

Then men screamed.

Dirk glanced back toward the arena wall as he climbed onto the final block below the balcony. A long sword protruded from the back of one of the soldiers there, coated with a thick layer of fresh blood. Short-Ass struggled to pull the sword out of the soldier's chest as he stood on a fallen stone below.

The men of Thebes clambered up the pile of fallen stones toward the soldiers, smiling and laughing now they had a chance to escape from death in the pit. The soldiers tried to swing their rifles low enough to shoot down the side of the wall, into the mass of approaching men.

But it was too late.

One of the men of Thebes fell back, shrieking and clutching at a dark red bullet-hole on his chest. But the others climbed on. Their daggers, swords and spears hammered into the soldiers' bodies as they reached the top of the wall. The soldiers who didn't fall screaming in the first few seconds turned and ran.

Dirk grabbed the railing around the balcony, and pulled himself up. He stared into the dark shadows for a second, until his eyes adapted to the light.

All he could see were some chairs lying on their sides, some scattered bowls and munchies, and half a dozen topless slave girls hunched down and whimpering in the corner.

Hitler was gone.

<30>

Dirk pressed against Nefert's side as the tank rattled and clunked along the street, following Hitler. He peered out the tank through the narrow vision port in the thick steel hull. The cloud of smoke from the tank's engine billowed around it and up the walls of the surrounding buildings, filling the air with its stench, and intermittently blocking his view.

Men and women screamed and shouted ahead of them as the tank twisted from side to side, banging into the walls of the houses and knocking rocks free, before it twisted back and turned toward the other side of the street to repeat the process. But the clatter of the engine and rattle of the tracks were so loud he could barely hear what the people were yelling.

A donkey whinneyed and raced ahead of them, pulling a cart piled high with fruit. The fruit rattled around the cart and banged against the wood, until the cart banged over a bump in the street and fruit flew over the sides.

The tank rolled on, squashing the fruit to mush.

A group of men ran across the street toward the open door of a building on the far side, then stopped as the donkey raced toward them. It twisted around, trying to avoid them, and the cart tipped over. The rest of the fruit scattered across the street, and the cart scraped against the stone as the donkey dragged it away as fast as it could.

A hand slapped Dirk's ass.

"Get out of the way," Rai said, from the seat beside his legs. "I'm trying to steer this thing, and I can't see where I'm going with your ass in my face."

Dirk slid aside, so she could look through the slit. "We must find Hitler. If we can't kill him, he will rally his soldiers and stop the revolt."

The tank shook as it slammed into the wall again. Dirk swung his head toward Sakhmet, who was sitting on a metal chair in the turret, with One-Eye curled up on her lap. He lay there with his tongue hanging out, dripping dog drool on her bare thigh below her loincloth.

"There is a revolt, isn't there?" Dirk said.

Sakhmet bit her lip, and glanced toward Rai. Then sighed.

"Not exactly."

The tank shook again, and Dirk grabbed the nearest pipe for support. Hot metal sizzled against his palm, but he ignored the pain. It wouldn't matter, if he couldn't stop Hitler.

Rai smacked her hand against his side. "I still can't see."

Dirk clambered over the pipes that ran between the tank's steam engine and the tracks, wincing as the hot metal brushed against his skin. He crouched as he reached the turret, then looked up toward Sakhmet.

"How not exactly?"

"We've got this tank."

"And that's it?"

Rai smirked. "We entertained the soldiers. Then we got them to show us how it worked. Then, when they got out, we jumped back in, and drove off."

"I think she drove over one."

The tank shook again as it smacked into another wall. "It's not my fault. I'm still learning."

"You did it deliberately."

Rai smirked again. "Maybe a bit."

Nefert pushed into the turret beside them, and peered out through a small vision port.

"There," she yelled, and glanced toward Dirk.

He wrapped an arm around Nefert's waist and stood beside her, then crouched to look out through the turret port. Hitler was disappearing down an alley on the far side of the street, with Spear pushing his wheelchair as fast as it would go. Hitler's girl followed close behind them, still holding her bowl, and munching from it. Hitler's dog trotted behind her, led by the topless Egyptian girl wearing lots of gold.

"Halt," Dirk yelled.

Then he grabbed the tank's gun to support himself as the tracks stopped moving and the tank slid to a halt, tearing up the surface of the street and throwing a thick cloud of dust into the air that spread all around them. Nefert clung to his arm as the motion pushed her toward the tank's metal wall.

Dirk looked up toward Sakhmet. "Turn the turret," he said, and motioned for her to turn it around to the right.

She grabbed a thick metal handle beside her, and grunted as she heaved against the weight of the turret. Metal grated on metal as the turret turned. Slowly. Dirk grabbed the handle nearest him, and added his muscles to hers. Nefert turned with the turret, dodging the hot metal pipes as she peered out through the vision port.

"Stop," she yelled.

The handles clattered as Sakhmet and Dirk released them. Dirk glanced through the port beside Nefert. Hitler was barely visible now, and would be at the far end of the alley in seconds.

They'd only get one chance to stop him.

He turned back to Sakhmet. "Fire."

Sakhmet grabbed a burning cord that dangled below the tank's gun, and swung from side to side as the tank moved. She pressed it against a deep, dark hole in the top of the gun.

And nothing happened.

"Fire," Dirk said. 'Before it's too late."

She pressed the cord against the breech of the gun again. Still nothing happened.

"It's not working."

"Did you reload it?"

"What's that?"

Dirk ducked into the thick cloud of smoke that billowed around the engine, and grabbed a shell from the rack on the side of the tank. He held the heavy, metal cone in one enhanced hand, and grabbed the powder bag beside it with the other. The tank was primitive compared to the kind he was used to, but guns hadn't changed much over the millennia.

He took one look at the breech of the tank's gun, then pressed the loading lever with his elbow. The breech flipped open with a metallic clatter, and he stuffed the shell inside, then followed it with a powder bag. The gun shook with the force of his muscular arms as he slammed it closed.

"Fire," he yelled.

<31>

Dirk crouched beside the tank's gun, and peered out through the vision port again. Hitler and Spear were almost at the end of the alley as Sakhmet pressed the burning cord against the breech of the gun. It hissed for a second, then the tank shook and rattled as the gun fired.

The stench of burning gunpowder joined the steam and smoke inside the tank. The shell whistled through the air, flying across the street, and into the alley. Hitler and Spear disappeared around the corner of the alley a split-second before the shell slammed into the building behind them. The walls erupted, tossing smashed stones across the alley. The clattered against the nearby walls and bounced down them to the sand.

Dirk slammed his hand against the wall of the tank, then wiped hot sweat from his burning forehead. Even his carefully engineered body wasn't built for fighting in a steam-powered tank in the heat of planet Egypt.

"Dammit. We have to get him."

Rai pushed hard against the levers in front of her. Steam hissed from the engine, and the tank's tracks rattled as they began to move again. Then the tank shook as the left front corner smashed into the wall of the house beside them. Rocks rattled off the metal hull, and the tracks ground over them until the tank was rolling along the street again.

The tank had to turn right somewhere. But how? Dirk leaned over to look as far as he could through the right side of the vision port in the front of the turret. All he could see were the scared faces of the Egyptians racing away from the tank.

"There," Nefert said, and pointed through the vision port. Up ahead was a wider alley to the right. Probably large enough for the tank to fit through.

"Right, right," Dirk yelled at Rai.

She pulled the right lever toward her, and the tread slowed, then reversed. The tank spun to the right, crushing a fruit stall against the wall behind it, and sending half a dozen fat, mangy rats scuttling across the street. Rai pushed the lever forward again, and the tank rolled toward the alley.

Dirk grabbed the turret handles and pulled himself up so he could peer out through all the vision ports around the turret. All he could see were the walls of the surrounding buildings, and the rapidly-approaching end of the alley. Sand spread out to the horizon beyond it.

"Faster," he yelled.

Rai pushed the levers all the way forward. Steam and smoke billowed from the engine, and the rattle of the tracks grew louder until Dirk turned down the volume in his enhanced ears, and Nefert covered hers with her hands.

Then they were at the far end of the alley, and out onto the open sand beyond.

"Left," Dirk yelled.

Rai pulled the left-hand lever back. Nefert squealed as the tank swung madly to the left, and she slid toward the far wall. Dirk grabbed her arm, and pulled her toward him.

The tank slid sideways across the sand, raising a cloud of sand that filled the air around it, so thick that he could no longer see anything through the vision port.

"Halt," he yelled.

The tank wobbled backwards and forwards as it came to a sliding halt on the sand. Dirk peered out of the port, and switched his eyes to infrared. But the sand cloud was so thick he still couldn't see anything beyond it.

"Forward, slowly."

The tank jerked as Rai pushed the levers forward. It rolled on through the sand cloud, until it reached the far side, and Dirk could finally see again.

Another yellow cloud billowed from the sand ahead of them. Something brown bounced up and down across the sand in front of the cloud as it raced away across the desert.

A truck.

Dirk zoomed in with his eyes. He could just make out Hitler in the back of the truck, sitting in his wheelchair. His girl sat on the truck bed beside him, still eating from her bowl. The dog and the Egyptian girl sat on the far side, staring at Hitler.

"Hitler," Dirk yelled, and pointed at the truck.

"They're heading for the slave camp," Nefert said.

And the truck was getting away from them, too. The tank might be able to drive over the worst terrain of Egypt, but it didn't move fast. Dirk's enhanced body could easily out-run it, and the girls probably could for a while. The truck was moving at least twice as fast as the tank, even while the wood and metal wheels slid on the sand, and Spear struggled to keep it moving.

Dirk reloaded the gun as fast as he could, then grabbed the wheels on the side of the breech. He'd been trained to shoot primitive weapons in the Space Marines, but nothing quite as primitive as this one. He spun the wheels to raise the muzzle of the gun, but who knew how far it would fire, or what angle it needed to be set at to hit the receding Nazis?

He took a guess, then elevated the gun a few more degrees.

"Fire," he said.

Sakhmet touched the burning cord to the breech of the gun. The powder hissed. The tank bucked as it bounced over a ridge in the sand.

Then the gun fired. The shell whistled through the air, and Dirk pressed his face closer to the vision port, as though he could will the shell to hit the truck.

Sand erupted just ahead of the truck, on the right. The truck twisted to the left, leaning over onto two wheels with the other two spinning in mid-air.

Then it fell back, spun to the right, and sprayed sand into the air behind the rear wheels as it rolled on.

Dirk grabbed another shell from the rack, and shoved it into the breech. The gun was smoking, and the tank filled with a cloud of burnt gunpowder as the breech opened. He paused for a second to give it a little time to cool, then shoved another powder bag in there.

He slammed the breech closed, just in case the charge did cook off in the boiling desert heat. An explosion that large in the confines of the tank would kill them all. He raised the gun barrel a few degrees more, then returned to the vision port.

Even over the rattle of the tracks, the crunching of the sand beneath them, and the hissing and clanking from the tank's steam engine, he could hear shouts from the slave camp. And gunfire. Something was going on over there. Pillars of black smoke rose from the site, but was that anything unusual? He'd only seen the place at night, and it looked like something from a horror movie back then.

A loud scream came from the camp, and he tilted his head to look toward it through the tank's narrow vision port. A fat man madly swung a whip as he ran across the sand, on fire. That probably wasn't an everyday occurrence, even here.

The truck was rapidly approaching the dark mass of the black pyramid that rose high above the desert, just outside the city walls. The truck twisted left and right now, but it was hard to tell whether they were steering that way deliberately, or it was just bouncing and sliding over the sand.

Either way, the tank's gun wasn't pointing that way.

"Right," he said.

Rai pulled the lever, and turned the tank to the right. Dirk grabbed the turret handle, and heaved on it to try to line up the barrel with the truck. He counted the seconds as the truck slid from side to side. Three seconds, near enough. The shell would need two seconds to reach them. And one second, maybe, for the gun to fire once he told them to.

He turned the turret another couple of degrees to the right.

"Fire."

Sand erupted around the rear wheels of the truck as the shell exploded beside it. The truck bounced into the air as the rear wheels rose while the front dug in. Then it tumbled end-over-end across the sand. Hitler's girl screamed, and her bowl went flying from the back of the truck, which flipped onto its side, then slid across the sand until it came to a stop just a few metres from the giant pyramid.

Dirk grabbed the lever to open the gun's breech again. The lever rattled as he pulled on it, but the breech stayed shut. He pushed the lever forward, and pulled it back again, as hard as his muscles could pull.

Metal ground on metal as the breech opened. A wave of heat blasted his face. Far too hot to fire again right now.

"Hurry," he said.

But Rai was already pushing the levers forward as far as she could. The tank wasn't going to move any faster.

The smell of burning oil filled the the tank as the engine rattled and chugged behind them. Water was condensing on the metal interior where steam was leaking out around the base of the chimney. This tank wasn't going to last much longer than its gun had. But at least it might get them to Hitler.

Spear climbed out of the truck, lay on the sand, and reached out his arms beneath it. He pulled Hitler out, and Hitler cursed and fiddled with his glasses as Spear pulled out the wheelchair. The two girls crawled out from beneath the truck, and Hitler's dog followed.

Hitler clambered back into the wheelchair with Spear's help. Spear pushed him across to the ramp that rose into the front of the giant pyramid, then up the shallow ramp, hunching over the wheelchair and heaving on it with all his strength to keep it moving. Then he rolled on into the dark pyramid.

Dirk stared at the pyramid through the narrow vision port. It much be at least a hundred metres tall, and just as wide. But the dark shadows on the sand around it didn't look like the ones from the half-finished stone pyramid when he'd first woken up on planet Egypt. It was almost as though they began a few metres above the sand.

And the sides of the pyramid had looked quite smooth from a distance, but the closer they came, the more strange objects he could see protruding from them.

And then there was the dark smoke beginning to rise from the top of the pyramid. From wide, oval openings near the peak, as though someone had built chimneys to keep the people inside it warm.

Or...

Oh.

Dirk glanced at Nefert.

"That's no pyramid."

<32>

This pyramid was mobile. Thick clouds of smoke and steam burst from the angled metal peak, and it began to move. Slowly, but inexorably and with increasing speed, it rolled across the sand toward the tank. The flickering, orange glow of the fires in the slave camp glittered from its sides. They weren't made of stone, they were made from thick metal plates, crudely riveted together.

Below the pyramid, metal tracks clattered and clunked as they crushed the sand beneath them. Tracks taller than Dirk's entire tank, and at least a hundred metres long. Probably more.

It was hard to tell just how big the pyramid was, until it rolled toward the wreckage of Hitler's truck, and crushed it into the sand as though it was barely an annoyance, let alone an obstacle. The pyramid bounced up and down for a few seconds on whatever suspension it might have as the treads rolled over the truck. Then it rolled on.

Dark cylinders protruded from rectangular holes in the sides of the pyramid. Hundreds of small ones where rifle barrels flashed as the soldiers inside fired at the slaves. A dozen or more larger barrels on each side, with turrets the size of the tank's main gun. And one that protruded from the top of each side, with a barrel the size of an old-style battleship's guns, thirty centimetres or more across.

Dirk shivered in the steamy heat of the tank's interior. He'd seen big tanks before, and fought in some. But nothing the size of this thing. No wonder Hitler expected to win his war against Thebes so easily. No weapons available on planet Egypt could defeat this monstrosity.

But he had to try.

He reloaded the gun, grabbed the turret lever, and rotated it to the right, until the crude wire crosshairs of gun sights were aimed directly at the pyramid. Not that he could really miss when the bulk of the thing filled the entire gun sight.

"Fire," he yelled.

The gun boomed, and the tank bucked. Shrapnel clattered from the outside of their tank's hull. Had Hitler hit them first? Dirk glanced left to right through the narrow vision port in the front of the turret, looking for any damage. Then he looked up, at the tank's gun.

The muzzle was a twisted, torn mass of metal, mangled into blackened strips which glowed a dull orange where they weren't covered with soot. Well, that was it. Back home, a shredder might fire a thousand times a second for an hour, but one shell a minute seemed too much for these Egyptian guns.

The shell whistled through the air, across the sand. Then it exploded on the side of the pyramid. Shrapnel clattered against the metal surface, and rattled down to the sand. But, beyond that, it had no noticeable effect. The pyramid tank rolled on.

And now they had nothing to shoot at it.

Bullets rattled from the outside of their tank as the riflemen inside it opened fire at them. One bullet dinged from the edge of the tank's vision port, and ricocheted away, barely missing Dirk's face. He ducked back.

"Reverse," he yelled.

Rai pulled the levers back. The engine hissed, and the tracks began to rotate backwards. The tank lurched as the tracks dug into the sand, and pulled them away from the pyramid.

Dirk peered out of the vision port as the tank rolled away in reverse. Wasn't the pyramid bigger than it was before? He stared at the front of the tracks for a few seconds.

They were coming closer. As slowly as the pyramid tank's treads appeared to move, they only looked slow compared to the enormous bulk of the thing. The pyramid itself was gaining on them.

Light flashed from one of the pyramid's main guns.

"Left," Dirk yelled.

Rai pushed the left lever forward. The tank twisted to the left just in time, as the shell from the pyramid whistled through the air past it, and exploded in the sand beside them.

Shrapnel tapped on the side of the turret, and bounced harmlessly off the steel plates. It wouldn't have been so harmless if it had been a direct hit.

"What are we going to do?" Nefert said.

What could they do? They were in a tank that couldn't fight, out on open sand. Running away was the only sensible option, but to where? Could they reach the slave camp before the pyramid caught up with them?

Or, maybe...

"Right," Dirk said.

Rai turned the tank again. Dirk waited until it was pointing directly toward the pyramid.

"Forward."

Rai glanced at him for a second, then pushed the levers. The metal of the tracks and gears groaned as they suddenly reversed direction, and the tank slid on the sand as the tracks fought for grip. Another shell from the pyramid flew over the top of the turret, and exploded behind them.

"What are you doing?" Sakhmet said.

"There must be some way into those treads for maintenance. Or a way to climb into the pyramid if that ramp fails. If we can get underneath the thing, we can try to get inside it and fight our way to Hitler."

Rai opened her mouth as though to speak, then slammed it shut and shook her head.

It was a crazy idea, but it was the best one he had. The one thing he could be sure of was that the big guns couldn't hit them if they got too close. They couldn't aim down that far.

Rai kept the levers pushed forward as far as they would go, and the tank raced toward the pyramid. Dirk's heart pounded as he prepared for battle. All they needed was a few seconds, thirty at most, and they'd be under the pyramid where no-one could shoot at them.

Steam hissed from the engine. It clattered and shook, and the pipes glowed faintly red.

As Dirk looked back through the vision port, a shell flashed toward him, and he ducked away. A loud thunk filled the tank as the shell scraped against the side of turret, then flew on and exploded in the sand.

They might have confused the gunners with their sudden change of direction, but that wouldn't last long.

"Faster," Dirk yelled. "And be ready to get out."

They'd have a minute at most to get out of the tank and find a way to stop the pyramid, or get inside it. That was all it would take to roll past them. Once it did, they'd be easy meat for the pyramid's gunners as it rolled away.

Rai grunted and groaned as she pushed the levers forward as far as they would go. The clattering from the engine grew louder and faster.

Then it stopped.

The tank twisted to the right as the right track locked up and the left rattled to a stop. Dirk jumped down from the turret into the tank as it slowly slid to a halt. Steam was oozing from the poorly-made welds in the pipes near the engine. He stayed as far away as he could from the clouds of hot steam, but it was rapidly filling the tank. He gasped for air as the hot droplets condensed on his skin.

He grabbed the starting handle on the front of the engine, and turned it. The engine stuttered for a second, before shards of metal exploded from the sides and clattered against the inside of the hull. The top of a piston protruded from a hole in the shattered steel.

This wasn't some Yokohama Industries fusion reactor. It was something primitive desert-dwellers had built by hand.

It was never going to run again.

Nefert leaned over in the turret and peered down at him. "What's happening?"

"The engine's done for. We have to get out of here."

Stationary, they were sitting ducks. At least out on the sand, they'd have some chance of escape.

Just not very much.

Dirk glanced out of the narrow vision port below the turret, but the pyramid tank was nowhere to be seen from the angle where their tank had come to a stop. It was certainly to be heard, though.

He could hardly miss the thunderous metallic clatter as the pyramid rolled toward them, the boom of more shells exploding in the sand around the tank, or the tapping of the bullets and cloud of shrapnel from the shell bouncing off the exterior.

Sakhmet opened the hatch and peered out. Then she yelped, pulled her head back down, and slammed it closed.

"What's wrong?" Dirk said.

Then he turned toward the vision port, and the deep clunk and clatter of the pyramid's treads. It was so loud now that the whole tank shook with the noise.

He peered out. Just in time to see the front of the pyramid's treads rolling straight towards them, barely three metres away.

"Take cover," he yelled.

Rai and Nefert backed into the corners of the hull. Dirk helped Sakhmet down. She grabbed One-Eye and hunched down beside Rai.

Dirk grabbed Nefert, and pulled her close. Then the giant pyramid was upon them.

Metal creaked and crunched all around them.

The seams on the tank's hull stretched. The sides bulged, and light showed between the panels for a second, before sand began to pour in.

Then the world went dark.

<33>

Hitler's pyramid tank rolled on over the desert sand, leaving only a smear of oil and a cloud of steam behind it where the thick metal treads had torn up the sand. A gerbil peered out of a thin brown bush with sun-dried leaves nearby, then hopped across the sand. It picked up a tiny black lump that looked like a seed, and chewed on it for a second. Then spat it out.

It hopped around the tank track, avoiding the thin pillar of steam and was still rising from the ground nearby, and sniffed more of the shattered lumps of coal.

Then jumped away as the sand moved beneath it. A mound grew in the surface of the sand, rising and spreading until it was taller than the gerbil, and twice as wide as the animal was long. The mound grew taller, until the sand fell away, exposing four long, dark fingers that wriggled slowly as they fought to dig through the ground.

The gerbil hopped over and sniffed them. Then it lunged forward and took a bite.

"Ow," Dirk yelled as his face broke through the sand just a few centimetres away. The gerbil took one look at him, then hopped away, back toward the bush it came from.

Dirk pushed his head up through the sand, and spat out the granules that had filled his mouth as he dug through it. Then spat again, as the remnants ground between his teeth.

Then something slapped against the back of his head. Something wide, warm and wet. Dirk twisted his head as far as it would go, but still couldn't see what it was. It slapped against him again, rubbing against his ear, and filling it with sticky goo. Dirk pulled his head away.

He twisted it again. The camel's big, pink tongue slapped against his face, and licked it from chin to cheek.

"Get away from here," Dirk yelled.

The camel just took a step back, and stared at him.

Dirk grunted and groaned as his muscular arms pushed against the weight of the sand above them. They burst from the surface of the desert, then he reached out and slammed his hands down onto the oil-smeared sand until his fingers sank in. He heaved until his shoulders rose above the sand, then pulled more until his chest followed. A thin cloud of steam floated up from the hole around him. A few seconds later, he pulled his feet out of the hole, then turned and reached down.

Rai's thin arms reached up toward him, and he grabbed her by the wrists. She squealed as he heaved against her feathery weight, and pulled her out of the tank's turret hatch, which the pyramid had pushed a metre below the surface.

As she crawled away from the hole, spitting out dirt, he reached down again, and helped Nefert out. Sakhmet followed, clutching One-Eye's stomach with her free hand. He panted, and dripped sand-filled drool from his lips.

"Now what?" Nefert said.

Dirk stared at the metal pyramid as it rolled on across the hot sand, toward the slave camp. The guns boomed, and shells exploded among the slave huts and tents. Shells fired back from artillery near the camp, exploding on the metal surface of the pyramid. But none seemed to do much more than to kill a handful of soldiers, whose rifles fell from the gun slits and slid down the side of the pyramid to the sand far below. All the while, the shells from the pyramid were exploding around the artillery positions, and destroying them fast.

"What can we do?" Rai said. "Nothing will stop that metal pyramid now."

Nefert pressed against Dirk's side. "The slaves are doomed."

"We can try," Dirk said. The only way to ensure nothing stopped the tank was to stop trying. He wasn't going to do that while he was still alive. Even if the fate of the universe hadn't depended on beating Hitler, Dirk's peace of mind now did. He couldn't let an asshole like Hitler beat him.

"You girls go to the slaves," he said. "Help them fight. Do whatever you can to try to stop the pyramid."

"How about you?"

They pyramid tank was approaching the side of the half-built stone pyramid that Dirk had watched the slaves working on after he first awoke in the camp with Nefert. The wooden scaffolding around the pyramid had collapsed, probably when a stray shell exploded there. But ramps of sand still ran up the sides of the stone walls, rising nearly a hundred metres into the air above the desert.

He glanced toward the camel. Then smirked to himself. "I have an idea."

<34>

One thing Dirk had already learned on planet Egypt was that camels stink. He'd seen plenty of them, and never found one that didn't. Riding this one merely reinforced that observation. Back in the Space Marines, he'd even ridden the giant land-worms of Sarcophagus IX, which were often considered to be the most disgusting creatures in the galaxy. But this camel smelled worse. And the spit would probably violate a dozen major galactic chemical weapons treaties.

He perched on the camel's furry hump, wobbling from side to side as the camel stood on legs almost as long as he was tall. Its tall, brown body twisted beneath him as the animal tried to adjust to his weight, and the sides of its furry chest rubbed against his legs, scraping against the thick, dark skin of his sun-adapted body.

The clatter of the pyramid tank's tracks echoed back to him from the hard stone wall of the half-finished pyramid, a couple of hundred metres ahead of them. The tank was getting close. Dirk didn't have a lot of time to prepare, if his plan was going to work.

With nothing else to hold onto, he clung to the fur on the side of the camel's neck. He kicked the beast's side. It just spat into the sand, and huffed. He kicked it again. It twisted on its wide hooves, and chewed.

The Delhi Llama had once told him that talking to animals was easy. You just had to treat them like your retarded kid brother, and they'd understand what you meant. Once you got into complex concepts, they just couldn't understand.

Dirk had tried that technique before, with little success. But it was worth a go.

He tapped the side of the camels' neck. "You run. We save universe. You hero. Get girl camels."

The camel's ears twitched. Then it went back to chewing whatever it had in its mouth.

"Hitler bad. We kill Hitler."

It didn't seem to understand. Or perhaps it just didn't care. As bad as Hitler might have been for the people of planet Egypt, he didn't seem to have done much harm to the camels. Probably helped them, to be honest, by building trucks and tanks that could do the camels' job and give them an easy life.

The camel might not want Hitler gone.

"You help, you free."

But it seemed pretty free already, just wandering the desert, eating anything it could find. Not a bad life for a wild animal.

Well, so much for that. Dirk kicked the camel's side again, as hard as he could.

Then he grabbed for the beast's neck as it lunged forward. It began to trot. He clung tighter to the camel's neck as it bounced up and down beneath him.

Hitler's pyramid tank rolled across the sand, with the thick iron treads crushing everything in its path. It had almost reached the half-built pyramid now, and the tank crushed the tents and huts on that side of the camp beneath it as it rolled onward. Slaves yelled and screamed as they ran away from the approaching monstrosity, then vanished beneath the heavy treads to emerge a moment later as a glob of red sand behind it.

Dirk kicked the camel even harder. It twisted beneath him, and swung its neck from side to side, trying to throw him off. He clung on with all his enhanced strength, and pulled on the camel's neck to aim it toward the sand ramp at the side of the half-finished pyramid.

The camel trotted up the ramp. Dirk kicked its sides again. It snorted, and spat into the sand. But it moved faster. It swung its hump, trying to toss him off, but he pressed his knees against the beast's side and clung on as the hump bounced up and down beneath him.

The top of Hitler's metal pyramid rose above the end of the ramp now. Dirk only had seconds before it would pass by, and he'd have no hope of reaching it from there. Even now, he needed the camel to run faster, if he was going to hit the side of the pyramid near the top.

He kicked it harder. It sped up, its hooves digging deep into the ramp and leaving a cloud of sand in the air behind them. Its breath became laboured as it climbed the steep angle of the ramp beside the stone blocks that made up the side of the half-built pyramid. Each step took it ever closer to the metal side of Hitler's pyramid that rose above the top of the ramp, blocking out the cloudless blue sky.

The camel raced toward the far end of the ramp. Its hooves dug deep into the sand, crunching it beneath them. The dark metal side of the pyramid came closer every second, growing larger and larger ahead of them. It was only a few metres away.

Then the camel seemed to realize that it was about to jump out into empty air with nothing but the hard iron plates of the pyramid tank to cushion its fall. In the rush to stop Hitler, Dirk hadn't really considered what would happen to his steed. Or that it might not be too happy about its fate.

It slowed down.

"Faster," Dirk yelled, and kicked it.

It went slower still.

For an animal that looked about as smart as a rock, it didn't seem so dumb any more.

"Run. Save world. You hero. Me hero."

It slowed down, and spat. The glob of goo sank into the sand, until it became a thick, green mass.

Dirk kicked it. Then kicked it again. It swung its neck back toward him, and the top of its head smacked into Dirk's chin. He pulled his head back, and kicked the camel again.

It wasn't having it.

Dirk had to get the stupid animal going. It was that, or the universe would be run by Hitler's descendants forever.

How could the fate of the universe depend on such a stupid desert animal?

Then something flashed ahead of them. Rifles fired from the side of the pyramid. Bullets slammed into the stone beside them. Shards of stone flew into the air, chipped away by the impact. The sharp edges tore bloody gashes in Dirk's arm and leg. The camel huffed and spat as the shards slammed into its side. Its neck twisted from side to side as it swung its head. A bullet cracked through the air beside Dirk. Then another scraped across the camel's nose before it smacked into the sand below them.

The camel began to run. Uphill, along the ramp toward Hitler's pyramid, as though determined to teach the soldiers a lesson for pissing it off. Or, at least, to spit and fart at them.

"Come on," Dirk yelled, and kicked the camel's sides again.

It twisted beneath him, then raced on.

Just a few more seconds. Dirk leaned forward over the camel's neck, and braced himself for the impact when he hit the side of the pyramid.

Then the camel stopped.

Dirk yelled as he slid from the camel's back, and flew over its head. He tumbled through the air with bullets hissing and cracking all around him. Ancient instincts sent his arms flailing around him as though he could fly.

On another world, with lower gravity, it might have worked. On planet Egypt, he had no chance.

It didn't even slow his fall by a millisecond.

<35>

Nefert led the way across the desert toward the slave camp, with Rai and Sakhmet close behind and One-Eye at the rear. Sand exploded into the air on all sides where some of the shells from Hitler's tank fell short of the camp. The three girls jogged toward the gate in the wall, where the guards now lay naked and dead, in dark, red circles where the blood had drained from their bodies into the sand. There was little the girls could do for the slaves back near Khatty's old pyramid, where the Pharaoh's metal pyramid was crushing and shooting them. But they could help the rest, if they got a chance.

Nefert ducked as a shell from the pyramid tank's gun whistled through the air above their heads. It passed over the top of the wall, and exploded on the far side. A cloud of sand, bloody body parts and shattered wood rose into the air, and slaves screamed.

They had to stop the pyramid, and fast.

She stepped over the bodies of the guards. One-Eye stopped to sniff them, but Sakhmet pulled him away. He followed them through the gate, and into the slave camp.

Beyond the gates, the camp was in chaos. Slaves ran in all directions, overseers swung their whips, trying to stop the slaves. The last of the soldiers fired into the crowd from the wall, and slaves fell to the sand, oozing blood.

Nefert grabbed the soldier's rifle. She swung it toward the soldiers on the wall, and fired. One soldier fell, screaming, and his body crunched on the rocks below. He groaned for a second until a slave raised a stone hammer, and smashed his skull.

Another soldier turned his rifle toward her. Then he too, fell with blood spurting from his chest. Nefert glanced behind her. A male slave had grabbed the rifle from the soldier she'd shot, and was using it to fire back. He fumbled with it, then raised it again. The rifle boomed. Another soldier screamed and fell from the wall.

Then bullets hammered into the sand around them as the remaining soldiers fired back.

Rai grabbed Nefert's shoulder. "Come on."

She was right. They had no time to waste on soldiers when Hitler's pyramid continued to inexorably roll their way. That was what they had to stop. They could kill every soldier, and it would make no difference when the pyramid crushed the camp beneath its treads.

She held the rifle as tight as she could as she jogged across the sand, toward the deep booms on the far side of the camp. The side where the slaves had been making big metal artillery guns for the Pharaoh's army.

A whip cracked in the sand beside her. A muscular overseer about as wide as she was tall stepped out from between two huts, and cracked his whip again. Thick drool dripped from his smiling lips as he stared at the girls.

Nefert pointed the rifle toward him and tried to fire it. But nothing happened.

The overseer laughed. "Pharaoh said to kill you all. But he didn't say we couldn't have a bit of fun first."

Nefert fumbled with the rifle. She'd seen Dirk and others use them, but how did they make it work?

Too late. The whip cracked against the wooden stock of the rifle, and she squealed as it pulled the gun from her hands. It clattered against the wall of one of the huts, and fell to the sand. She lunged toward it, but the whip cracked again. She squealed as it wrapped around her ankle.

The overseer chuckled as he pulled her toward him.

She dug her fingers into the sand, trying to stop herself. But her fingertips just dug narrow trails in the ground. She kicked her legs, but she just slid faster.

Sakhmet ran between the two nearest huts, and disappeared. One-Eye barked, and followed.

"Hey," Rai yelled. As the overseer glanced toward her, she pouted and smirked, then shook her chest so her breasts wobbled from side to side.

For a second, he stopped dragging Nefert. His gaze lowered from Rai's face to her chest.

Then Sakhmet screamed as she jumped onto him from the roof of the nearby hut. She slammed down on his back, wrapped her legs around his waist, and slapped her hands over his face. He released the whip and reached up. Then screamed as Sakhmet dug her fingers into his eyes.

The overseer swung his tanned, muscular arms up toward his head. He grabbed Sakhmet's arms, and tried to pull them away. She squealed, and One-Eye raced toward him. Then jumped. The overseer screamed a hideous scream as One-Eye's jaws clamped down on his loincloth.

Rai grabbed a rock from the ground, and ran toward the overseer. Nefert dug her toes into the sand and pushed herself up, then grabbed the rifle. Rai smacked the rock against the overseer's head with a loud crunch. He twisted around, swinging his arms high, trying to knock her hands away. Rai swung the rock again, and his arm blocked her blow. With his other hand, he reached up and tried to grab Sakhmet's arm to pull it away from his face.

Nefert fumbled with the lever on the rifle. Something shiny and metallic fell out, and she pushed the lever back again. Then aimed it toward the overseer. One-Eye swung away from the overseer's groin as the man swung from side to side, trying madly to dislodge Sakhmet or the dog. Red blood spread across the thin material of the loincloth, around One-Eye's mouth.

Nefert pulled the trigger. The rifle boomed, and more blood burst from the overseer's chest.

Then his knees gave way, and he slumped down on the sand. Sakhmet released him and rolled aside. Rai swung her rock a few more times, smacking it against the overseer's head until he stopped moving.

One-Eye shook his head madly from side to side, twisting his jaws on the bloody loincloth. Sakhmet grabbed him and pulled him away.

Then a dark, triangular shadow spread across the sand around them. The hissing, clanking and crunching of the metal pyramid filled the air, and its bulk was blocking out the sun.

Rai slapped her hand on Nefert's shoulder. 'We have to go."

Slaves were screaming on the far side of the camp as they tried to escape through the wall nearest the river. The gate on that side was furthest from the metal pyramid, and the closest to freedom. But those trying to escape were caught in a crossfire from the soldiers on the walls and in the metal pyramid. Some of the slaves crouched low behind stones and huts, others threw rocks at the soldiers. A few fired captured rifles at them. But most just screamed and died.

Nefert and the others ran toward the thunder and flames of the artillery guns on the far side of the camp. The slaves had been building them for the Pharaoh, and now the slaves were turning them against him. For all the good that might do.

Bullets cracked through the air and smacked into the sand and the huts. Shells exploded, many of them near the row of booming artillery guns, which had little protection aside from the huts they were trying to hide behind. Which didn't do much when one of the pyramid's shells hit one, and blew the walls apart.

There wasn't much time.

Then they were almost at the artillery. She could see the guns now, lined up between the huts and tents about half-way across the slave camp.

But every time the pyramid's guns boomed, less huts and tents remained after the shells Hitler's men fired exploded between them, and threw leather, rocks and body parts into the desert air.

The girls ducked as a shell threw sand high above them, and left Nefert's ears ringing. She could see the men around the nearest of the slave-captured artillery yelling at each other, and at them. But she couldn't hear what they were saying over the slowly-fading ringing noise in her ears.

She covered her ears, but the buzzing only grew worse.

Then another shell flew over her head. It slammed into the gun, and blew it apart. Pieces of metal smashed into the huts beside the girls, and a rain of sand splattered on their heads.

The men who had been firing lay dead beside it. Nefert's feet slapped down into the blood-soaked sand as she stepped over the bodies, and they left red footprints behind her as she strode onward.

Osiris stood at another gun, stripped down to his loincloth, and covered in sweat which rolled over his flab and dripped to the sand below. His chubby stomach flopped down as he crouched and grabbed a shell from the pile beside it, and stuffed it into the metal tube. Then picked up a long, thick stick and pushed it down the tube.

He tossed the stick aside, then stuffed a finger in one ear, and touched the end of the burning rope to the back of the gun with his free hand.

It boomed. So loud that the shouts and screams of the slave camp were barely audible over the buzz it left in Nefert's ears.

Osiris grunted as he picked up another shell from the stack near the gun. Nefert grabbed his arm.

"We have to stop the metal pyramid."

"What?" Osiris yelled.

"I said..."

Osiris turned his head around. "Sorry, I can only hear on this side after all that racket."

"We have to stop the metal pyramid."

"What do you think I'm trying to do?"

A loud boom came from their right. The shell hit Hitler's pyramid, and exploded. Metal rattled against metal, and some of the rifles that had been pointing out of the pyramid clattered down its metal sides, toward the sand.

Then the pyramid's guns boomed once more. A shell hissed through the air above their heads, then it slammed down into the sand beside another gun a few dozen cubits to the right. Nefert ducked and covered her face as a thick cloud of sand flew toward them.

Then she opened her eyes. A severed arm slammed down on the sand beside her. A head followed, with the eyes open as wide as they would go.

A random mass of blood-soaked body parts followed.

Smoke rose from a crater in the sand a few cubits from where the other gun stood. But it still looked intact.

A pile of shells sat in the sand on the far side of the gun. A pair of severed feet stood in the sand beside them, with blood oozing from the ankles, where all that was left of the legs were a pair of shattered white bones.

Osiris covered his ear again, and his gun fired. The shell whistled across the camp toward the metal pyramid. This time, it passed a cubit above the sharp peak of the pyramid, and slammed down into the desert behind it. A shower of sand tapped against the metal wall of the pyramid, then slid back down to the ground.

Nefert grabbed an shell from the pile. She strained as she tried to lift it, but it wouldn't move, no matter how hard she tried. Rai and Sakhmet crouched down beside her, and stuffed their hands into the gaps below it. They pulled until their cheeks grew red, but it rose barely an inch before they dropped it with a gasp and clatter.

A male face peered out from a hole in the wall of a hut thirty cubits away. His eyes met hers for a second, then he ducked back.

"Help us," Nefert said.

The man peered out again. His face rose slowly, and he glanced toward the pyramid where it towered above the wall around the slave camp. The wall shook as the pyramid's metal treads slammed into it. Stones fell, and the soldiers who had been standing on them screamed as they flew through the air, and smacked down into the sand.

The pyramid didn't even slow as it pushed the stones aside and crushed any slaves, soldiers or overseers who were too slow to get out of its way. Even the stone huts barely caused it to wobble slightly as it squashed them down into the sand.

"What can we do against that?" he said.

"We can fight."

<36>

Dirk's enhanced Space Marine brain detected the prospect of imminent death, and switched into its *fast-but-dumb* mode, trading computational power for rapid response, and allowing it to operate faster than even Dirk's own reptilian hind-brain. The world seemed to slow around him as the shift occurred. His skulltop computer projected his calculated trajectory into his optic nerves. The dashed green line it created curved scarily away in front of him, and met the side of the pyramid about half-way down.

As he tumbled, he rotated far enough to see the camel stare at him from the ramp beside the pyramid. It stood there with its hooves right against the front of the ramp, slowly chewing. And upside down, because Dirk's head was below his feet.

Dirk's back slammed into the metal side of the pyramid, He grunted as the impact knocked the wind from his lungs. His arms flailed again, trying to find anything he could grasp onto, but all his fingers touched was flat metal.

He slid, head-first, down the sharply angled metal side of the pyramid, toward the ground far below. The motion was barely perceptible at first as his brain raced, with its ancient lizard-brain instincts desperately hunting for a way to survive. But he was going to continue sliding until his head slammed into the ground, if he didn't find a way to stop it.

He threw his arms out and pressed his fingers against the metal surface. It was built from plates riveted together, but the gaps between them were too small for his fingers to find any kind of grip. As he slid downward, an open, rectangular gun slit passed by, with a rifle protruding through it. But it was still too far away to grab.

He pressed his right heel hard against the metal. He winced as it bumped over the gaps between the plates, tearing away a chunk of skin. But it slowed him down on that side, and he began to turn.

His body was sliding across the tank now, as well as down. Slowly, barely fast enough to see in his accelerated state, but he was heading toward the gun slits.

Just not fast enough.

If he didn't find something to stop his descent, and fast, he was going to slide all the way down to the sand. The rattle and clunk of the metal treads grew louder as he slid toward them. If he fell that far, even if he survived the drop to the sand, he wouldn't survive being crushed beneath the metal. He didn't have a tank's hull to protect him this time, just his own skin and bones. They wouldn't do much against the weight of a huge steel pyramid.

He slid past a row of rifles, coming so close to the gun slits that he could see the bemused eyes of the soldiers staring out at him as he passed too close to shoot, but too far to grab the slit and try to stop his fall.

He stretched as far as he could. The tips of his fingers found the corner of one of the slits, just for a second. Then they lost their grip, pulled free by his momentum as he slid down the metal wall.

But it moved him further to the right. And the next row of gun slits was approaching fast.

He pressed his heel harder against the hot metal hull of the pyramid, and reached out as far as he could with his right arm, stretching it toward the forest of guns protruding from the slits. He pressed his right hand against the metal, and his body turned further, until he was sliding almost sideways.

The guns were just centimetres away. Barely out of reach.

Then something tore behind him. His loincloth caught on a row of poorly-installed rivets that protruded from the metal. His body twisted further as he slid past the next row of gun slits.

The soldier to the right leaned forward and stared at him through the slit. His gun twisted as he moved, and the barrel leaned a few centimetres toward Dirk.

Just close enough to reach.

He grabbed the gun. The hot barrel burned against his palm, but he shut down the pain. The soldier behind the gun slit yelled as Dirk's weight hauled on the barrel. His legs twisted sideways, and his body spun around. Dirk grunted with the sudden pain as all the force of slowing his slide passed through his arm to the rifle barrel. Then it pulled him to a stop. The gun clattered against the hard edge of the gun slit as it twisted in the soldier's hands.

Then it slid free.

Dirk felt himself falling, but his brain was still working fast enough to react. He grabbed the edge of the gun slit, and held on, as the rifle slid through it, then tumbled to the ground.

His legs dangled down the side of the pyramid below him. His foot slammed against something long and heavy. Another rifle, below him this time. He kicked at it, until the soldier holding the gun yelped and dropped that one, too.

But he wasn't going to save the slaves by knocking out one rifle at a time. The other soldiers were shooting at the camp non-stop, and the big guns were booming above him.

He had to get inside.

He looked up as his brain began to slow, now sure that he wasn't immediately about to die. As the world sped up, some of his reasoning powers returned. Ten metres above him, one of the big tank guns protruded from the side of the pyramid. There was no way through these tiny gun slits, but if he could get up there, perhaps he'd find a way in.

Between him and the gun stood a forest of rifle barrels, booming intermittently as the soldiers reloaded them and fired at the slaves.

He glanced down. He must still be thirty metres above the sand, and that was a long way to fall, bouncing from the hull plates until he slammed into the sand. But, really, what choice did he have?

He grunted as he heaved on the edge of the gun slit, and pulled himself up. His body flew upwards for a split second, and he reached out toward the next rifle between him and the big gun. His fingers wrapped around the barrel, and he clung onto it for a split second. Something banged on metal inside the tank, and the rifle slid through the slit. But he held it long enough to swing himself up again, grabbing another rifle above him and slamming his toes down on the base of a gun slit.

He swung from gun slit to gun slit without stopping for a second, leaving a mass of moaning and groaning soldiers in his wake, and a dozen or more rifles clattering down the side of the pyramid, toward the sand.

Gears ground together as the turret twisted in the side of the pyramid, then stopped. Dirk stared down the barrel, which was wider than his own muscular arms. For a second, his Space Marine training returned, and he mused about the wisdom of firing unguided shells from a smooth-bore barrel.

Then he realized it was pointed right at him.

He ducked, and clung onto the gap between two metal plates as the gun fired.

<37>

Nefert stared out across the sand as Sakhmet and Rai slammed the big stick into the artillery gun's barrel, forcing the next shell down the tube. The male slave grunted as he heaved on the rear of the gun, and it scraped slowly across the sand, to get a better angle on the metal pyramid as it crushed the slave camp.

Not that they could really miss from this distance. Hitler's metal pyramid towered above them, almost blocking out the sky. A rain of bullets hammered into the huts, sand and the few slaves who were brave enough to leave what little protection the huts and tents might provide.

The pyramid fired with a flash of orange flames, and another shell whistled through the air. This one was so big, she could see it as it flew toward the camp. A black lump that slid across the sky as though it was on an afternoon stroll. It grew larger as it fell toward the sand. Then larger still.

It was coming right for them.

Nefert slammed down onto the sand, and covered her head with her arms. Rai and Sakhmet dove down beside her. One-Eye circled around the gun, barking.

The shell smashed into the hut to their left. Sticks and rocks scattered across the sand as it exploded, and blew the hut apart. Chunks of wood from the roof smashed into the side of the gun, and bounced from it as they fell back to the sand.

Nefert looked up. All that remained of the hut was a smoking crater in the sand, and a few burning sticks scattered around it.

They were doomed. She should have known they couldn't win. Should have been happy to be just a bit of entertainment for the overseers, until a baby popped out and they made her a cooking slave instead. She could have lived to at least twenty that way. Maybe even old enough to see her kids grow up.

Now she was going to die, here on the sand.

No. A brave death was better than giving herself to men she hated for the rest of her life. She would die a free woman.

If only Dirk had been there to die beside her, she could go happily with him to the underworld.

Their gun fired. The shell hammered into the side of the pyramid, blowing a couple of dozen rifles from the gun slits. But that still wasn't enough.

She grabbed another shell, and the male slave helped her load it. She shook her arms to relieve the strain of the weight as Sakhmet pushed it in.

The metal pyramid was almost on them now. It had smashed through the walls and left a trail of squashed huts and people across the sand behind it. Bullets dinged as they bounced off the metal shield around their gun, and cracked as they flew through the air above the shield, before coming to a stop in the sand behind them, or slamming into the slaves trying to escape through the river gate.

Rai slapped the burning cord down on the breech of the gun. Nefert covered her ears. It boomed and shook, twisting on the sand. The shell burst from the barrel in a blast of flame, and flew through the air toward the pyramid.

It exploded near the top of the pyramid this time. The brief flash ripped through the black paint, but had no other effect that she could see, other than to piss them off.

The pyramid's guns boomed in reply.

Another big, black shell flew their way.

She dove for the sand again.

And, this time, the world exploded around her.

<38>

Dirk's enhanced ears shut down to protect themselves as the tank's big gun fired. He could feel the wind blowing his hair as the shell passed just centimetres above his head. The muzzle blast from the gun blew hot gas and debris across his dark skin, smearing him with half-burned gunpowder and glowing ashes. His face wobbled as the blast hit his skin, and blew his hair all around his head.

As he pushed himself on, his foot slid on the edge of the gun slit where he stood, and he lunged upward, grabbing the nearest rifle, and propelling himself on toward the turret.

The tank shook as another round exploded near the pointed peak of the pyramid. Dirk slammed down on the metal, as close as he could press himself against it, as shrapnel filled the air above him, clattering against the hull plates and bouncing down to the ground.

Then he moved on. He grabbed the next gun barrel above him, and winced at the heat coming from the metal where the soldier behind the gun slit had been firing at the slaves. He twisted the gun around to loosen the man's grip, then swung the barrel around, until he heard a grunt and crunch as the butt smacked into the soldier's face.

Then he pulled the rifle out through the gun slit, and tossed it aside, so it clattered down to the sand.

He worked his way up the steep incline toward the turret one gun at a time. Then grabbed the turret and peered in.

Two men moved behind the turret's gun slit. They'd pulled the cannon back into the turret, and were now busy pushing the next shell down the barrel. For all the effort Hitler and Spear had put into their enormous tank, they still hadn't mastered building breech-loading artillery yet.

Dirk whistled, then ducked down in front of the turret.

He could just hear the clatter of feet on metal inside. He waited a second, then popped up and looked in. One of the gunners stared out.

Dirk punched him in the face. The gunner didn't make a sound as he fell back, and slumped to the floor of the turret. Not that anyone inside was likely to notice, they must be deaf if they'd been shooting that thing for so long with no hearing protection. Dirk would be, if his ears weren't augmented to handle the noise of firing Space Marine weaponry. Even their handguns were louder than this antique cannon.

Dirk pushed his head in through the gun slit. The gunner who was preparing to fire the gun glanced toward him, and his eyes grew wide for a second, before he turned toward a rifle that hung from the turret wall. Dirk pushed harder as the man swung the rifle toward him. Dirk's shoulders squeezed through the slit, and his belly began to follow.

The gunner raised the rifle, and fired.

Just as Dirk's hips slid through the slit, and his body slumped down to the floor. He winced as the rifle bullet tore a long, red graze across his calf, before it slammed into the metal frame of the turret, and ricocheted. He covered his head with his hands as the bullet bounced off the roof of the turret, then the wall.

He looked up as the noise of the ricochet faded away. The gunner stared at Dirk for a second, making no attempt to chamber another round in the rifle.

Then the gunner's jaw dropped open as he looked down at the circle of red spreading across his chest, around the swastika that had been painted on his shirt. Blood oozed from the hole where the ricocheting bullet had slammed into his heart.

Then he collapsed, moaning and groaning, and lay spreadeagled on the hard metal floor of the turret.

Dirk grabbed the gunner's rifle, and cycled the action. There was a door at the rear of the turret, and he pulled it slightly open, then peered out into the interior of Hitler's metal death machine.

<39>

The corridor behind the turret was loud, smokey, and packed with men. A couple of dozen stood at gun slits in the metal walls, with a couple of metres between them. They aimed their rifles out of the slits, and fired as fast as they could. Each shot added a new cloud of foul-smelling smoke to the haze that filled the air around them. A haze thick enough that they would have a hard time even seeing who was moving through the corridor.

The soldiers had removed their shirts in the stifling heat of the tank's interior, and stood in only their loincloths and bare feet. Those at the gun slits fired and cycled the bolts on their rifles until the guns were empty. Two more men walked along the line from soldier to soldier, handing out more ammunition that they stuffed into the guns, so they could start firing again.

Hitler might not have any machineguns, but he didn't need them with hundreds of men firing their guns as fat as they could. The constant fire from the gun slits must be tearing up anything on the ground that survived the cannon.

One of the medium-sized guns near the top of the pyramid boomed, and the soldiers wobbled as the pyramid itself tilted under the recoil. Dirk grabbed the edge of the doorway, and stabilized himself as the tank tilted back on its suspension, then bounced back to something approximating vertical. But even that was only an approximation.

One of the soldiers in the corridor dropped a round as he tried to load his rifle, and it rolled away to the right, eventually coming to a stop near the far wall. He crouched and leaned over to grab it, then loaded it into the rifle and fired again.

The whole floor of the corridor was tilted a few degrees to his left. The constant firing of the guns must have unbalanced the tank, or perhaps it was just rushed into action before it was ready. Either way, Hitler would have to do some really serious maintenance work on his killing machine before he could use the thing to attack another city.

But that was the only good news Dirk had.

He was alone in a tank full of Hitler's men. He'd make a guess that Hitler and Spear would be somewhere near the top of the pyramid. In his experience of dealing with vicious, violent assholes, that was the kind of place they'd want to watch and gloat when they were dealing out the death and destruction to all around them. That was where he had to go.

But there were hundreds of men between here and there.

He backed into the turret and grabbed the dead gunner's legs, then rolled the man over, removed his swastika loincloth, and wrapped it around his own body. Then he waited until the big gun fired again, and slid out into the corridor.

The soldiers were too preoccupied with hanging on as the tank leaned under the recoil to wonder where a gunner was going. Dirk wiped sweat and steam from his forehead. In the heat inside the tank, few people would be able to tell him from the Pharaoh's men who'd taken off the rest of their uniforms. At least that would give him some opportunity to move through the tank and figure out how to get to Hitler.

Dirk kept his face low and stayed as close to the wall as he could. He clasped the gunner's rifle in his left hand, and almost pressed against the wall. Much of the corridor was dark, but beams of fading desert sunlight shone through the gun slits, and cast glowing rectangles on the floor around the shadows of the soldiers. He crossed them as fast as he could, but the corridor was barely a metre wide, and his shoulder nudged the soldiers' backs as he pushed past them.

The soldiers grunted and glanced at his back as he barged past them, then they turned back and fired their rifles out of the gun slits, toward the slave camp.

They could be shooting at Nefert, or one of the other girls. Maybe they'd shot some already.

Dirk shivered at the thought.

He paused for a second. He really shouldn't care about that right now. This was war, and his job was to kill Hitler. The girls could take care of themselves. Dealing with these men would just get him into a fight. One he couldn't win against the number of Hitler's soldiers who filled the pyramid. Beat Hitler, and he would no longer have to worry about them. He just had to find the man fast.

He settled for clenching his fists and his lips, and vowing to kill every one of them if anything happened to the girls.

The soldier beside him fired another round. Then howled He glance toward Dirk, with a smile on his face. "Got one."

The soldier turned back to the gun slit, and cycled his rifle.

To hell with subtlety. Dirk grabbed the man's legs, and heaved on them.

The man shrieked as Dirk pushed the soldier's head and shoulders through the gun slit. His rifle slid from his grip, and clattered down the outside of the tank. And he followed. He screamed as he bounced down the tank's hull, knocking a couple more rifles out of the gun slits below before he smashed down into the sand with a loud crunch.

Dirk clenched his fists and swung around, ready to take on the rest of Hitler's men. But they were too preoccupied with shooting to notice what he'd done. And the booming of the guns in such a confined space must have deafened them. If Dirk's ears didn't have built-in hearing protection, it would have deafened him, too.

He grabbed the next soldier, and tossed him out of the gun slit. Then the next. The others were still too busy shooting to notice the fate of their comrades. And every soldier Dirk tossed overboard meant three or four out of action as the falling men hit their rifles and they tumbled to the desert sand.

It was a small thing, a tiny part of the ongoing battle, but it felt good to be able to do something to help. The men firing from the slave camp were brave. But they'd need a miracle to disable the tank that way.

And the pyramid's big guns fired in return, shaking the tank more than the slaves' shells had. Paint flaked from the ceiling, and fell onto the heads of the men in the corridor. At this rate, there wouldn't be much of it left by the end of the battle. The iron walls were already smeared with steam and powder residue from the fighting.

Dirk grabbed the next soldier, and lifted him from his feet.

Then a voice called out. "You, Nubian. What in Ra's name are you doing?"

<40>

A tall, brown-skinned man wearing an officer's peaked cap pushed his way past the soldiers in the narrow, smokey metal corridor at the side of the tank. The officer stared at Dirk with barely a blink, and the scowl on his face grew more angry with every step. The smoke swirled around the man as he moved, as though even the air was scared of him, and wanted to get out of his way.

The soldier struggled in Dirk's grip, twisting and turning and trying to break free. But the soldier was a rifleman trained for shooting rather than swinging a sword, and his muscles were a fraction as large as Dirk's. In the end, the soldier settled for swinging his elbows back and trying to smack them into Dirk's stomach.

"Let me go."

The officer stomped onward, until his thudding footsteps against the metal almost drowned out the sound of the riflemen firing. "What in Ra's name are you doing?"

Dirk released the soldier, patted the man's shoulder, and rubbed the grey mass of powder residue from his skin. "Just checking the men, sir."

"You are a gunner. Why are you not at your gun?"

Dirk patted the front of his loincloth. "Sorry, sir, but nature called. I have a small bladder."

"If you need to piss, you can piss in your turret."

"The gun is broken. The Pharaoh has asked us to fire too many shots too fast. It needs some time to cool down before it will work again."

"If it needs to cool down, maybe you could piss on it."

Dirk shrugged. "That's not proper procedure, sir."

The officer peered past him. "Where are the other men?"

"What other men?"

The officer pointed past Dirk's shoulder. "The other men who should be killing the Untermensch from back there."

Dirk shrugged. "I guess they abandoned their posts."

The officer reached down to the leather belt around his waist, just above the loincloth. He pulled a roughly-made pistol from his belt. Dirk had seen enough roughly-made pistols in his time to know they could hurt just as much as a well-made one.

"Why would they do that?" the officer said.

An incoming bullet pinged from the edge of the gun slit, then slammed into the wall between Dirk and the officer, and ricocheted into the floor.

"The slaves are getting to be better shots, sir."

"If the men ran, they will be executed. Where did they go?"

"I think I saw one go down below."

The officer waved the pistol toward Dirk. "You. Return to your post. I will find the cowards."

"Let me help you, sir."

"I thought you needed to piss?"

"Perhaps I can find somewhere that way."

The officer shook his head, and lowered his gun. He turned away, and strolled along the corridor toward the empty gun slits where Dirk had tossed the soldiers outside.

Then the wall of the tank shook as a shell exploded on the hull. Hot gas burst through the gun slits, but did little more than singe a few hairs on the nearby soldiers. Shrapnel clattered against the metal hull, and a chunk about ten centimetres across slammed into Dirk's arm. But, by the time it had bounced through the gun slit and hit him, it only had enough energy left to leave a jagged, shallow scratch across his skin.

Dirk grabbed the nearest gun slit for support, and slammed the rifle butt into the back of the officer's head. The officer's pistol fired as he fell toward the floor, and Dirk ducked as the bullet ricocheted from the wall and bounced along the corridor. A soldier up ahead groaned, then collapsed at his post with blood spurting from his neck. But the rest ignored the noise and injury, as though they thought the slaves had shot him.

Dirk waited until the soldiers had returned to their routine of firing, cycling their guns and reloading. Then he grabbed the peaked cap, and slapped it on his head. It sat there, perched on the top of his skull, wobbling. Damn thing was a couple of sizes too small, but it would have to do.

He grabbed the officer's arms, pulled him into the shadows, then shoved him through the gun slit. The body thudded down to the sand, then disappeared beneath the treads.

Where now?

He turned, and followed the corridor back toward wherever the officer had come from. He'd already seen the corridor in the other direction, and there didn't seem to be any point going back that way. The soldiers moved aside as soon as they saw him approach, then glanced at his hat. They didn't care what his face looked like, so long as his clothes looked like an officer.

He followed the corridor to the corner of the pyramid, then turned. Another corridor led that way, but the men weren't shooting so fast, since their gun slits faced along the slave camp, not toward it. They only fired now and again, and saluted Dirk when he approached.

Somewhere, there must be a way to get deeper into the tank. These men had to have come up here somehow, and had to be able to get back down when required.

He stared into the shadows between the shafts of light that shone through the gun slits, and tried to pretend that he was just examining the tank for damage.

There it was, just ahead of him. An alcove in the wall, that ended at a metal rectangle with shiny hinges.

A door.

<41>

The door opened onto a scene that would have made a good substitute for Hell. Dirk had fought the Thoria there, down in the core of the galaxy with the sky glowing by the light of stars being torn apart by giant black holes. The air behind the door was even hotter than the desert outside the pyramid, and as sickeningly humid as the swamps of Subcutaneous V. There were no windows in the dark, iron walls to let the heat out and bring some cooler, less humid air in. Or to let in any light.

He stood on a platform about half-way up a room that rose perhaps forty metres from the wide metal floor to the narrow metal ceiling. Every three or four metres, a platform ran around metal walls that angled inwards as they followed the shape of the pyramid's exterior. The metal dripped with thin streams of murky water where steam was condensing on top of a thick, accumulated layer of soot, and washing it away.

The only illumination came from the flickering flames of the open fires burning below a row of thirty-metre-tall iron boilers in the middle of the room. The orange glow of the fires cast giant shadows across the walls as men moved down below. Gangs of male slaves were chained to the thick metal girders that supported the boilers. They picked up black rocks from a huge pile in the centre of the room on wide shovels, then tossed them into the flames to keep the fires burning.

One of the slaves screamed as a white cloud of steam hissed from the join between two pipes, and played across his skin. He pulled back against the chains, and raised his blackened fingers toward his face, which was a mass of bulging red blisters raised by the hot steam. Chains rattled as two of the nearby slaves tried to grab him, but their chains pulled tight before their arms could reach the man.

And it was too late. An overseer lunged forward, and cracked his whip. It wrapped around the blistered skin of the burned slave's neck, and pulled tight. The slave reached up and grabbed the leather whip cord, and heaved against it, trying to pull it free. But the overseer pulled harder. He smirked as the slave gasped for breath, then tumbled to the floor. The slave jerked for a few seconds, then stopped.

The overseer relaxed his grip, and flicked the whip free. He rolled the burned slave over with his foot, and looked up at the slaves who were staring at him. "It was for his own good."

Dirk clenched his fist around the rifle. If he could afford to give himself away, he'd shoot that asshole. But he had bigger fish to gut.

If he was going to kill Hitler, he had to even the odds. The few soldiers he'd dealt with so far weren't going to make much difference when there must be hundreds more where they came from. He needed something big. Something that would put a monkey-wrench in Hitler's plans, and distract his men.

A cough came from behind him, barely loud enough to hear over the clanking, rattling, hissing and whipping noises from down below that echoed from the hard, iron walls.

Then again.

Louder this time.

Dirk tightened his grip on the rifle, and slid his finger into the trigger guard, ready to shoot.

Then a hand tapped his shoulder.

He turned, slowly, and looked into a dark face. Not black-skinned like his own, but coated with a thick layer of soot that looked like it would go right through to the bone, and smeared with a shiny layer of oil, sweat and steam.

The man carried no weapons, unless you counted a thick iron wrench. Which could do some nasty damage to a man if it hit them in the right place. A leather pouch was strapped around his waist, hanging in front of his loincloth. The firelight glistened from rods of oily metal in the pouch. Some spanners, screwdrivers, and assorted other tools. He held a roll of papyrus in his hand with strange squiggles marked across it.

"What are you doing here?" the engineer said.

"The Pharaoh asked me to check the status of the engines."

The engineer wiped sweat and soot from his forehead. It smeared across his arm, and he wiped that on his loincloth. But the soot was too ingrained in his skin to make much difference. His forehead just became a little less dark than his cheeks.

"Tell him the engines are as good as you can expect after bringing them into action a day ahead of schedule, and running them flat out the whole time. If he wants them to work better, maybe he should try listening to us now and again. But, no. No matter how much we tell him that he's going to break them, will he listen? Maybe when the Underworld freezes over."

Dirk nodded. He'd known plenty of engineers in his time in the Space Marines. Men who kept the Marines' ships running. Fixed their suits. Overhauled their weapons. And he'd never known one who had anything good to say about the people who gave them their orders.

"Is that all?" the engineer said.

Dirk bit his lip for a second as he thought. "If a slave was to try to sabotage the pyramid, how would he do it?"

The engineer's eyes narrowed. Maybe Dirk had gone a step too far. "And why should I tell you that?"

"The Pharaoh is concerned that a slave might break free down there and try to destroy the pyramid. Are you refusing to answer his question?"

The engineer gave Dirk a *damn-you-soldiers-are-stupid* look, and sighed. Then he tossed his papyrus on a nearby metal bench, and motioned for Dirk to follow him. His feet clattered across the iron grating of the floor, and he grabbed a tubular railing as he approached the edge and looked down.

Dirk stopped beside him, and looked over. The engineer pointed toward a mass of pipes and metal cylinders that hung from the roof of the room. Wide pipes from the boilers went into the bottom of the gizmo, and ten times as many narrow pipes stretched out from it, spreading all around the room. Many disappeared through holes in the walls, heading for the other parts of the tank.

"The weakest spot," the engineer said, "is the main steam regulator over there. But it's far above the level the slaves could easily reach. We have to bring in our biggest ladders to perform maintenance on it."

"If it was damaged, what would that do?"

"It would fail to control the amount of steam entering the tracks. Pipes would burst, and the pistons in the engines could seize or break. It really wouldn't be a good day."

"Doesn't sound like it."

"But, like I said, it's much too high for the slaves to reach. The soldiers and overseers could stop them well before they could do any damage."

Dirk nodded again. That was true. Even if the slaves climbed up the girders between the floors, they'd still be metres away from the regulator. They'd have to find a pipe that would hold their weight, and slide themselves across it.

And, while doing that, they'd be easy pickings for a soldier with a rifle. There was no way they could get across the pipe fast enough, before the soldier could shoot them.

"Thank you," he said, and nodded sagely. "Everything seems to be in order."

"Good. Then I'll get back to work. Because I have a lot of it, and you're really getting in my way."

Dirk waited for the engineer to return to his desk, then swung the rifle up. He aimed quickly at the join between the regulator and one of the pipes, then fired. The gun cracked, and the slaves looked up. The bullet hit the iron pipe with a heavy thud, and punched a hole in the metal. Steam began to hiss out in a thick, white spray. He cycled the action and fired again, blowing another hole in a nearby pipe.

"What are you doing?" the engineer yelled, then stared at Dirk for a second. "Why are you wearing an army officer's hat and a gunner's loincloth?"

Dirk fired again, and blew a hole in the regulator. The metal around it began to bulge under the pressure of the escaping steam. The engineer grabbed his arm. Dirk twisted away, pulling against the engineer's thumb to break his grip. The man might have built some muscles hauling big hunks of iron around, but he was no match for the good work of the Space Marines' bioengineers.

The engineer grabbed him again.

Dirk swung his elbow, and slammed it into the engineer's face. That was enough. The man went down with barely a whimper, and smacked onto the floor.

He was keeping Hitler's machines going, he didn't deserve to die for that. His skills might come in handy for the Egyptians once Dirk had killed Hitler and set them free.

He grabbed a cable that dangled from the wall, and tore it free. Then wrapped it around the engineer's wrists and pulled it tight. The engineer struggled as Dirk grabbed the man's ankles and wrapped the other end of the cable around them, until he could no longer move.

Then Dirk raised the rifle and fired again. The bullet smacked into the regulator, and punched another hole. Steam billowed into the air. Dirk cycled the action again, and hoped there were still bullets left.

He raised the rifle to fire. Then a curved panel on the side of the regulator exploded outwards, followed by a huge cloud of steam. The panel thumped and rattled against the boilers as it tumbled down. The nearby slaves jumped aside as it fell toward them and smashed into the floor.

As the slaves heard the shots and saw the destruction they'd caused, they glanced up toward Dirk. He smiled and nodded back at them.

"Get back to work," an overseer yelled. His words were louder than the hiss of steam, and echoed from the walls until they filled the room.

He swung his whip toward the slaves. It cracked across the back of one slave, who tried to grab the cord as the overseer twisted his arm and pulled it back.

Dirk swung the rifle down, and fired.

The overseer's whip cracked for one last time as he fell backwards with blood oozing from a bullet hole in his chest. His head smacked into the metal base of one of the boilers, with a sickening crack. He slumped down into the fire, leaving a thick smear of blood behind him on the iron. His hair wiped a trail across the soot-smeared metal as he fell, then caught light as he collapsed onto the burning coals.

One of the slaves grabbed a set of keys from the overseer's belt. He unlocked his own chains, then passed them around to the other slaves nearby. In seconds, a dozen of them were free.

Another overseer peered around a nearby boiler. Dirk raised the gun again, and shot him in the head.

He cycled the action, but the magazine was empty. He tossed the gun over the rail to the nearest slave, who used the butt to thump an overseer in the face.

In a moment, the initial fight was over, as the last of the overseers working down below fell under the onslaught of a dozen slaves, who beat him and stomped him until he stopped moving. They looked at each other for a second, then glanced up at Dirk.

"Destroy whatever you can," he said. "Then raise hell."

<42>

Dirk didn't need to tell the engine-room slaves twice. They yelled and laughed as they swung the shovels against the pipes until the joins began to spew steam. Then swung them harder, until they broke apart. They stepped back, and dodged out of the way as the steam clouds passed them, and rose toward the top of the room.

Burning black rocks fell from one of the boilers as the slaves hammered against the support girders holding it above the fire. Flames rushed in lines across the floor as oil ignited where it had dripped and accumulated in gaps between the metal plates. The nearby slaves yelled and dodged aside. The boiler twisted as the narrow iron girders began to bend. Then it tilted toward the floor, slowly at first, but rapidly accelerating.

The boiler smashed into the floor, and the seams burst. Slaves jumped aside or onto the nearby machinery as hot water exploded from the boiler, putting out the fires before it sank down through gaps between the floor plates.

Wherever the water had gone, something below them began to rattle and clatter, and Dirk grabbed a nearby girder for support as the tank lurched from side to side.

The slaves slammed into pipes or fell to the floor as the tank swerved to the left. They clambered to their feet again and smashed more of the pipes and boiler controls.

Gears began to grind below them, and the tank swerved to the right, then back. The constant vibration and rattling of the tank's tracks faded as the slaves continued their work, rushing to destroy as much as possible before the soldiers now appearing on the platforms up above could stop them.

Dirk left them to it. He had to find Hitler. He glanced up. Metal ladders led from the floor of the engine room to the roof, through holes in the platforms placed every few metres around the boilers and pistons. He could barely see the top of the nearest ladder, but climbing it should take him closer to Hitler. That was all that mattered.

Slaves were climbing those same ladders on the far side of the engine room, taking over all the platforms they could reach. The clambered up as fast as they could even while soldiers fired down at them, then swarmed across the platform with any weapons they could find to beat the soldiers to death.

Dirk grabbed the nearest ladder, and climbed a step.

Then stopped as a door clunked open. A soldier stepped in through the doorway. He paused for a second as he stared at the chaos around him. Then pulled his sword from his scabbard, and waved it toward the slaves.

"Halt," the soldier yelled.

Then the blade of a shovel slammed into his face with a metallic crunch. His eyes widened and his jaw fell as the slave pulled his shovel back, then the soldier collapsed onto the floor. The slave raised the shovel again, and slammed the blade down on the soldier's neck. His head came free and rolled aside, while his blood spurted from his neck, splattering the nearby pipes and spreading in a pool all around him.

The slave laughed as the soldier's head rolled away across the platform, then gave it a good kick. It flew into the air, bounced off a nearby boiler, and smacked down to the floor below, smashing its nose. The slaves down below kicked it again.

This time, it landed in the flames below the boiler. The hair caught light almost immediately, and the burning flesh added the scent of roast pork to the mix of burning rocks, oil and steam in the air.

Dirk grabbed the soldier's sword, and hefted it in his fist. Poor balanced and overweight compared to what he was used to, but it would have to do. It was long and pointy and would look good sticking out of Hitler's guts. That was all he needed.

More soldiers appeared at other doorways, but the slaves laid into them with shovels, wrenches, and any other tools they could find. Sharp or heavy, either could do the job in a close quarters battle. Rifles fired from the doorways, but the slaves gave as good as they got, painting the engine room walls with the soldiers' blood.

Dirk began to climb the ladder. The fighting grew louder as he moved up rung by rung, toward the peak of the pyramid. He passed half a dozen platforms where soldiers and slaves were fighting for their lives, before he reached the top. Those slaves would keep Hitler's men busy while Dirk saved the universe.

Then he stopped. The ladder ended at the roof of the engine room. He ignored the sounds of fighting as he looked around him. Some poorly-made screws held a hatch in the roof half a metre from the ladder.

He shoved the point of the sword into the slots on the screws, and turned the blade until the screws came loose, then fell away. The hatch twisted away from the roof as he removed more of the screws, then fell away as the last one came out.

Metal clanked far below, and someone yelled.

Dirk pulled himself up into the hole behind the hatch, as slowly as he could, to minimize noise. He blinked for a second as his eyes grew accustomed to the bright light beyond. The hatch opened onto a room about ten metres wide near the top of the pyramid, with a balcony on one side which gave a view of the desert around them. The bright light of the sinking sun shone in from the balcony, and into Dirk's face.

Hitler stood beside a panel of gauges, switches and lights that stretched from floor to ceiling in the west wall. Some of the lights glowed red, some of the others were flashing. The needles on the gauges swung from side to side, seemingly at random. Whatever they indicated about the pyramid tank, it didn't seem to be going well.

The topless, brown-skinned girl crouched near Hitler's feet, with her face pressed against the metal floor. The suited man Spear fiddled with a console of switches and knobs that rose from the floor in the centre of the room.

"Mein Fuhrer," Spear said. "We cannot kill all the slaves. We must have them to build the weapons for our new Reich."

"We will find more slaves."

"We will have to bring them from the mines, and that will reduce production of iron and coal."

"When we capture Thebes, we will have all the slaves we could want. These must die to pay for their rebellion."

Hitler's girl leaned against the railing on the balcony.

"When can I get back to my bloody pool?"

"Soon, my little Blindinger. But we must kill the Jews first."

Hitler fiddled with the switches on the panel. Spear lunged toward his hand, but Hitler glared at him, and he pulled back.

Then something exploded down below. Dirk grabbed the edge of the hatchway to support himself as the pyramid shook from side to side.

Hitler slammed his fists against the control panel. "What the fuck is wrong with this thing?" He glanced toward Spear. "You have failed me for the last time, you Jew-loving asshole."

Hitler's dog dozed lazily beside the console. She opened her eyes for a second and stared at Dirk as he climbed into the room, then closed them again and went back to sleep.

No-one else was looking his way. Hitler was engrossed in the control panel, and the others were engrossed by Hitler.

Dirk stretched his fingers, took a firm grip on the sword, and prepared to save the universe. Then he put his free fist to his mouth, and coughed.

The cough echoed around the room, from one metal wall to another. But no-one responded.

He coughed again. This time, Hitler looked away from the panel, then adjusted the spectacles on his nose. He squinted through them at Dirk.

"You," Hitler said, as he pointed a wrinkled, shaky finger toward Dirk. "Untermensch. We killed you in the desert."

"Reports of my death were..." Dirk said, then tried to think of the right word. What was it? It was on the tip of his tongue, but with the heat and the steam and the strain of the battle, he just couldn't get it to come out.

Hitler stared at him with little piggy eyes as Dirk thought. He didn't have time for this.

"... wrong."

It would have to do.

"No matter," Hitler said. "This time they will be right."

"This time you die," Dirk said. He raised his sword, and pointed it toward Hitler. What part should he cut off first? With the fate of the universe at stake, the head would probably be the best choice. It had always worked for him before.

Well, except with species like the Vulgans that didn't keep their brain in their head, so hacking it off was just a flesh wound. But he was pretty sure Hitler did. He looked the type.

Dirk twirled his wrist, so the sword swung in a circle in his hand. The sunlight reflected from it, casting a glittering glow over the room. Hitler just stared at it.

Then he turned, and hobbled away to his wheelchair.

Dirk took a step to follow. Spear stepped out from behind the console, between Dirk and Hitler. Dirk swung the sword toward him, and Spear watched it move for a second. Then took the safer option, and hid behind the console.

Dirk raised the sword high above his head, then brought it down hard, point first. It slammed into the console, and sparks sprayed around the room. The gauges swung wildly, and lights began to flicker. He twisted the blade, tearing into whatever wires and cables were inside the console.

Smoke rose from the console, and the lights went out. Hitler's wheelchair squeaked as he rolled across the control room as fast as he could push it, toward an arch on the far side.

Dirk heaved on the sword. It twisted inside the console, and flames burst from the metal around it. He ducked back as the fire singed his eyebrows. Hitler was moving faster than Dirk had ever seen him move before. Pushing the wheels as though his life depended on it.

Which it probably did.

As the flames died away, Dirk swung back and grabbed the sword. It slid from the console as he heaved on it.

He lunged across the control room, toward the archway where Hitler was rapidly disappearing. A clay pot smashed against the wall beside Dirk's head, spraying him with nuts and munchies. Hitler's girl picked up another bowl from the floor, and threw it his way.

Dirk ducked, and it slammed into the wall beside him.

But the distraction had worked. Hitler rolled through the archway, and gears ground above it. A thick iron door began to descend from the roof of the control room to fill the arch.

Dirk raced toward it, dodging another bowl of munchies that barely missed his head. Say what you might about Hitler's girl, but she wasn't a bad shot when she was angry.

The door was almost closed. Dirk threw himself toward it, holding the sword out ahead of him as he slid across the metal floor of the control room. The blade slid through the archway as the door ground down toward it.

Then the door slammed shut. The sword crunched beneath it, but the blade held the bottom of the door a few millimetres from the floor. Just enough. Dirk crouched and pushed the tips of his fingers beneath it. He grimaced and grunted as he forced his fingers in as far as they would go, until his fingertips felt the empty air on the far side.

Then he heaved on the door.

<43>

Hitler's metal pyramid rolled into the middle of the slave camp, trailing a thick cloud of black smoke from the chimneys, and accompanied by a cacophony of clunking tracks and grinding gears. It crushed everything in its path down into the sand, and left behind a trail of shattered wood, broken stones, twisted metal, and blood. Flames glowed among the debris, where it had knocked over the fires used to melt the steel, and they had set alight the wood and cloth among the rubble.

The soldiers continued to fire from the slits in the sides of the tank, shooting at the remaining slaves as they cowered in the temporary safety of whatever cover they could find around the camp. The pyramid's guns boomed, and threw clouds of sand, rubble and debris into the air all around the camp where their shells landed.

But as the tank crushed the huts and the guns blew them up, with every moment that passed, the amount of cover the slaves could hide behind grew less.

Deep down in the shadows below the tank, something stirred beneath the rubble. Nefert pushed aside the remains of the hut wall that had fallen and protected her from most of the blast of the shell that hit their gun, and the pile of ammunition beside it. She spat sand from her mouth, and wiped it away from her lips.

Blood oozed from a gash on her forehead, but she was still alive. And something moaned and groaned beneath the remains of the gun. The base of the pyramid was perhaps a dozen cubits above her, and let in little light as its bulk blocked out the sun. But she could see a face in the rubble.

Sakhmet looked out at her, and stretched her arms past the pile of bent metal that had once been an artillery gun. Nefert grabbed her and heaved. Sakhmet slid across the sand, and pushed herself low against it as she slid out beneath the twisted and jagged hulk of the gun's armour.

The pyramid shook above them as its guns fired once more. The explosion from the guns pushed the pyramid back on its tracks for a second, and the tracks rattled and clunked as the pyramid recoiled, then rebounded. The cubit-wide springs that supported the mass of metal above them creaked and groaned as the weight of the pyramid shifted.

But, for whatever reason, it had stopped, right above them. Now, the Pharaoh's soldiers couldn't shoot at them. And they still might be able to fight back.

Nefert clambered over the piles of debris around her, and looked up at the walls and ceiling of metal at the base of the enormous tank. Metal bars, curved at each end, protruded from the walls every couple of dozen cubits along.

She climbed onto the remains of a hut wall, grabbed one of the metal bars on the side of the tank, and looked up. The bar she held was only a dozen cubits off the ground, and more of them protruded from the wall of metal higher up.

Close enough together that they could climb.

Of course. As Dirk had said, there had to be some way for the Pharaoh's men to get into the tracks and the base of the pyramid to work on them. They'd seen the big ramp when the Pharaoh escaped into the pyramid earlier, but surely they wouldn't use that all the time, not just for repairs.

"What are you so interested in?" Rai said.

Nefert grabbed the rungs of the ladder, and heaved herself up. She climbed up past the tracks, until she reached a door in the metal. She pulled it open, and peered inside.

Warm air billowed out into her face, bringing the stench of hot oil with it. She could see little detail in the shadows, but the light that reached them below the pyramid reflected off shiny metal things whose purpose she could barely even guess at. Dirk would know, but Dirk wasn't there. Either way, they looked important.

She clambered higher, until she reached the top rungs of the ladder. There was a door in the metal floor of the pyramid. She pulled that open, and pushed herself up as far as she could, until she could push her head inside, past the thick metal skin of the pyramid. The passage beyond would barely be large enough for her to climb into. The air was full of smoke and steam, but it was too dark to see what was inside even if the air was clear.

She pulled her head back, and glanced down toward the survivors of the exploding guns.

A familiar face stared up at her, as Rai helped a male survivor out of the debris. A chubby face, whose hair was now burned off on one side.

"Osiris," she yelled, and clambered down the ladder.

<44>

Dirk heaved again as he tried to lift the metal door, straining his bioengineered muscles to their limits. The muscles bulged on his arms and shoulders, stretching until his veins stood out like whips buried in a mountain of flesh. Gears grated and metal groaned somewhere in the archway around the door, and the smell of burning oil filled the air around him as the gears fought against his strength.

The door rose slightly as his muscles strained further.

But then it stopped.

Hitler was on the other side. Somehow Dirk had to lift the door and get through it to kill the man. Or find another way through the metal archway around it. He glanced to both sides, but there were no hatches in the wall that he might be able to use to get through it this time. The door was the only way.

Something thumped into his shoulders, and smashed against his straining muscles. Chunks of brown clay clattered to the floor around him.

"Leave him alone," Hitler's girl yelled at Dirk. She picked up another brown bowl of munchies, and tossed it toward him.

This time, Dirk lowered his head, and the bowl smashed against the wall, instead of his back. Nuts and dates flew through the air in a cloud behind the bowl, and clattered to the floor all around him.

Dirk imagined robins singing on the balcony railing, and bunnies hopping across the metal floor of the control room. Then gerbils bouncing across the desert, dancing and spinning as they did so. He sucked in a deep breath and strained his muscles, but the door barely moved another millimetre.

A thud echoed from the metal walls as the topless girl punched Hitler's girl in the face. Hitler's girl put one hand on her cheek as it began to bulge from the impact, and swung a punch back. The topless girl dodged, and swung her leg, knocking Hitler's girl's legs out from under her.

She smacked down on the floor, and groaned.

The topless girl grabbed something from Hitler's girl, then shuffled toward Dirk, on all fours with her face on the floor.

"Let me help," she said.

"I don't think so."

The chi power oozed into Dirk's arms and legs, and he gave the door one more heave. The gears gave way with a snap that echoed around the control room for what seemed like minutes. The door slid up another four or five centimetres.

Then stopped.

He heaved against the weight of the thick metal door, and the motors that were trying to push it down again against his muscles. But the motors were winning.

The girl reached up and pushed a key into a lock near the door. Steam hissed somewhere in the door frame, and a thin haze burst from the seal.

Then the door rose, until the gears crunched, and it stopped about a metre from the floor. The mechanism was broken, but there was still enough room for him to climb underneath.

Dirk glanced toward the girl. She smiled at him, then dropped to the floor and placed her head in front of his feet.

"Thank you," he said.

He grabbed the sword from beneath the door. The blade was a little bent in the middle, but it would still be better than a pointy stick.

The girl put her hand on his calf. "Marry me, oh great one."

Dirk crouched, and slid under the door. "Maybe later."

The edge of the door scraped against his back, but he forced his way beneath it. Then the gears rattled and crunched, and the door slammed back down into the floor.

There was no way back now.

And no way out for Hitler, either.

A staircase led down behind the door. Metal steps in a dark metal stairwell. It smelled of smoke and steam, and groans and thuds echoed against the walls from down below. Dirk crouched and held the sword ready to strike as he descended, peering into the dim light ahead of him.

The steps ended at four doors in a narrow corridor. Dirk raised his sword ready to strike, and pushed one open. Behind it was a bedroom with steeply angled walls and a big, pink bed. Desert sunlight shone in through grilled windows in the walls, casting long, thin stripes across the floor.

He tried the next. Another bedroom. And the next. A dog's straw bed in the middle of a narrow room.

Finally, the last.

He could hear moans and groans through the thin gaps around the edge of the door. Someone was inside.

He slammed the door open with his shoulder, and rushed in, ready to fight.

Totenkopf lay on the bed, wearing only a thin loincloth. Three brown-skinned Egyptian girls lay beside him, wearing nothing but frowns.

Dirk slammed the point of the sword into the bed beside Totenkopf's head. Chunks of straw and a cloud of straw dust exploded into the air as the sword slashed through the thin cloth covering it.

"Where's Hitler?"

Totenkopf raised a shaky hand, and pointed toward the far side of the room. Dirk pulled the sword away.

He felt a strange urge to punch the man in his vile, half-smirking face. Totenkopf had helped Hitler to enslave the people of planet Egypt, and now he was abusing these poor girls. Worse than that, he'd shot Dirk when he first arrived on planet Egypt.

He shouldn't, though. He had other things to do. And, if Totenkopf hadn't shot him, Dirk would never have met Nefert and her girls. So maybe it was for the best.

Screw it.

He swung the butt of the sword. Totenkopf's nose crunched as the metal smacked into it. The man screamed and fell back, with blood bursting from his broken nose.

Then Dirk hurried toward the door.

The last he saw of them, the girls were beating Totenkopf with anything they could find, as he writhed and squealed on the bed, begging them to stop.

Just not begging very hard. Somehow, Dirk really got the impression that the man kind of enjoyed it.

More steps. This pyramid must be a mass of floors, each one larger than the last as the sides of the pyramid spread further apart the closer they came to the ground. He'd seen Hitler's control room and their living quarters, but what came next?

Dirk crept down the steps. Hitler might be running from him, but, in that wheelchair, he couldn't have gone much faster than Dirk had. It must have bumped down all these steps.

The steps ended at a single door, already open. The air grew thicker with steam and smoke as Dirk descended. He swung the sword ahead of him, trying to waft some of the haze away from his face. But it just replaced the steam with smoke and the smoke with steam. The air was full of it, and more joined the clouds every second.

He ducked into the corner beside the door, then leaned out around the edge and peered into the smokey haze that filled the room beyond. A closet. The corner of a bed. And...

Hitler's wheelchair sat in the haze a couple of metres away.

Empty.

Maybe the asshole had fallen out of the thing as it rolled down the steps. It was surprising that he'd managed to get this far in it. Now he'd be crawling around the floor of the room, trying to escape, and Dirk just had to stick a sword in the man's back and save the universe.

He stepped into the room, and wafted the haze away.

Something appeared out of the haze as Dirk moved into the room, becoming clearer with every step he took. Something tall, dark and humanoid.

A clunky iron exoskeleton, whose helmeted head reached almost to the ceiling. A boiler a metre across and two metres tall puffed steam through pipes to the pistons which pumped back and forwards on the sides of the suit. The metal was painted black, with highlights in gold leaf that glittered in the narrow beams of light that shone through the haze from tall windows around the room. The highlights traced the outline of eagles and other Nazi symbols on the chest and arms of the suit.

Spear's attempt to create something like a Space Marine's battle suit, from the look of it. And one he'd put a lot of effort into, from the look of the decorations. There was probably enough gold on the suit to cover Dirk's Space Marine salary for a few millennia.

Dirk had spent many years inside those suits, and wouldn't have survived as many years as he had without them. The suit let him carry the kind of heavy weapons the Marines needed to shoot through the suits the other guys were wearing, and provided some kind of protection against their weapons. Not to mention protection against the hazardous climate of many of the planets he'd fought on.

That Spear had built a primitive version of his own was hardly good news. Dirk had torn unarmoured men apart with the suit's bare hands in close combat during his time in the Space Marines. It was a messy way to go, and he didn't fancy this guy doing that to him.

As Dirk entered the room, one of the exoskeleton's metal feet rose high into the air, then slammed down onto the metal floor, turning the suit sixty degrees toward him. The other foot followed, turning the suit until the chest was pointing toward Dirk. Then the thick metal helmet tilted up, until Dirk was looking into its visor.

He couldn't see much of the face behind the helmet, but he could see the dark, piggy eyes. There was no doubt that Hitler was inside it.

Steam billowed from the engine on the back of Hitler's iron exoskeleton. It might not be high-tech, but a steam engine was sure to be stronger than even Dirk's enhanced body.

And, somehow, he had to beat it.

Pistons hissed and scraped as Hitler raised an arm. He made a fist of his iron-clad fingers, and punched the nearest wall. The thud of the impact echoed around the compartment, and Hitler smiled as he pulled the hand back. The wall had bent beneath the blow, leaving an indentation a few centimetres deep.

Yeah, that was definitely more than Dirk's hands could do.

"Now you die, Untermensch," Hitler said. "You and all your kind are about to see your last day on Earth."

The metal floor shook as Hitler took a long step toward him, and slammed the iron feet of the suit down. He wasn't just stronger than Dirk now. He could move fast with the extra couple of metres the suit's hydraulic legs added to his gait.

Unless, perhaps, Dirk could sever the hydraulic pipes that provided power to the limbs. Or somehow put out the fire in the steam engine. Dousing it with water would do, but where would he find it in the desert? The nearest water he knew of was in the river, which was at least a kilometre from where he'd jumped onto the tank. There was no chance of that.

He clenched his fists, for what good that might do, and readied himself to save the universe.

<45>

Osiris grunted and groaned as he climbed up the ladder through the shadows beneath the pyramid, toward Nefert. She was hunched up in the base of the pyramid, where the hatch opened into the interior above the track. His face glowed red, and sweat dripped from his hair, down his forehead, and onto his bare chest. He held an artillery shell over his shoulder, and it banged against the metal wall of the tank's tracks as he climbed.

"Careful," Nefert yelled.

He pulled it further way from the metal side of the tracks. She was right. The last thing they needed was for the shell to explode now, before they pushed it in place. She'd managed to bring together a dozen or more of the slaves who'd ended up trapped below the pyramid when it stopped moving, and one exploding shell could kill them all.

Rai and Sakhmet backed away from the bottom of the tracks. They were helping the other slaves lift more shells from the pile that had survived the attack on the guns by the metal pyramid, then carry them up the ladders, and stuff them into the hatches on the treads and the base of the pyramid.

One-Eye raced around on the sand, barking and yelping at the girls down there. He snapped playfully at Sakhmet's ankles, and she giggled as she stepped aside.

Osiris heaved against the weight of the shell.

"Ra's fat nuts," he muttered as he climbed another rung, then pulled his left hand away to wipe sweat from his forehead. He slapped his wet hand down on the final rung, and pulled himself up.

He shoved the nose of the shell in through the hatch. Nefert grabbed it, and pulled as Osiris pushed. Between them they got it through the hatch and shoved it safely into the tunnel. Osiris gave it one last shove, pushing it further into the tank, then wiped his brow again.

He peered into the metal tunnel as Nefert shoved the shell as far along as it would go. Who know what was above there, but he couldn't imagine it would take kindly to having these shells explode right below it.

He took a deep breath, blew it out, then put his feet and hands on the side of the ladder and slid down. Sand crunched beneath his bare feet as he landed beside the tracks, then stomped across to the rapidly-shrinking pile of shells.

"Be careful," Rai said.

Osiris grunted as he grabbed the shell and tossed it onto his shoulder. "There's a war on, you know."

"That doesn't mean you should get yourself killed."

He climbed the ladder again. Nefert jumped down, because there would be no more room in the tunnel for her after they pushed another shell inside. Osiris grunted and groaned as he pushed the shell in there, then heaved against it to push it as far as he could into the tunnel.

"Hey," a muffled male voice yelled. "Help me."

Osiris pushed the panel back in place to seal the shells inside the tank. Then slid down the ladder.

He and Sheba grabbed the rocks that had once been the wall of one of the slave huts, and now lay in a pile on the sand. Then slowly pulled them aside. A moment later, a filthy, brown foot appeared beneath them, then a set of hairy legs. Nefert pushed aside the rocks nearest her.

A head rose from the sand below them.

A familiar bald head. The bald man who had refused to fight that morning.

The one who'd turned Nefert in to Hitler, rather than fight.

He pushed himself up on his elbows, then crunched his jaws together, and spat out a mouthful of sand.

Baldy slumped down on his knees on the sand as Sheba pulled his arm toward her. He twisted his wrist away, and tried to push away the rocks over his legs. She grabbed his ear, and twisted it until he groaned.

Nefert stomped across the sand, then stopped in front of him, with her hands on her hips. She pouted and narrowed her eyes as she stared at him.

"You refused to help me earlier today. Why should we help you now?"

"Please, I was wrong. I didn't realize you meant what you said. Just get me out of here. I'll fight. We all will."

Nefert nodded toward the pile of shells. "Get moving."

The other slaves, male and female, stared at Baldy, then moved the rocks. He lowered his face, then grabbed one end of a shell, and helped them carry it toward the pyramid's treads. For all his complaints earlier, maybe he could be of some use to the slave revolt, after all.

Osiris dug deeper into the sand. Another hand appeared where the slave hut had once stood. The fingers wriggled, and he and the slaves pulled on the hand. Big-Ears' face burst from the ground, spitting sand.

The pile of shells shrank as the slaves carried them away, one-by-one. Then, finally, they were all gone, stuffed into whatever holes they could find in the pyramid.

Now they just had to explode.

"Everyone, get away from here," Nefert said.

Osiris peered out at the desert beyond the pyramid. Sand erupted in clouds and spurts across the remains of the slave camp, as Hitler's men fired their rifles and the pyramid's guns at anything that moved.

"They'll kill us,"

"They'll have much more important things to worry about very soon. And you may die if you stay here."

Nefert picked up the burning cord from the gun.

Rai grabbed her wrist, and pulled it back.

"Dirk is still inside."

"Then he needs all the help he can get."

Nefert tried to pull her arm away, but Osiris grabbed the cord. "He won't be happy if he beats the Pharaoh and you're not around to celebrate with."

"I'll trust in God to protect me."

Osiris pulled the burning cord from her fingers.

"No. You'll trust in me."

<46>

Dirk stared up at the shiny metal mask over Hitler's face. The dark, evil eyes stared back at him from the slits in the mask. His own face reflected from the shiny gold plating. He raised his fist in front of his face, but it was minute when compared to Hitler's huge, metal hands. Nor would his mangled sword achieve much against the thick iron armour.

Hitler's voice boomed around the room, amplified by the suit. "Ready to die, untermensch?"

Facing death to save the universe from a homicidal asshole in a big, metal suit. It was just like a day in the Space Marines. Except Dirk didn't have a big, metal suit of his own to protect him from Hitler's blows.

"Come and get it, you Nazi asshole."

Hitler raised his foot, and swung it toward Dirk. The metal floor of the room clanged as the heavy, iron foot slammed down upon it. Dirk couldn't see Hitler's face, but he was pretty sure there was a big smile on it right now. If Dirk didn't think of something fast, he was going to end up as a big red splat on the floor.

The other foot stepped forward, with a clunk that echoed back from the long staircase of metal steps behind Dirk. He could still turn around and back away from this monster. But the universe needed him.

He hefted the sword in his hand. It probably weighed a hundredth as much as one of Hitler's metal hands. It was like a mosquito trying to kill a dinosaur. But he was a whole lot smarter than any mosquito he'd ever met. Even the Mosquito People of Ophiuchus Delta, who'd fought a long, guerrilla war in the jungle, kidnapping colonists and sucking their blood.

The suit was big and bulky, but there were gaps between the hand-fashioned metal panels. Big ones, in places. If he could get the sword through there, into something important behind the armour, he might have a chance of taking Hitler down.

The suit stopped moving. The engine hissed and filled the hot, humid air with a cloud of steam. The two men sized each other up for a moment.

Then Hitler swung his fist. Dirk ducked and rolled, and the fist swung past him, hammering instead into the archway around the door. The metal arch bent under the impact, which left a dent the size and shape of Hitler's metal knuckles.

A gap opened between the plates around Hitler's ankle as he began to twist around, looking for Dirk. Dirk swung his sword toward it, but Hitler stepped back, and the blade found only empty air.

The fist slammed down. Dirk rolled aside, and the floor of the room shook as the fist smashed into it at speed. Hitler stared down at the floor for a second, then pulled his fist back.

Dirk pushed himself to his feet, and jogged behind Hitler's leg. The metal foot rose to take a step back, but that just gave Dirk a clear shot at the gap around the ankle.

He swung his sword arm out, and lunged toward it.

Then the whole pyramid shook as the thud of an explosion rattled through the hull. Dirk's blow went wide, and the sword blade slammed into the metal below Hitler's knee.

Rivets bulged from the joins between the metal plates of the walls. A dozen or more burst from the plates in the ceiling, and clattered down onto Hitler's metal suit. More creaked and groaned in the floor. The plates twisted and bulged as the walls adjusted to the new forces that were trying to pull them apart.

Someone down there had found a way to fight back, at last.

Hitler wobbled on his metal legs as the floor shook. His back slammed into the wall, and his suit creaked. But he smashed his metal elbows against the wall and pushed himself back up onto his feet. They clunked as he turned back toward Dirk. Hitler raised his metal hands in front of his chest, and flexed the fingers toward Dirk.

"Come to me, Untermensch. I'll tear your mindless head from your black body."

Then he took a long step forward, and another, clunking across the metal floor faster than Dirk could run. Hitler's flailing arms slammed into the huge, enamelled bath on that side of the room, and tore it from the floor.

Dirk ducked as Hitler swung his arm again. Hitler twisted his blow at the last second, and the tips of his metal fingers slammed into Dirk's side.

Dirk's feet left the ground under the impact, and the sword slid from his grip as he flew through the air. It tumbled across the floor until the blade jammed into a gap between the twisted metal plates.

Then Dirk's back smacked into the wall. The impact slammed his spine against the metal, knocked his breath from his lungs, and left him gasping as he slid down to the floor. He sucked in half a dozen rapid, deep breaths as Hitler's metal feet clunked across the floor toward him.

Hitler swung his arm toward Dirk's head. Dirk dodged aside, and the metal hand smashed into the wall where he'd just been. Hitler pulled his hand back from the centimetre-deep crater in the metal where Dirk's head would have been if he hadn't moved so fast. And that head would have been splattered all across Hitler's metal fist.

Hitler pulled his arm back. Glass shattered as his metal elbow slammed into a lamp on the far side of the room. Dirk ducked and lunged forward as the arm swung toward him again. It smashed through the closet in the corner of the room, and scattered clothes across the floor.

A flaming oil lamp wobbled on a table beside the closet. The flame flickered as it shook from side to side.

Dirk grabbed it, and tossed it toward Hitler. It smashed on the metal helmet, spraying burning oil across the visor.

Hitler's metal legs whined as he backed away. He reached up and grabbed the sides of the helmet, and pulled it away from his head. Then tossed it aside. It smashed down onto the Pharaoh-sized bed, whose legs creaked under the weight. Then rolled off the mattress, and on across the floor.

Hitler lunged toward Dirk, raising his knee almost to chest level. Then swung his leg for a bone-smashing kick.

Dirk rolled over as the metal foot swung down. The floor plates shook under the impact, and a plate tore free, scattering more rivets across the room.

Dirk grabbed one as Hitler turned toward him. He pulled his arm back, took aim, and threw the rivet as hard and as fast as his bioengineered muscles could unleash it.

Glass cracked and shattered as the rivet smashed into Hitler's glasses. They pushed back into his face, and the rivet ricocheted off the frame. It thumped into his nose, which twisted and cracked under the impact.

Hitler reached up toward his face, but the metal framework around his head blocked the big, metal fist. He flicked his head from side to side, trying to move the glasses. They tilted on his nose with his motion.

Dirk threw another rivet. It smashed into Hitler's cheek, and he raised his head as he yelled with pain. Blood dripped down his face from the gash where the edge of the rivet had slashed his skin. Hitler's head twisted from side to side, splattering blood across the wall beside him.

The glasses slid down Hitler's nose, then off his ears. They tapped against the metal framework around his head as they fell, then tumbled to the floor.

Hitler reached up again. "Where are those fucking glasses?"

Then he twisted as though looking for them. His feet slammed down onto the metal floor.

And crushed the twisted remains of his glasses beneath them. As he lifted the foot again, all that remained were a few shattered glass shards and a mangled metal frame.

Dirk rolled away as Hitler swung madly from side to side, swinging his arms, punching the walls, and slamming his feet down onto the floor all around him. Dirk dodged each of the blows, but his legs were beginning to grow weak from all the exertion of the last hour, despite his bioengineered strength.

Hitler swung around again, smacking his foot down with every step, until he was almost facing away.

The boiler on the back of the suit was glowing red at the base. All this running and punching must be pulling so much power from the steam engine that it was beginning to overheat. Dirk didn't know much about steam engines, but he'd seen a Shredder overheat one time, and it was a really bad day for the gun crew when the superconducting barrels blew apart.

He pushed himself to his feet.

"Come on," he yelled. "You're going to take over the world, and I'm just a Nubian. Are you scared of me?"

Hitler's mouth opened into a rabid yell, and he swung his arms. His feet smashed against metal as they pounded across the floor toward Dirk. He pushed hard against the wall behind him, and slid across the floor, between the exoskeleton's feet as the metal hands smashed together just where he'd been standing.

Hitler turned again. Dirk ducked as the exoskeleton's arms swung through the air above him. Then glanced toward the steam engine. Thin white clouds of steam were oozing from joins where it didn't look like steam should be oozing.

"Too slow, asshole."

Hitler swung again. Dirk dodged to the right, and kicked off from the wall. As Hitler raised his foot to turn toward where Dirk had been, he slid past. The foot stomped down again. A row of rivets bulged from the top of the boiler.

"What are you waiting for?" Dirk yelled.

Hitler turned again. His face glowed red with anger, and his eyes were bulging from his face.

He raised his leg to stomp forward. But it stopped half-way. Hoses burst free behind the metal plates, and a cloud of steam erupted from the gaps between them.

Hitler screamed.

Then the boiler exploded. Boiling-hot water sprayed out across the ceiling and walls, hissing and steaming where it touched the metal. Dirk ducked beneath the bed as the water poured down onto the straw mattress.

Hitler screamed again. Louder, this time. And longer.

Dirk peered out just in time to see the boiling water and red-hot coals spray across Hitler's body. Hitler's skin turned red, then began to slide off his bones. His hands pulled free of the metal arms of the suit, and left the skin behind. The red claws that remained reached up toward his face, and the flaming moustache on his top lip. He slapped at is, as though trying to put out the flames, but the skin came away beneath his fingers.

Then the knees of the suit gave way, and it slumped down onto the floor.

<47>

Dirk raced back up the metal steps toward the control room at the top of the pyramid, leaving Hitler's bloody, smoking body behind him. He'd saved the universe, but he still had to save himself. And there was only one way he knew to do that.

The steps shook beneath him as something else exploded far below. He slid to the side, and his shoulder slammed into the metal wall of the stairway. He pushed himself back up to his feet. The stairs now sloped to the right, and he stumbled up them, putting his hand on the wall to support himself as his feet slid across the metal.

The metal door to the control room was open again at the top of the steps. But something exploded below him again, and his stomach rose into his chest as the pyramid slammed down a metre or more. The metal door shook, then slid down into the archway, and slammed into the top of the steps.

He had no way out through there.

Squeals and thuds came from the room to the left, where he'd left Totenkopf with the slave girls. Scraping and clunking came from a doorway to the right.

The floor rattled. The dark faces and bare chests of the slave girls peered out from Totenkopf's room, then they squealed as the pyramid shook again. They took one look at each other, then raced down the steps. Hopefully they knew a way out.

Dirk peered into the doorway on the right. A familiar, suited figure was hunched over on the metal floor.

"Spear!" Dirk yelled.

Spear was fumbling with the time vortex gizmo that had brought him to Egypt. He adjusted the controls on the side, and the air wobbled above it, before the vortex opened. From where Dirk stood, he was looking at the vortex almost from the side, and could see little more than an elongated, haze oval.

Dirk pulled himself through the doorway, but the pyramid shook again, and his body slammed into the right side of the doorway, then the left.

By the time he regained his footing, it was too late.

Spear stepped through the vortex, on to wherever he was going. He glanced back at Dirk, then leaned back through the vortex, and grabbed the time portal gizmo. He smirked at Dirk for a second, then picked it up, and pulled it through the portal. With one flick of the switch, the portal shrank to a tiny circle of dazzling white light. Then it was gone.

Dirk raced across the room, in the vain hope that there might still be some faint remnant of the vortex left that could send him back home. But he passed through the space where the vortex had been, and just came out the other side.

So that was that.

The pyramid shook again, and the walls rattled at the thud of an explosion far below. And again, by a larger explosion this time. Dirk's Space Marine training hadn't spent much time on steam power, but he was pretty sure the engines shouldn't be doing that. The sooner he got out of there, the better.

There was a window in the side of Spear's room. Metal shutters covered it, but one hung loose where the explosions had torn the locks away and loosened the hinges.

Dirk pulled the other shutter open, and looked out.

He stared down the inclined sides of the pyramid. Many of the iron panels had been blown out from the inside. Some were just twisted lumps of dark metal, while others lay in pieces scattered across the sand below. Thick clouds of smoke and glowing flames burst from the gaps where the panels had been.

Down below, a few rifles were still firing, but most of the soldiers seemed to have figured out that the battle was lost, and abandoned their posts. Aside from the flames, the bent metal and the thick smoke from holes over what looked like a fiery inferno inside the tank, he had a clear path to the sand of the slave camp.

The pyramid shook again. Two panels exploded from the side of the tank and tumbled through the air, leaving behind a burst of orange flame that raced up the side of the pyramid. He pulled his face away from the window and covered it with his arm as the flames rushed past the window, then faded.

Then twisted to the left as the top of the pyramid exploded. Piece of metal clattered down the sides, followed by chunks of the console displays with their gauges still swinging from side to side with the motion.

Screw it. What choice did he have?

He climbed onto the windowsill, picked the safest looking route down the side of the pyramid, then jumped.

<48>

Dirk slammed down onto his ass on the steeply-angled side of the pyramid. The dark metal and rivets raced past him as he began to pick up speed. He'd done this before when he jumped on board, but it had been a whole lot easier when the sides of the pyramid were still intact, and flames weren't bursting from the holes where panels had been torn away by the explosions.

Another explosion raised from the hull a few metres below him. The edges twisted as it rose from the surface with flames bursting around them. The rivets tore and flew through the air, clattering against the hull as they fell toward the sand, bouncing from the pyramid's metal surface on the way.

Then the edges of the panel gave way as it lost most of the rivets, and it exploded outward. The shards that remained of the panel tumbled through the air, twisting and turning ready to slash any flesh they contacted as they bounced from the lower levels of the hull, and knocked some of the few remaining rifles from the gun slits.

That missing panel left behind a gaping hole full of flames.

And Dirk was heading right toward it.

He grabbed the twisted metal edge of a nearby panel where it had bent away from the pyramid tank's hull. The metal cut into the palm of his hand as he put his weight on it, but his body twisted toward it, and away from the flames.

He slid on. The rivets hammered against his back and ass as he slid over them, but the cuts and scrapes in his skin would be a small price to pay for survival.

The ground approached rapidly. The chunks of stone, shards of metal and twisted steel plates in the debris grew in size as he raced down the side of the pyramid toward them.

He pressed his heels against the metal, and the momentum pushed him up onto his feet for a second. He pushed against the tank's hull with his hands and feet, and threw himself into the air three or four metres above the ground, as far as he could from the pyramid, and the debris scattered around it.

The sides of the pyramid exploded behind him as he flew toward the sand. He tumbled in the air, then landed chest-first in the desert and sank half a metre into the sand. He pushed himself up, pulling his face free and gasping for breath as his head rose from the sand into the hot, desert air.

The surviving slaves ran from the explosions, racing in all directions across the sand from the pyramid. Some hid behind the remaining huts, others made for the walls, and clambered over them, or forced their way out through the gates.

One-Eye raced over and licked Dirk's face. Dirk pulled himself to his feet, grabbed the dog, and jogged across the sand as chunks of metal exploding from the remains of the pyramid smashed into the sand around him.

"Wait," a female voice yelled.

The topless girl with the gold jewellery lay on the sand, and raised her hand toward him. Dirk grabbed it with his free hand, and pulled her to her feet, then helped her to run. She might have been with Hitler, but she didn't seem a bad sort. And she'd helped him to beat the asshole. He owed her one.

"Marry me, great one," she said.

"I'll think about it."

She wasn't bad looking. Not so great when compared to the genetically-engineered college girls of his time, but she was darn pretty by the standards of the girls he'd met on planet Egypt. He could do a lot worse.

But his heart just wouldn't be in it.

Besides, he had to find the strange man who'd sent him there, and return to his own time. Planet Egypt had been fun to visit, but he had a life waiting for him out there among the stars. Not to mention a college-girl orgy.

Even though he'd missed his chance to escape through the vortex with Spear, there must be some way home. Even in the worst of times in the Space Marines, he'd always found a way to get back alive. Planet Egypt couldn't be any harder than that.

She followed him anyway. With Hitler gone, she probably didn't have anywhere better to go. The surviving ex-slaves stared at her as she passed, and she stepped closer to Dirk, as though scared of what they might do to her now her power was gone.

Osiris sat on the sand, leaning against a pile of rocks that had once been a slave hut. He held a mug in his hand, full of deep, brown liquid. In all the chaos of the battle and its aftermath, he'd somehow managed to find himself a drink.

"Where's Nefert?" Dirk said.

"I don't know," Osiris said. "She was helping me to set off the shells that we used to blow up the pyramid. When the tracks broke away and the whole thing crashed down, I lost sight of her."

Dirk's heart jumped.

He'd kind of got used to the girl.

Had she given her life to save Dirk? And the universe?

It was a brave thought, but he'd still rather have her there alive beside him. And, ideally, if he was going to be stuck on planet Egypt for the rest of his life, her writhing beneath him in his bed at night.

He cupped his hands and yelled. "Has anyone seen Nefert?"

The now ex-slaves glanced at each other, then shook their heads. Dirk turned on the spot, staring out across the desert. He could see many ex-slaves moving in the rubble that used to be their slave camp. And many dead bodies, mangled by bullets, explosives or more antiquated weapons, or crushed beneath the treads of the tank.

Nefert could be one of them.

He turned toward the pyramid. If that was the last place Osiris had seen her, that's where she was most likely to be.

And one of the bodies scattered around the base of the shattered pyramid was moving toward him.

Dirk strode that way.

Yes, someone was moving. They were crawling across the sand toward him. A man whose body was bloody and burned anywhere the skin wasn't covered by the remaining cloth of his torn, dark suit.

A bright red face lifted up from the sand. Most of the skin was burned away, exposing bloody muscles and sinews beneath it. One eye was closed behind eyelids stuck together with blood, the other dark eye stared toward Dirk.

Who could hardly mistake that face for any other.

Hitler cackled. "Now, untermensch. You die."

<49>

Hitler cackled again as he raised one burned, wobbly hand from the sand, and pointed toward Dirk. Then Hitler's other arm gave way, and he collapsed back into the sand.

He pushed himself up, and cackled again. Whatever was left of the man had clearly gone completely insane. Which wasn't surprising when most of his skin had been burned or boiled away by the exploding boiler.

That had to hurt.

Dirk grabbed a rifle from the hands of a soldier who lay dead on the sand with his chest crushed by a rock and his head smashed into a bloody mess a metre from his severed neck.

He swung the rifle toward Hitler and pulled the trigger. The gun clicked, but nothing happened. He cycled the bolt, but the magazine was empty.

Hitler raised his hand again. But, this time, it clutched a small, dark pistol with a bulbous grip and a tiny barrel. A pistol of a kind he had seen before, when he first arrived on Planet Egypt. In the Space Marines, the gun would have barely been considered a weapon, but on Planet Egypt it could kill.

The pistol cracked as Hitler pulled the trigger, but his hand was wobbling so much that the bullet whizzed through the air above Dirk's head, and smacked into the wall around the slave camp instead.

Dirk tossed the useless rifle aside. He grabbed a rock from the ruins of a slave hut, and held it high in front of him. Just in time, as Hitler's next shot slammed into the rock and tore chunks away.

Dirk's arm muscles strained as he held the rock ahead of him like a laser shield. Another bullet smacked into the rock, tearing away a chunk near the top and ricocheting off into the sand. The splinters rained down on Dirk's foot.

He stepped forward as more pistol bullets hammered into his impromptu shield. Two. Three. Four. An old gun couldn't hold many more than that.

Then another bullet smacked into the left side of the rock shield. A loud crack filled the air, and the chunk of rock Dirk's fingers held broke away. The rock shield twisted in his grip, and he tried to hold on. But another bullet hammered into the rock, and it fell from his hands.

Hitler's skinless face smirked as he aimed the gun between Dirk's eyes.

Dirk still held the last chunk of the rock in his left hand. He tossed it at Hitler. It slammed into Hitler's arm just he fired, and the bullet went wild, cracking through the air above Dirk's shoulder. Hitler's wrist snapped under the impact, and the gun fell to the sand.

Dirk grabbed the pistol, and swung it toward Hitler's head. This time, he'd make sure the asshole was dead.

Then another face appeared from behind the rock pile at Hitler's side. A face smeared with soot and sand.

A face Dirk recognized.

Nefert.

Blood had run down the left side of her face from a gash in her forehead, and matted her hair. Her eyes bulged with hatred as she stared at Hitler. But otherwise she looked intact.

She smiled at Dirk, then yelled a crazy yell as she grabbed a fist-sized rock and jumped down from the debris pile, toward Hitler's writhing body in the sand. He looked up just in time to see her flying toward him.

But too late to do anything.

Nefert yelled as she slammed the rock down on Hitler's head. The other ex-slaves crowded around her, swinging whatever weapons they could find. Hitler's bones crunched as the ex-slaves he had oppressed for so long smashed them into a bloody mess in the sand.

He wasn't coming back from that one. Unless he was built like the Vorkins from Ignominius Four, whose DNA could find its fellow cells even if they were splattered across a battlefield, and rebuild their bodies. That had made a pretty damn nasty fight, when the dead would return to life unless they were completely obliterated.

But Hitler didn't have the Vorkins' pointy skulls, or their fourth eye in the back of his head. At least, not so far as Dirk had seen. It might have been hidden under that funny hat Hitler had worn on the throne. But he'd seen no sign of it as Hitler crawled across the sand toward him just moments ago.

So, most likely, that was that.

Dirk tossed the pistol aside. He could finally relax after all these months. He'd saved the universe, more or less. He'd put right the mistake that his relative had made so long ago, and history should now follow the course it was supposed to follow.

Not that he could really remember much from his history lessons at school, but he didn't remember anything about the Pharaoh of Planet Egypt in the military history lessons he'd taken in Space Marine training.

And the freshly ex-slaves seemed to be relaxing now, too.

Rai giggled, then jumped on Osiris as he knocked back the last of his wine. He slumped down to the sand beneath her, and she straddled him, then pulled up his loincloth. Then she leaned forward and planted a big kiss on his stubbled face, before he grinned and pulled her loincloth away. She squealed as he rolled over on top of her, and his flabby stomach pressed down on her thin, girlish body.

Hitler's dog strolled across the sand. A thin stream of smoke rose from a burned patch on her side, but she didn't seem to be worried about it. She sniffed the bloody mess that had once been her master, then strolled on, toward the wall.

One-Eye looked up, then climbed to his feet and trotted over to her. He sniffed her, then mounted her. His tongue dangled from his lips as he lay on her back for a few seconds, hammering away at her ass.

After he finished, he trotted back to Sakhmet. Hitler's dog followed close behind, wagging her tail. Guess Sakhmet had two dogs to look after now. But she seemed to enjoy it.

Another explosion shook the pyramid tank, and a shower of rivets fell from the sky, clattering as they slammed into the rocks and debris, or raising yelps and groans when they hit the slaves. With a sigh of tearing metal, the peak of the pyramid collapsed, and fell into the flames below.

Silence spread across the crowd of slaves as they turned to watch the pyramid collapse. Metal creaked and groaned as more rivets gave way under the weight, and the joins between the hull plates began to tear, until the whole pyramid peeled apart like a hundred-metre tall black metal banana.

The ground shook as the plates fell, and Dirk coughed as the impact lifted a thick cloud of sand into the air, that spread until it filled the entire slave camp, and the world disappeared into the yellow haze.

Then all that remained of Hitler's giant, steam-powered death machine was a fire crackling beneath a pile of iron plates and pipes. A fire so tall and bright that he could still see it through the sandy haze.

The noise of the collapse faded, and the haze disappeared as the breeze from the river blew away the last of the sand cloud that hadn't already settled to the ground.

As the yellow haze faded away, it exposed the crowd of hundreds of slaves who stood around him, staring at Hitler's body and the burning funeral pyre of the pyramid tank that had been intended to conquer the world.

They turned toward Dirk.

"Pharaoh! Pharaoh! Pharaoh!" they chanted.

<50>

Dirk lounged on the bank of the Nile in the fading daylight, with his back against a nice, warm, rock. He stared out across the glittering water as the sun set behind him. Hitler's tank was still burning in the slave camp, and the tall stream of smoke cast a long, twisting shadow across the water. Hitler was dead, the slaves—those still alive, at least—were safe and free.

The universe may or may not have been saved, but he had no way to find out. And there was nothing more he could do.

He lowered his legs over the riverbank, and dipped his feet into the cool river water. He sighed as the cold seemed to suck the pain from his toes and soles. His body had been subjected to much since he arrived on planet Egypt, and this was one of the few chances he'd had to relax.

His stomach rumbled. He hadn't eaten since last night. He could do with something to fill it. Something big, meaty and bloody. But he'd probably have to make do with another plate of stringy, gamey camel. That was about the best thing anyone ever had to eat around here.

One-Eye lay on his back beside the rock. Hitler's dog dozed in the shadows beside him.

Dirk reached over and rubbed One-Eye's stomach. That dog didn't even seem to care what he had to eat. Just about anything would do. Dead, alive, or in between.

Even if it had been rotting in the hot sun for a week.

Even Dirk's bioengineered Space Marine stomach would still have a hard time not getting sick eating rotten road-kill. But nothing seemed to faze One-Eye's guts.

Laughing and squealing came from behind him. He peered around the rock. Sheba and half a dozen other ex-slave girls laughed as they carried Hitler's girl high above their heads. She squealed and swung her arms madly at them, but they just raised her higher. They raced out between two sand dunes, then across the sand track between the dunes and the water.

She struggled harder as they stopped at the river bank. Then tossed her into the water.

"There's your pool," Sheba shouted, then chortled.

"I'll get you," Hitler's girl yelled as she floated away down the river, twisting and turning in the current. Then she turned away from them in the water, and began to swim downriver.

Maybe he should do something about that. She might be a nag, but she'd never really done anything to harm him,

Then again, maybe he'd be better off leaving her to find her own new life on planet Egypt. She was swimming faster than he could swim without his bioengineered strength. It didn't look like she'd have much trouble escaping from anyone who wanted to cause her trouble.

Then a hand grabbed his shoulder.

Nefert leaned over the rock. "What is the matter?"

"Spear got away. Now I've got no way to go home."

"Nubia is only a few weeks by camel. But why would you go? Why not stay here? Be Pharaoh?"

Here on planet Egypt? He opened his mouth to tell her what a crazy idea that was. Then stopped, and stared out at the glittering river water again.

The river water turned red as the body of a Nazi guard floated past, its head in two pieces where an axe must have cut through, with its limbs bobbing up and down beside it. Then a crocodile's jaws lunged up from the water, and the body was gone, leaving just a slowly dispersing patch of blood.

What did Dirk have to go back for, anyway?

His girlfriend would only bitch at him, the way she always did. The swim team girls would use him until he could be used no more. He had no job, and he'd never get a good reference from his job at BastadoCorp after he got their mining ship blown up. Even if it wasn't really his fault.

Nefert crouched beside him, and motioned for him to lean forward. As he did so, she slid her hands up his back, and began to massage his bioengineered shoulders.

Ah, that felt good.

She leaned forward, and pressed her breasts against his back.

That felt even better.

"I have something important to tell you," she said.

"What?"

"I think we have a little Dirk on the way."

Oh, yes. Maybe he should have thought about that. When he joined the Space Marines, they implanted a birth-control gizmo in his body which was supposed to ensure that no little accidents would get in the way of his duty to the Marines. But that was over a decade ago. How long did those things last?

Obviously not that long.

Could he go back to the future and leave his kid here on planet Egypt? What if he took Nefert with him? She was smart and resourceful, but could she adapt to life in space?

And, if the strange man returned him to the time he'd left, it could make the whole orgy thing a bit complicated.

He'd have to talk to the strange man about it. Maybe he'd have some ideas. He must be used to sending people to different times and places. It seemed to be his job.

"You don't mind?" Nefert said.

"I don't mind."

She wrapped her arms around his waist, and pressed against him until her breasts squashed against his back. "Good."

Something moved beside the rocks across the water. Dirk peered toward it. Something humanoid, and short. Barely taller than Dirk's waist.

Was that the strange man from the future? If so, he'd picked an awfully bad time to come and take Dirk back there.

No. A hand rose toward the sky and waved at them. It was just a kid, playing in the water. Whoever the strange man had been, he clearly had no intention of taking Dirk back.

His future was on planet Egypt, now.

He could still hear the freed slaves chanting for him. He could say on planet Egypt, become their leader, maybe try to bring some kind of civilization to them.

He'd done enough for the universe, and it didn't seem to care what happened to him.

Pharaoh Dirk and Queen Nefert. He could handle that.

ABOUT THE AUTHOR

Edward M. Grant is a physicist and software developer turned SF and horror writer. He lives in the frozen wastes of Canada, but was born in England, where he wrote for a science and technology magazine and worked on numerous indie movies in and around London. He has travelled the world, been a VIP at several space shuttle launches, survived earthquakes and a tsunami, climbed Mt Fuji, assisted the search for the MH370 airliner, and visits nuclear explosion sites as a hobby.

Find him online at **www.edwardmgrant.com,** *or subscribe to his new release mailing list at* **www.edwardmgrant.com/list**.

ALSO BY EDWARD M. GRANT

PETRINA

A stripper, a hitman, his target, and a monk with a severed head in his bag. It's a typical passenger manifest for the crew of the space freighter 'Big Momma'.

Russ is hiding from 'Nam flashbacks. Alex may have met her dream guy. Max is tempted to throw them all out the airlock.

They only have to survive a three week flight from the Heavenly Retreat habitat—The Sleaziest Place In The Solar System™—to the remote asteroid, 482 Petrina.

But someone doesn't want them to get there.

SPACE WEASELS

Vicious, congenitally bureaucratic, and proud of their resplendent flame-red uniforms which give them a five minute life expectancy in combat, the Flaming Space Weasels wiped out most of Dirk Beretta's fellow space marines at the battle of Din Bin Foo... then served them for lunch with a nice Merlot.

In the aftermath, Dirk quits his job as poster boy for the space marines, to drown his sorrow in cheap booze and cheaper women. But when a gang of pirate Weasels come hunting fresh meat for the kibble factories, his brand of pig-headed determination and excessive violence may offer the chance for redemption... and revenge.

A 7,000 word science fiction short story.

FADE TO GREY

How do you repair a dead planet?

Maintenance Bot M-3 was always proud of the smooth and reliable operation of the starships it maintained as they travelled the galaxy searching for life on unexplored worlds. It lived for the desperate struggle against the forces of chaos and decay, fighting against time to complete repairs before disaster struck.

But this job may be beyond even its capabilities.

A 15,000 word science fiction novelette set in The Future's universe.

ROBO-ZOMBIE

Darren's Robo-Rat project would have saved countless lives, allowing rescuers to go places no human could survive. If only the zombie apocalypse hadn't interrupted its funding.

Now he's trapped on a hotel roof in Saskatoon with his boss, while the girl he loves fights zombies far below. But Rob the zombie, a case of electronics, and a cordless drill may offer a chance to rescue her after all...

A 7,500 word science fiction horror short story. With remotely-controlled zombies.